Palma Harcourt was bo
and educated at St
worked in variou
travelling widely and living in several
world. Her experiences have provided her with
background material for her thrillers
with diplomatic settings.

Also by Palma Harcourt

PALMA HARCOURT

A Fair Exchange

Futura
Macdonald & Co
London & Sydney

A Futura Book

First published in Great Britain in 1975
by William Collins Sons & Co Ltd

This Futura edition published in 1984

Copyright © Palma Harcourt 1975

All rights reserved
No part of this publication may be reproduced,
stored in a retrieval system, or transmitted, in any
form or by any means without the prior
permission in writing of the publisher, nor be
otherwise circulated in any form of binding or
cover other than that in which it is published and
without a similar condition including this
condition being imposed on the subsequent
purchaser.

ISBN 0 7088 2498 6

Reproduced, printed and bound in Great Britain by
Hazell Watson & Viney Limited,
Member of the BPCC Group,
Aylesbury, Bucks

Futura Publications
A Division of
Macdonald & Co (Publishers) Ltd
Maxwell House
74 Worship Street
London EC2A 2EN
A BPCC plc Company

For my parents

This book is fiction. Naturally, some geographical locations and the names of some official and other appointments exist in reality. However, any apparent relationship between the characters in this novel and persons who hold or have held these appointments is entirely coincidental.

CONTENTS

Part One

WASHINGTON DC

Chapter One

'Ah, Derek! So glad you could manage to come.'

'My pleasure, sir.'

'Yes.'

The Ambassador studied his watch in silent rebuke and, before I could stop myself, I too was looking at the time. I hadn't realized it was so late. I shouldn't have played that extra game of squash. But how was I to know that on a thundery May evening the Washington traffic would be more snarled than ever? Perhaps I should apologize.

A First Secretary wasn't supposed to be the last arrival at a dinner party given by his Ambassador, and there were already about twenty people, chatting and drinking and eating tit-bits in the long, beautifully-proportioned drawing-room. For that matter, in such a major post as Washington, a First Secretary wasn't supposed to be a guest at all – or not as frequently as I was. I stifled my apology.

After allowing me an impatient minute to greet my hostess the Ambassador began to lead me on a round of introductions. His plummy voice interrupted conversations and his huge frame inserted itself and me into uninterested groups.

'May I introduce Derek Almourn, one of the First Secretaries at our Embassy. Lord Almourn, his father, is a former colleague of mine and an old friend.'

Out of the corner of my eye I noticed the Minister turning away his head, but not before I had seen his mouth twitch with amusement. I didn't resent it. I liked and respected the Minister. The Ambassador I neither liked nor respected. There were two reasons for this. The first was that he was a political appointee and I have never understood why a plum job should be awarded as politicians' largesse when able, even brilliant, career diplomats are available;

the Ambassador, I considered, was neither brilliant nor particularly able. The second – and by far more important – was the way he used me, because I was Francis Almourn's son. That he was an awful liar and nothing would have made my father acknowledge him as a friend was beside the point.

'I believe I had the pleasure of meeting your father once in London, Mr Almourn. He was Minister of Defence at the time,' said the White House aide.

'I never understand how you can be a lord and yet be a member of your British Cabinet.' This from the Texan, adviser on oil to the President.

'The Prime Minister chooses his Cabinet from both Houses,' I said. 'But by tradition most of the high offices can't be held by peers.' And, to my alarm, I found myself explaining – to them and a couple of senior Senators who were all going out of their way to be pleasant to me, because I was, indeed, the son of an important man – some of the idiosyncracies of the British parliamentary system.

'So you can't be a lord and a British Prime Minister at the same time?'

'Not any more,' I agreed, smiling at the Texan drawl. 'Not unless you renounce your peerage.'

And that my father had unequivocally refused to do. I don't know what it had cost him; he had never consulted me. But, when your party and your country are clamouring for you to accept the highest office in the land, it can't be easy to turn it down and agree to serve under a lesser man. Most people had thought him mad to value a three-hundred-year-old title above the Prime Ministership, but I approved. Even though I don't think much of politicians I give unstinted approval to Francis Almourn. I am also very fond of him.

'We-ell, that's very interesting, Mr Almourn. You've not thought of going in for politics yourself, I suppose?'

'No - er - no,' I said absently, though, in fact, it's the last thing in the world I should want to do.

But my attention had been caught and riveted by the latest guests to arrive. I hadn't been the last, after all; how glad I was

14

not to have apologized. The Ambassador and his lady were clearly delighted by the new arrivals. There was much hand shaking and pecking of cheeks and general animation. I stood and watched.

'Senator Charlton and his beautiful wife.'

'His wife?'

The Texan gave a huge belly-laugh and I had to laugh too. I had given myself away completely. The Senator and his wife were part of the background for me. I couldn't take my eyes off the girl.

'And their charming daughter, Miss Lynn Charlton.'

I watched as the Ambassador brought them around. I had remembered who Charlton was now. He was the Democratic Senator for one of the New England states, liberal with a small 'l', a moderate in politics, the kind of man whom Republicans and Democrats alike welcomed on committees because he had a reputation for 'objective pragmatism', in other words for good old English compromise. As a result he was always busy and often in the news, usually accompanied by his wife.

And his daughter? For a moment her cold fingers lingered in my hand as the Ambassador introduced me in his customary fashion. For once I didn't resent it. Lynn Charlton had clearly never heard of Lord Almourn. She gave me a small, cat-like smile and followed her parents to the next group of guests. I was devastated.

In spite of some pressure from my mother and even more pressure from other people's mothers I was, at thirty-one, still a bachelor, for the simple reason that I had never met anybody whom I wanted to marry. I had known birds whom I liked to be with, to dance with, ride with, swim with, go to plays and concerts with, to make love with – but not one I had ever fancied as my wife. Either they had been unwilling or, if they had been willing, it had been for the wrong reasons, because they thought I was a good catch. And I was sensitive on that point.

Across the room I could see Lynn Charlton talking to the Minister and wished I had the nerve to join them. But I could imagine the great guffaw of laughter from my Texan companion that would follow me and the sardonic grin of the Minister if I

15

suddenly appeared at his elbow. It didn't matter; there would be time later.

I made my excuses and wandered off to join a trio of blue-haired matrons, who immediately engulfed me in their conversation. They were talking about a little Italian dressmaker who ran up copies of dresses for next to nothing. Two of the matrons were boasting, the third was angling for an introduction, which she wasn't going to get.

'What does your wife do, Mr Almourn? Does she buy all her clothes in Europe?'

'I'm not married.'

'Then what are you doing talking to three old women like us when you could be with Lynn Charlton?'

'Such a beautiful girl! That lovely long hair, the colour of ripe corn.'

'And those huge violet eyes.'

'And clever too. Did you know she's studying for her Master's at Georgetown University?'

The two of them sang her praises, eager to change the conversation from introductions to dressmakers, and I listened avidly, sipping my second whisky. Before dinner parties such as this I usually ration myself to one drink but tonight merited another whisky.

The Ambassador's social secretary was moving among the guests, murmuring to each of the men the name of the lady whom he was to take in to dinner and pointing her out if he greeted the information blankly. I wondered who would be lucky enough to get Lynn. Dinner was announced as the social secretary hurried towards me.

'Derek, you'll never guess.'

She was a nice girl and I liked her. 'I hope it's you,' I said.

'No, you don't.' She shook her head. 'Not when you're to take in Miss Charlton!'

I couldn't contradict her but to hide my delight, I said, 'I'll never again think an unkind thought about His Excellency.'

'Be thankful for once that he's so fond of the ruddy aristocracy,' she murmured.

16

I made a face at her. 'It pays off sometimes.'

And this was one of the times! By the end of the fish course Miss Charlton and I had completed all the standard questions and answers, such as how did I like Washington and had she ever been to Europe. By the time we had finished the *boeuf en croûte* we were on first-name terms. With the salad we both turned reluctantly – I hoped she was as reluctant as I was – to our neighbours on the other side.

Mine was a rather pleasant French woman, a doctor, now married to an influential Congressman, who talked at length about what she insisted on calling *Indo-Chine*. She was knowledgeable and objective. Another time I would have been fascinated. Now she must have seen my eyes glaze because she suddenly lost interest in me and left me to concentrate on the *zabaglione*. I waited for Lynn.

'What have you been talking about?' she asked.

'The part played by the French in Vietnam,' I said. 'Dien Bien Phu and all that.''

'But that's history.' She was impatient. 'It's the part the Americans are playing right now that's important.'

'You feel strongly about the war?'

'Who doesn't?'

Ask a silly question and you get a silly answer. I hadn't met an American who didn't have strong views on Vietnam. Lynn, however, had spoken with particular vehemence and I wondered how I could change the subject. I was too late. I had to listen to yet another lecture on South East Asia.

'The French were fighting an old colonial war,' Lynn said. 'It was right they should have lost. It was right too that the Americans should have gone to help bring order to the country. The French had left it in a dreadful mess. But we shouldn't have gotten involved in the fighting and we certainly shouldn't have let it escalate as we did. We shouldn't have used saturation bombing and defoliation and – and napalm. Some of the pictures – it's ghastly what we've done to those poor peasants. And we go on and on doing it. You know, I don't believe this war is ever going to end unless we organize people to demand peace and freedom and . . .'

This was, I assumed, a repetition of Senator Charlton's line, but a simplistic and somewhat naïve version. From the wisdom of my thirty-one years I reminded myself that Lynn was a college student and very young. Besides she showed a real compassion. I could sympathize with much of what she had been saying. And she was no extremist. She was fully aware of the brutality and horror inflicted by the enemy. But the difference was, as she said, that she felt herself responsible only for the American conscience.

She was still busy explaining, the grapes on her plate untouched, when our hostess decided to collect the ladies.

'I hope I haven't been boring you,' she said earnestly as we all stood up.

I pulled back her chair. 'I was fascinated. Will you have dinner with me tomorrow night and tell me the rest?'

Lynn laughed. 'Tomorrow? Yes, that'll be okay. Will you pick me up about seven? We live in Rock Creek Park. The address is in the phone book.'

'Thank you.'

For the next thirty minutes I drank port and took part in the male conversation or I suppose I did. I was in a haze of happiness which cut me off from those around me. I could only think of Lynn Charlton and the fact that she had promised to have dinner with me the next day. And there was still the rest of this evening.

Here I was wrong. The evening was about to fall apart. The gentlemen trooped back into the drawing-room, chatting and joking among themselves, masculinely confident of a warm greeting from the ladies. But the talk and laughter faded and we stood, in a cloud of cigar-smoke, gawking.

The ladies presented a most unladylike tableau. Lynn and the matron who had failed to get the address of the Italian dressmaker stood facing each other like two fighting cocks, their talons ready to strike. Lynn's mother stood behind her and a little to her left, as though she were a second, and the matron was similarly supported by one of her friends. The Ambassadress, the Minister's wife and the social secretary had withdrawn slightly to underline the fact that the fight was all-American, even though it was taking place on what was technically British soil and, as if to substantiate this, the wife of the Canadian Ambassador was gazing fixedly at a painting by Sutherland. The rest of the women were unashamedly watching. The atmosphere was nine months pregnant and God knows what it was going to produce.

If Lynn hadn't been involved I would have enjoyed the scene, especially in its present setting.

'My dear child, you don't understand.'

'It's you who doesn't understand, Mrs Unger. And I'm not your dear child. I'm not a child at all. I'm twenty-one years old and – '

'Lynn, darling, please stop.'

'Yes, you're twenty-one. That just proves my point. You're still very young. And foolish.'

'My brother was not much older when he was sent to Vietnam. Nobody said he was too young to risk his life or – or worse – flying a chopper. If you're old enough to fight for your country you ought to be old enough to have some say in what happens.'

'And, if you'll pardon me, ill-mannered too. You students, you think you can do what you like and say what you like.'

'All those stupid marches!'

'Demanding the President should do this and do that. Stupid!'

The two matrons had ganged up on her now. 'Stoopid!' they repeated. 'Stoopid!' The American pronunciation made the word sound more of an invective than it was.

'Perhaps I am young and foolish and – and ill-mannered – all the things you say,' Lynn said fiercely. 'But I'm not selfish and cruel like you. You don't care about the people who are being killed and maimed and tortured. Not even about the Americans. And if people like you must have their way this war'll go on for ever and my brother'll rot in a Vietnamese prison camp until he's – he's as old as you are.'

'Lynn!' her mother protested.

But Lynn had come to an end. Her voice broke, and tears streamed down her cheeks and she ran from the room. Senator Charlton, almost as white-faced as his daughter, went after her. The social secretary followed, giving me a despairing look as she hurried past. I wished I could help but there was nothing I could do.

'I apologize for Lynn,' Mrs Charlton said. 'She and Lloyd have always been exceptionally close. She misses him very much and she worries about him – desperately. For that matter so do I and my husband. I'm sorry.'

'My dear, we understand. Of course we understand. I was only saying to my husband the other day how dreadful it is for people who have sons . . .'

The Minister's wife, suddenly garrulous, slipped her hand under Mrs Charlton's arm and led her to a near-by sofa. I became aware of the Minister standing beside me. He grinned at me sardonically.

'My wife,' he murmured, 'is a wonderful woman.'

'She is indeed, sir,' I said.

'Then what are we waiting for, young Almourn? Into the fray!'

Exuding charm he bore down upon the two angry matrons and I followed him. The Ambassador and his lady also went into action. The guests responded. Coffee and liqueurs re-circulated. But nothing could resuscitate the spirit of what had never been a very good party.

Senator Charlton reappeared briefly to say good night and claim his wife; Lynn did not reappear. Very soon after the Charltons had gone the rest of the guests began to drift away. I waited until only the British were left, partly from a sense of duty and partly out of gratitude for having been introduced to Lynn. I didn't expect the Ambassador to let down his hair and comment on the events of the evening in front of me. I said my goodbyes and thank-yous and, not missing the trick, he told me to remember him to my father when I next wrote.

'I always do, sir,' I said untruthfully, and made my escape into the balmy Washington night.

I had promised to pick Lynn up 'about seven' but it was after eight when I arrived, angry and anxious, at the Charltons' house.

Normally I am a methodical, punctual person but this evening everything had gone wrong. First, when I had made the date with Lynn I had forgotten that the chap who was my immediate junior at the Embassy was giving a cocktail party. I couldn't stand him up so I was forced to arrive on the dot and leave as early as was decent. By then, however, I was running late.

Next, due to my own stupidity, I took a wrong turning and impatiently driving on, got lost. At last I stopped the Jaguar under a lamp-post to consult a map. I had found where I was and was thrusting the map back into the door pocket when there was a sharp rap on the window and I looked up into a black grinning face. There were two of them, both young, both negroes, both grinning widely. Maybe they had seen me looking at the map and wanted to help but I didn't think so. I didn't like the look of them. And this was Washington, a city with one of the highest crime rates in the world, where muggings were a commonplace. As I hesitated the taller youth tried the handle of the Jag but the door was locked; I had lived in Washington for over a year and had been well briefed. Automatically I slammed down my foot on the accelerator – I was taking no chances – and the car shot into safety.

But I was shaken, so shaken that when I reached Rock Creek Park, one of the élite and safer districts, I hesitated about getting out of the car to examine house numbers. Instead I drove at a crawl, peering among the trees, until finally I found the Charltons' imposing residence. This consumed yet more time. I was now very late and very unsure of my welcome.

A woman in a neat grey dress, whom I took to be the house-keeper, opened the front door and showed me into what appeared to be a library. I waited – for fifteen minutes.

'Hi, Derek!'

'Lynn! I'm most terribly sorry. But I had to have a drink with some people and then I lost my way and was nearly mugged and – '

'I wasn't expecting you to come at all.'

'Why not? You said you'd have dinner with me tonight.'

'That was before I made such a scene at your Ambassador's

party. I thought after that I'd be *persona non grata* to everybody from the British Embassy.'

'Of course not. We were all on your side,' I said, stretching the truth a little. 'And anyhow Her Majesty's Government doesn't choose my friends.'

Lynn gave me her small, secretive smile. 'I'm sorry. If I'd known you were going to come I would have called you. You see, I forgot. I already had a date.'

I could scarcely blame her. I had done the same thing myself. But I was horribly disappointed. For the first time I took in what she was wearing. Purple slacks, some sort of crocheted top, and a shawl to match the slacks. She hadn't dressed like that for me. And she had a bag slung over one shoulder. She was ready to go out. I tried to return her smile but I had rarely felt so miserable.

Lynn took pity on me. 'I'm going to a meeting of "Double PF" – People for Peace and Freedom. It's a sort of committee affair but there'll be food and wine. You're welcome to come if you'd like to, Derek.'

'Thank you, but – '

I had just said that HMG didn't choose my friends. I had failed to say that it did choose my enemies. And if protest groups in the country in which one was *en poste* were not actually enemies, they were most definitely untouchables. No involvement in politics was a rule which applied even more stringently abroad than at home.

I felt that I had hesitated too long. Lynn was looking at me enquiringly, expecting an answer. 'But won't they mind if you bring along a stranger?' I said.

'Oh, it's very informal and anyway you're not a stranger. You're my friend.'

Two minutes later we were on our way.

Lynn had insisted on taking her own car because we were going out of the District of Columbia, and, as she said, it was easier to drive than to direct me. She drove fast but well. I was just beginning to relax and enjoy myself when she surprised me by saying we had to pick up somebody called Virginia. I cursed silently. The evening was not living up to my expectations.

'Who's Virginia?' I asked.

'Virginia Urse. She's my closest friend and one of the most wonderful people. I don't know what I would do without her.'

'I'm impressed. Miss Urse must be something special. Is she at the university with you?'

'Oh no! She's much older than I am. At least thirty. (I winced.) And she's Mrs Urse. She's married. Or rather she was. Her husband was one of the first Americans to get killed in Vietnam.'

'I see. And she's a member of Double PF?'

'Yes. That's where I met her. I was nearly out of my mind at the time. Lloyd, my brother, had been reported missing. He was a helicopter pilot and all we knew was that his chopper had crashed. I was making myself sick worrying about him, wondering if he was dead or crawling around the jungle someplace, wounded maybe, or being tortured in some village. And then the relief to know he was a POW in Hanoi. I shall always be grateful to Virginia for – for – ' suddenly her vehement gratitude trailed away and she ended the sentence with a weak – 'for showing me how I could work for peace.'

There was a short uneasy silence between us as Lynn swung the car into the circular drive of the apartment block where Virginia Urse lived. Virginia herself was waiting for us in the front hall.

She was a tall, dark woman with light-coloured eyes. My first impression was that she was what the Victorians would have called 'a fine figure of a woman' but I was soon to discover this was an illusion. She wasn't really handsome. Her bone structure was bad and she lacked elegance. But there was something about her, a self-assurance, a strength of character, a purposefulness that dimmed even Lynn's beauty. I disliked her on sight.

What was more I felt she had sensed this and therefore was going out of her way to be pleasant to me. For instance she insisted on sitting in the back of the car so that I could be beside Lynn. But she leaned over Lynn's seat, breathing down her neck, and I had to twist myself around to answer her. Lynn, concentrated on driving, took almost no part in the conversation.

'I'm glad you came, Derek. Lynn was afraid that after last night's contretemps . . .'

'My sympathies were all with Lynn.'

'And why not? You British had the sense to keep out of this bloody war.'

'Yes.'

'Was your father part of that decision-making?'

'I wouldn't know.'

What I did know was that although it was only about twenty-four hours since I had met Lynn, Mrs Urse was already well-briefed on me and the Almourn family. I resented this. And I resented how, as she went on to talk to me about the Vietnam war and the matrons at the Ambassador's dinner-party, she made us chums in defence of Lynn.

I blamed her too for spoiling my evening when, in fact, the evening was pretty tattered before she joined us. Nor was I grateful for the difference her clout made to my reception when finally we arrived at a white clapboard house where the meeting was being held. As it was, the People for Peace and Freedom didn't exactly greet me with open arms. I suppose they had a right to be suspicious. After all I was a stranger, a foreigner and the one chap in the big, rather bare room wearing a suit and a tie. Because of Virginia, however, they were prepared to tolerate if not to welcome me.

A white-haired man, old enough to be my father, brought me a cushion – there was a shortage of chairs – and a rather pretty girl produced a glass of red wine. I sat on the floor beside Lynn. Proceedings were about to begin.

Virginia read the minutes of the last meeting. The white-haired man, whom people called the Professor, made a short speech in which he said that the war in South East Asia was no nearer an end, that negotiations in Paris were achieving nothing, and that more pressure must be put on President Nixon to declare, if necessary, a unilateral peace, the only condition being that all American POWs must be released. Action was what was needed, he maintained, to force the President's hand, but what action? He asked for suggestions.

If I expected something startling at this point I was disappointed. Nobody suggested kidnapping Dr Kissinger or planting a bomb on the White House lawn. It was all very dull, very predictable, very boring – and very harmless; it reminded me of the occasional political meeting I had attended when I was up at Oxford. I finished my second glass of nasty red wine – I was yearning for something to eat – and shifted my position on the cushion so that Lynn could lean more comfortably against my shoulder and it was a casual gesture to put my arm around her. There were compensations.

Nevertheless, I was glad when the meeting ended. I stood up and pulled Lynn to her feet. For a moment we were isolated. Virginia and the Professor seemed to have disappeared and the rest of them – a baker's dozen or so – were milling around, still arguing. Nobody was interested in us.

'Lynn, I have to go to a reception for some NATO characters tomorrow night. I can't get out of it. But would you have dinner with me on Friday?'

'I can't, Derek. Sorry. I'm going away on Friday.'

'Going away?'

She laughed. 'To Rehoboth – on the Delaware coast. We have a summer house there. Mum and I are going to open it up for the season.'

'How long will you be away?'

'Till Monday. I have to be back then. I've got classes most of the day.'

'And in the evening? Will you have dinner with me? Please!'

'Okay. I should like that.'

'Thank you, Lynn.'

'You're welcome, Derek.'

Virginia had reappeared. She stood in the doorway and clapped her hands. Supper was ready. Would we all come and please bring our glasses. I followed Lynn. It was going to be a long weekend.

On Monday evening I took Lynn to the best French restaurant in Washington. The food was superb, the wine excellent, the bill astronomic and Lynn looked more desirable than ever. I was very happy.

After dinner we drove along beside the Potomac. The moon shone on the water and the cherry blossoms and us. I asked Lynn to marry me. And she refused. To be kind to me she said that she wouldn't even think of marriage until Lloyd, her brother, was safely back from Vietnam.

That was in May.

Chapter Two

In July, Lynn and I became engaged.

It happened one Friday evening after I had driven down from Washington to spend the weekend with the Charltons at their summer place in Rehoboth. Lynn was alone in the house; her parents had gone to have drinks with some neighbours. And I knew as soon as she came out to the car that she was in a happy mood.

'Hi, Derek.' She kissed me warmly.

'Hullo, Lynn.'

'You're earlier than I expected. That's great.'

'I trusted to my CD plates and broke all speed limits to get to you.'

'You must have been lucky! The police have been cracking down on speeding diplomats lately. They mayn't be able to fine you, but they sure hold you up and give you horrid warnings.'

'They must have known I was on my way to you.' I teased her. 'Here! Some chocolates for you and some diplomatic scotch for your parents.' I gave her the parcels and picked up my suitcase.

'Oh, thanks, Derek. You know where your room is. Have a wash-up and change if you like. I'll be on the porch with some beer.'

'Okay. I won't be long.'

The temperature had been over ninety when I left Washington and the humidity unbelievably high. But on the Delaware coast, with a light breeze off the Atlantic, it was fifteen degrees cooler. By the time I had had a quick shower and changed into slacks and a cotton shirt I felt wonderful. I went to find Lynn.

It was two months since I had asked her to marry me and she had refused. Since then I had spent every available minute with her – every minute that she and that damned woman, Virginia

27

Urse, and People for Peace and Freedom would spare her. It was obvious what I felt about her. On the other hand I hadn't tried to force her, and I hadn't repeated my proposal. For the moment at any rate I was prepared to respect her decision to wait until her brother was safely home. Now, on this lovely evening as we lay side by side on the chaises longues, sipping our beer and listening to the quiet summer sounds of the garden, I felt wonderfully content.

'Derek.' Lynn said suddenly. 'I want to talk to you – seriously.'

'Good,' I said, totally unaware of what was coming.

'Don't sound so – so bored. It's important!'

'Sorry.'

'Derek, if you still – still want to marry me and I – I think you do, I want to too.'

'What?'

But she didn't need to repeat it.

Some while later when I was dimly getting used to the idea that Lynn had actually promised to marry me it occurred to me to ask her what had made her change her mind.

'Lloyd,' she said, to my surprise. 'I haven't told you yet, have I? It's fabulous! We've had another letter from him. They're not really letters. Messages. Dad says they're rather like the Red Cross messages people used to get in World War II. It didn't say much, except that he was well and conditions weren't too bad and he sent us all his love. Then there was a sort of PS.''Tell Lynn to be happy.'' And that decided me. After all, Virginia has been getting at me for ages. She thought that if I wanted you I should grab you while I could. So – I proposed.'

'And I accepted.'

I kissed her. I didn't exactly like the idea of owing my happiness to Lloyd's intervention, still less to Virginia Urse's championship, but it would have been churlish to carp. Lloyd was my brother-in-law-to-be and Virginia – well, temporarily I should have to put up with Virginia, but Lynn and I wouldn't be living in Washington for ever. As for Senator and Mrs Charlton, I liked them both and they couldn't have been nicer to me.

The Senator immediately insisted that I telephone my own

28

family about the engagement and, forgetting in my excitement the time differential between the US and the UK, I proceeded to arouse my sleeping parents. However, they too rallied to the occasion and duly gave us their blessing. So the evening ended in a welter of mutual congratulations and I told myself I was a lucky man.

Altogether it was a splendid weekend. Lynn said she would write it up in red ink in her diary and that was the way I felt too.

On Monday morning, later than I should have been, I drove back to Washington. I breezed through the Embassy and up to my office where I came to a full stop. The Minister was sitting with his feet on my desk.

'Morning, Derek.'

'Good morning, sir.'

'There is, in fact, little good about it. You've not yet read the telegrams, I assume?'

'I've just – '

'Quite. And you didn't by any chance speak to your father over the weekend?'

'As a matter of fact I did. On Friday night – the small hours of Saturday in London.' I smiled widely as I remembered the circumstances.

'He wouldn't have known then,' the Minister said at once. 'The PM was out of the country. He didn't get back until Saturday evening, their time. And on Sunday morning John Day-Brune was arrested – for treason.'

'John Day-Brune? For treason?'

My mind was still full of Lynn and sun and sea and sand. The brutality of the Minister's words shocked me without penetrating. I couldn't absorb them at once. If he had admitted to being a traitor himself I shouldn't have been more overwhelmed. I forced myself to take in what he had said.

But John Day-Brune?

John Day-Brune was a multitude of things. He was an expert on international affairs and as such was an adviser to the Cabinet. He wrote books and lectured and very occasionally appeared on television. He attended international meetings at the highest level and both at home and abroad his pronouncements on foreign relations were treated with respect. He knew everybody and must have been a repository of secrets. He was a traitor.

'There's no doubt?'

'None. There has been a NATO leak for some while. Our Intelligence people set a trap and it caught Day-Brune. No possibility of doubt. They were very careful.'

Of course they would have been careful. Day-Brune was a public figure, a member of the Establishment. He had the right sort of background and the right sort of friends. Photographs of him chatting up the Queen Mum in the paddock at Newmarket, or with some foreign princeling at the Eton and Harrow match, or in the Royal Box – as likely Covent Garden as Ascot or Wimbledon – appeared in all the glossies. He lunched in the best clubs and dined in the best houses. He had private means, in addition to his not inconsiderable salary. He had, as far as I knew, no chip on his shoulder.

'Why?'

'That is an esoteric question,' the Minister said bitterly. 'The Americans want to know what he has done and how much he knows. I've already had enquiries from the White House, State and CIA, not to mention the *Washington Post* and the *New York Times et al.* Which accounts for the fact that I've taken refuge in your office.'

I didn't need to ask him why my office. I knew the answer to that. Junior as I was, I was probably the only member of the Embassy staff, other than himself, who had a personal knowledge of Day-Brune. Indeed the last time I had met Day-Brune he and the Minister had been my father's guests at dinner.

'Did you know him well?' I spoke without thinking.

'We were at prep school together. At the age of eight I thought he was the greatest thing on two legs there had ever been. It's strange how such things colour the future. Over the years I may have tempered my opinion but I never had reason to reverse it, until now. Somehow the personal betrayal is far more shocking than the actual treason.'

30

'Yes!'

'Your father would understand.'

'Yes,' I repeated. 'I'm sorry.'

'Let's hope you never do.'

He pushed himself to his feet as the telephone rang. 'I've called a meeting for eleven in my office. I want everybody remotely connected with the NATO desk.'

'Yes, sir.' The telephone rang again and I picked up the receiver. The Minister had left the room. 'Hullo!'

'Derek?'

'Speaking.' I sat down; the chair was warm from the Minister's bottom.

'Oh honey, you'll never guess what has happened. The greatest thing! Just after you went this morning a friend of Dad's, who's somebody important in NBC, called to say they've got some film.' Lynn was almost inarticulate with excitement. 'It's an official release from Hanoi but it was taken by American cameramen. The North Vietnamese invited an American reporter and his crew to tape some interviews and things in a POW camp. And this friend at NBC says that Lloyd's in one of them. Oh Derek! You can imagine. We've blown our minds. They're showing a special half-hour programme on TV tonight at eight, so come early and – '

'I'm not sure I'll be able to, Lynn.'

'Why not? This is important, Derek! More important than some old cocktail party. We'll be able to see Lloyd and hear him speak maybe.'

Oh God! I turned a metaphorical cartwheel. I had been thinking about Day-Brune and working late at the office – there was bound to be a heap of extra work – not about cocktail parties. Now Lynn had reminded me. There were NATO meetings scheduled for tomorrow and, as a preliminary, Canada was giving a reception in honour of the delegates from the Northern Flank countries. We, the British, would be expected to attend in force in order to give the impression that, although it was unfortunate and deplorable, this business of Day-Brune was not a major disaster. That no one would believe us was irrelevant. To show the flag on such occasions was part of the game; and the game was played for real.

'Derek! Derek, are you still there?'

'Yes.' I sighed. 'Darling, I'll do my very best. I promise.'

'Okay, honey. It's eight o'clock, remember. 'Bye.'

In the event I made it, thanks to our Minister's wife. Catching me looking surreptitiously at my watch as the party ground down the evening she asked after Lynn and I told her not only about our engagement but also about Lloyd Charlton's television appearance. Immediately she grasped the point.

After congratulating me she said, 'My dear boy, of course you want to be with the Charltons at this time but to duck away tonight just isn't on, is it? Unless – ' She gripped my wrist. 'Derek, could you bear it for once? You know. Lord Almourn's son, a First Secretary at our Embassy, engaged to Senator Charlton's girl and his son a POW in Vietnam, on the telly – the TV I mean – any minute now. You know the sort of thing? It'll be a wonderful conversation piece. So safe! Everybody'll bless you. It'll distract them from all the rattling skeletons. What about it?'

'It makes me cringe,' I said truthfully, 'but if you think it'll help, by all means go ahead. The things I do for my country!'

'Rubbish!' she said. 'It's Lynn you're doing it for. Give me five minutes and you'll be on your way to her.'

It was nearer fifteen than five but otherwise she was right. The Canadian Ambassador saw me to the door himself and shook hands again. Behind him the noise swelled comfortingly as the NATO representatives, thrusting Day-Brune to the back of their minds, got down to enjoying the party. Our Minister must have been relieved; thanks to his wife's cleverness the British had pulled a fast one. And I was free.

Rejoicing in this minor victory, I extricated my Jaguar – luckily the Canadian residence is also in Rock Creek Park – and in no time was swinging into the drive of the Charltons' house. As I did I narrowly missed hitting one of those plain vans that, according to the ads, deliver anything, at any time, anywhere in the District of Columbia. I swore. The front door was just shutting. I leaned on the horn, the door re-opened and, still carrying the parcel that the van had delivered, the housekeeper came out on to the steps.

'Good evening, Mr Almourn. Hurry, please. It's almost eight.'

'Evening, Mrs Baldwin. Here, let me take that for you. It looks heavy.'

'Thank you. It's for Miss Lynn. The family's in the TV room, waiting.'

The grandfather clock began to take deep, asthmatic breaths prior to striking the hour and Mrs Baldwin trotted across the hall ahead of me. She needn't have bothered. The programme hadn't begun yet. Nevertheless, the Charltons were already watching the television screen and appeared absorbed in the commercials. Mrs Charlton managed to give me a smile and the Senator gestured to me to help myself to a drink but Lynn ignored me. I put the parcel down on a table, poured myself a whisky and sat myself next to her on the sofa. I kissed her and absently she returned my kiss. I could feel her tension. I prayed that Lloyd Charlton would appear looking strong and healthy and reassuring. I rather wished myself somewhere else.

The commercials ended. A famous news commentator, all world-renowned phlegm and capped teeth, explained in what circumstances the film had been taped and how it was authenticated. He warned us not to expect too much.

Then suddenly we were in the prison camp. We saw a dirt compound, surrounded by huts. About half-a-dozen prisoners were taking exercise. They marched around and around in a circle. They did not speak or have any contact with each other. There were more guards than prisoners. All the guards were young and, in spite of being armed, looked more vulnerable than the prisoners. Two of them smiled from a close-up; it would have taken a hard heart to hate either of them. The same two suddenly produced a ball and the prisoners, joined by a few others, kicked it about, apparently with enjoyment. At no time were the faces of the prisoners recognizable.

To me the whole thing stank of communist propaganda and reminded me unpleasantly of John Day-Brune.

Next we saw the inside of a hut, wooden bunks, wooden table, wooden chairs, one prisoner reading what could have been a letter. There were no spare garments lying around, no pin-ups on the walls, no tin mugs or packs of cards. As a result the hut looked un-

33

inhabited and unreal. It occurred to me that if they were going to dress a set for a prison camp scene the North Vietnamese could have learned a lot from watching the *Colditz* series on the telly.

With a whirring noise the film ran down. The commentator reappeared and told us not to go away; more was to come. I hoped it would be better than what had gone which had been pathetic and inevitably a bitter disappointment to the Charltons. They barely spoke or moved during the three minutes of the most inappropriate commercials, except for the Senator who, mumbling encouragement, got up to pour himself another bourbon and branch water, his favourite tipple.

The programme resumed. Once again the commentator fore-shadowed what we were about to see, an interview with four prisoners of war, one of whom surely had to be Lloyd. The tension in the room increased. As before, the commentator continued, the North Vietnamese had co-operated and seemingly had not brought any pressure to bear on the men. Nevertheless, we should all remember that the very fact they were POWs meant that they were not completely free to speak their minds.

'Oh, who cares?' Lynn said desperately. 'Why doesn't he get on with it. It's the film we want.' She was leaning forward, biting her lower lip, and willing her brother to appear.

At last the film started.

Four men sat on the far side of a wooden table. They were dressed in Mao jackets and, except for one whose head was bandaged, they appeared fit and well. They gave their names and ranks in turn. The youngest was Lieutenant Lloyd Charlton.

I didn't need to be told his name. I would have known him without that. Lynn's sharp indrawn breath as the camera focused on him was enough. Besides he was very like his photographs, which meant like his sister, the same bright-coloured hair, the same set of eyes and mouth. He gazed out of the screen at us, handsome, serious, self-contained.

The POWs agreed that they had not been badly treated. They were given adequate, if monotonous, food. They grinned, and said they dreamed of steaks and French fried. They had adequate amenities and adequate exercise. The captain pointed out that they were prisoners of war; they couldn't expect the camp to be the St Regis or the Ritz. The lieutenant with the bandaged head said there was a shortage of drugs but what there were were shared impartially between the Americans, who were after all the enemy, and the North Vietnamese casualties; he himself had been well cared for in hospital. The major, who was the senior officer, said that he regretted the American bombing of Hanoi not least because it would lengthen the war and what every POW wanted was for the war to end so that he could go home to his folks. The captain and the lieutenant nodded vigorously.

It was, alas, all propaganda for the communists, more subtle than in the other films, but propaganda nevertheless. Only Lloyd, who had volunteered nothing and let the others do most of the talking, seemed to dissociate himself from it.

'What about you, Lieutenant Charlton?' the interviewer said. 'Do you think we ought to stop the bombing?'

'That's up to the American people,' Lloyd said unexpectedly. 'They must do what's best for the United States and not worry too much about us. Our country must come first.' He spoke quietly, casually, throwing away the lines.

The next moment the interviewer was saying that the POWs would now say goodbye. The screen went blank and the commentator returned to wrap up the programme. But nobody wanted to watch him. Senator Charlton was switching off the television set. Lynn and her mother were crying and laughing and hugging each other. Mrs Baldwin, the housekeeper, was wiping her eyes. The Senator blew his nose loudly.

'Well, Derek,' he said to me, 'now you've seen my boy what do you think of your future brother-in-law?'

'You must be very proud of him, sir,' I said. 'In his position it must have taken a lot of cold courage to make that statement about leaving decisions on bombing to the American people. The communists can't have liked it much.'

'I know. I am proud. Very proud. And his country will be proud of him too, you'll see.' The Senator lowered his voice so that the women wouldn't hear. 'I only hope the commies didn't punish the boy for it afterwards.'

35

'I shouldn't imagine so,' I said. 'If they had really hated his remarks they wouldn't have let him make them.'

There was, unfortunately, another explanation, that the communists hadn't wiped Lloyd's statement because it demonstrated the POWs freedom to say what they liked and thus added authenticity to the rest of the programme. If this were so, they might well have made Lloyd pay later for his rashness. I could only hope such an explanation wouldn't occur to the Senator.

'I shouldn't worry too much, sir,' I said.

The Senator was staring at me. 'I don't follow,' he said. 'What do you mean – let him make them? Nobody *let* him do anything. Lloyd had the guts to say what he believed, what he thought the people at home should be told. None of this propaganda stuff. I don't understand why you should want to deprecate what he did, Derek.'

'I'm not,' I said hurriedly. 'I'm not, sir. But the film was cut and, if they had wanted to, the communists could have wiped what he had to say.'

He shrugged. 'So what? I don't know what you're suggesting.' He poured himself a slug of bourbon, added some drops of branch water and drank it down.

'I'm not really suggesting anything,' I said, wondering how we had suddenly got at cross-purposes.

'Then if you don't mind my saying so, Derek, you should think first before you make stupid comments.'

I did mind. But there was nothing to be gained by saying so, especially to Senator Charlton, especially on such an occasion as this, and especially as he had so confused me by now that I didn't know what we were arguing about.

Opportunely Mrs Charlton interrupted us and sent the Senator to fetch champagne. 'You'll find it already in the refrigerator, Ken,' she said. 'I put in a couple of bottles earlier. I was hoping we would want to celebrate. We'll have it in the garden, shall we? Supper in about a half-hour.' And when the Senator had gone obediently on his errand, she said to me, 'You mustn't mind Ken, Derek. You see he feels particularly strongly about Lloyd because our son need never have gone to the war. Lloyd had student status

– he was studying for his doctorate – he could have been deferred. Probably indefinitely. Other boys have been. But he was afraid people would say he had got out of the draft because his father was an influential senator and he wasn't having that. He was determined to go to Vietnam.'

'I didn't know that,' I said, interested. 'I sympathize with him.'

'I'm sure you do, Derek. But you must learn to sympathize with Ken, too. It has made it very hard for him.' She smiled to take the sting out of the reproof. 'Now let's go into the garden and drink to Lloyd, shall we?'

Lynn was on the telephone. 'Yes, Virginia,' she said. 'Yes, I know I'll have to pay for it some time. I gave my word ... Yes ... Yes. Of course it's worth it. But don't let's spoil this evening, please, Virginia.' She sounded a bit waspish. 'Okay, Virginia. 'Bye then. See you tomorrow.'

She put down the receiver and turned to us, frowning. The bloom of her happiness seemed to have faded. 'That was Virginia,' she said unnecessarily. 'She was watching the programme and she called to say how fabulous she thought Lloyd had been and how happy she was for us.'

'That was very kind of her,' Mrs Charlton said.

'Very,' I agreed without enthusiasm.

'If you owe her something, Lynn, you must pay her.'

Lynn ignored her mother. 'Virginia *is* kind, Derek.'

'I know, darling.'

'And it's so much worse for her. We know Lloyd's alive and well but her husband isn't ever going to come back.'

'I know, darling,' I said again. And to change the subject I pointed out the parcel on the table. 'Have you seen that, Lynn?'

'You brought me a gift?'

'I'm afraid not, darling.'

I explained how I and the parcel had arrived on the doorstep at the same time and Mrs Charlton told me to bring it along. Lynn could open it on the patio; if the packing made a mess, she said, it would be easier to sweep up.

The parcel was about two feet long by a foot wide. It was wrapped in thick brown paper with Lynn's name and address printed on it in capital letters and was adorned with several red and white labels saying FRAGILE. I carried it carefully. It was cumbersome to hold and quite heavy.

In the garden, which consisted of a large patio and a pocket-handkerchief of brown grass surrounded by flowering shrubs, I waited, clutching the parcel, while Lynn and her mother arranged the metal furniture to their satisfaction. It was very hot and humid. I was glad when the Senator arrived with the champagne and, having parked the parcel, I could sprawl in a chair – but not for long.

We were to have a little ceremony. We all stood. The Senator urged the cork from the bottle with a practised ease that I could envy and filled our glasses. We raised them to Lloyd.

'To our dear son.'

'To our dear son. God bless him.'

'To my dearest brother. May he come home very soon.'

'To Lloyd,' I mumbled, wishing I hadn't chosen this evening to be so out of tune with the Charltons.

We drank. It was an emotional moment, relieved by the house-keeper who came bustling out with the telephone; the evening was to be inundated with congratulations from friends who had seen the television programme. Mrs Charlton took the call. The Senator and I tried to relax; he appeared to have forgotten our earlier differences. Lynn decided to open her parcel.

'What's that you've got there, Lynn? A wedding gift?' the Senator asked.

'I don't know. I suppose it must be. I did call some of the kids when we got back from Rehoboth but that wasn't till noon. Whoever it's from must have reacted at speed.'

She had torn off the outer paper to reveal the distinctive wrapping of one of the posh shops on Connecticut Avenue. Attached to it was a small envelope, which she tossed into my lap.

'You open that, Derek. If this is a wedding gift it's for both of us.'

I extracted a card from the envelope. 'It's from somebody called Bruno,' I said. 'He has written: *To wish you every happiness, Lynn, and to remind you of me always. Bruno.* Who's Bruno?'

'Bruno?' Lynn repeated.

She didn't answer my question. She made a big thing of removing the final cover and lifting from its polystyrene bed our first wedding present. She held it out so that we could see it and presumably admire. Her hands shook a little, I noticed.

It was a porcelain figure of a brown bear standing around eighteen inches high on his hind legs. It looked and doubtless was an expensive *objet d'art*. I thought it hideous.

'It's a – a bear!' the Senator said, obviously sharing my opinion.

'Very appropriate coming from Bruno,' I said. 'It *will* remind you of him, darling.'

'Who is he, Lynn?' Mrs Charlton had finished her telephone conversation. 'Have we met him? I don't remember anybody called Bruno.'

'You don't know him.' Lynn spoke abruptly. She sounded very tense. 'I don't really know him myself. He's just a – a man connected with the Double PF.'

She turned her back in order to stand the figure on the table and I didn't see exactly what happened. I suppose that it could have been an accident. Her hand could have slipped. But I think that, though she denied it afterwards, she dropped the damned thing on purpose. At any rate, the bear bounced off the corner of the table and shattered on the patio.

'Oh dear!' Lynn said with what seemed to me complete insincerity. 'I am sorry! Derek, our first wedding gift.'

I grinned at her. 'Not to worry,' I said. 'I never liked Bruno much.'

She gave me a lop-sided grin in return. Then suddenly, kicking aside broken bits of bear, she leaned over my chair and kissed me on the mouth. 'I love you,' she said earnestly, 'very much. Don't ever forget that, Derek, please.'

And I promised that I wouldn't.

If it hadn't been for niggling thoughts of John Day-Brune I would have enjoyed the rest of the evening.

Chapter Three

I was very much in love with Lynn and we had survived a hectic engagement, a Washington wedding that had resembled nothing so much as an international convention and a honeymoon in South America – one of our many wedding presents that I most appreciated – without even a lovers' tiff. But just before Christmas, when we had been married about two months, we had a shattering row.

It was a Saturday morning. Nevertheless I had to go in to the office. As usual there was a pile of work waiting to be done. John Day-Brune, who had been sentenced to thirty years imprisonment for treason, was now languishing in his cell but the repercussions of his treachery continued to make themselves felt in an ever-widening circle of minutiae. As memorandum was followed by memorandum it often seemed that nothing would ever be quite secure again – and the harder we worked to stop the gaps.

Lynn complained at the amount of time I spent at the Chancery but she couldn't really complain of being lonely or bored. She had her family and her friends and there was still a lot to be done to the large apartment we had rented way up Massachusetts Avenue. In addition there were coffee parties for the new bride, luncheons for the new bride, teas for the new bride and, if she wanted a change of scene, there were always her People for Peace and Freedom.

It was the Double PF that was the cause of our present row.

'I don't care what you say.' Lynn was angry. 'I am going to march. If you were half-way decent you would be marching too. After all, Lloyd's your brother-in-law!' She was sitting up in bed watching me dress.

'I couldn't march even if he were my brother.' I looked around for my trousers; considering that Lynn was wearing the most transparent of nightgowns I don't know why I should have felt at such a disadvantage without them. 'Don't you understand that as a British diplomat I cannot take part in a political rally in a country to which I'm accredited – or in any other for that matter. And as my wife you can't either.'

'I can and I will! I'm an American! And it's not a political rally. It's a peace rally. Don't *you* understand, Derek? After all those talks in Paris and all Kissinger's secret missions and all Nixon's promises we're back where we started – bombing North Vietnam. The war's no nearer being over than when Lloyd was drafted.'

'Well, that's not the fault of the Americans.' I punched my tie-pin viciously through my tie and into my finger. I suppressed a yelp of pain. 'Why don't you blame the North Vietnamese and the Vietcong?'

'Because I can't do anything about them but I can do something about the Americans. And I'm going to. If the President sees enough of us marching on the White House he'll know he has got to stop this war. America's a democracy. People count here. And the people are for peace.'

I had heard this argument before. It hadn't convinced me then and it didn't convince me now but I let it go. Personally I didn't care a damn who marched on the White House, providing Lynn wasn't among them.

I buttoned my waistcoat, put on my jacket and sat myself on the edge of the bed. I had decided to try a different tack. Neither a plain request nor a direct order had achieved a thing.

'Now look, Lynn,' I said. 'If, as you hope, this turns out to be a huge, public demonstration there's bound to be some violence. You could get hurt.'

'And you would weep buckets of tears, wouldn't you, Derek? But not for me. For yourself! If you're so afraid for me how come you never objected to me taking part in that happening at the Lincoln Memorial last September? I can tell you why. It didn't matter if I got hurt there, did it? I wasn't married to Her Majesty's god-damned British Embassy then. I was just the daughter of a United States Senator who had a brother in a POW camp in Hanoi.'

'That's not fair,' I said.

Nor was it. I hadn't known about the happening until it was in the past tense and there was nothing I could do about it. Nevertheless, there was more than a grain of truth in what Lynn said. My main reason for not wanting her to go today was because of possible repercussions at the Embassy. The British Foreign and Commonwealth Office was not a great believer in Women's Lib. and if Lynn collected some undesirable publicity over this march it would be the same as if I myself had put up the black. She was my wife now, and as far as HMG was concerned I was responsible for her.

Lynn didn't see it that way. And she hadn't finished with me either. She went on to tell me what she thought of me. I was stuck-up and stuffy and I didn't like her friends. Look at the way I treated Virginia! And Lloyd! I didn't care about Lloyd, even though he was her brother. All I cared about was becoming a British Ambassador and what an ambition that was. Ambassador of a second-rate power! She laughed loudly.

'Shut up!' I said, startling her. By now I was angry too. 'Why the hell did you marry me if you had such a low opinion of me and my country?'

'Because I loved you and because − because. What does it matter why I married you? I did, didn't I?' Lynn sat up in bed and hugged her knees to her breasts. 'Get out!' she cried. 'Get out! I hate you, you and your striped pants!'

Involuntarily I looked down at my dark grey trousers. 'I'm not wearing striped pants,' I began − as if it mattered.

'You always wear striped pants! You never take them off. Even in bed you wear the god-damned things.'

That eminent Canadian diplomatist, the late Lester Pearson, worded it more admirably when he said that 'striped pants are not so much a state of apparel as a state of mind', but there was no doubt what Lynn meant. And if she had said it on purpose to hurt me she had succeeded.

I slammed out of the bedroom, collected my coat and my briefcase and saw, out of the corner of my eye, what I always thought of as 'Bruno's bear'. Oh yes, he was here with us, standing menacingly on a not too conspicuous shelf in a corner of our living-room. He was not, of course, the original animal which Lynn had smashed. This was his twin; a considerate Bruno, having somehow heard of her 'accident', had provided him for us. And Lynn had decided that after all she liked the bear and insisted he should be on show. Personally I hated the damn thing.

However, in spite of everything, I am not particularly proud of what I did next.

I put down my briefcase, picked up Bruno's bear by his hind legs as if he were a weapon and went back into the bedroom. Lynn was still sitting up in bed, hugging her knees; she hadn't moved since I left her. She looked small and pathetic. But I threw the bear at her with as much force as I could bring myself to use.

'Here!' I said. 'I'm sure you'd rather have Bruno in bed with you than me.'

Lynn screamed. But the bear, to my chagrin, bounced off the pillow on to the carpet. It wasn't even chipped. I stormed out of the room and out of the flat. I was shaking with some emotion, presumably anger. I felt as if I wanted to be sick – throw up, Lynn would have said.

By the time I reached my office in the Embassy, however, I was comparatively calm and, as the morning wore on, I began to reproach myself. I tried to see myself from Lynn's point of view. I was ten years older than she was; sometimes it was a positive generation gap. I was English and she thought of England as the British travel agencies choose to depict it, ancient, tradition-laden and of no importance except to tourists. Finally, I was a diplomat and so, by Lynn's definition, a stuffed shirt or a pair of striped pants. Yet she had married me. Why, was a mystery.

For the umpteenth time I put out my hand to the telephone and at last I dialled and let it ring, willing Lynn to answer. Nothing happened. I imagined the empty flat and wondered where Lynn might be. Reluctantly, but she was my best bet, I telephoned Virginia Urse. Virginia said that Lynn wasn't picking her up until one o'clock. I don't know if she was lying. Next I telephoned the Charltons and the housekeeper said that the Senator and Mrs Charlton were in New York for the weekend and she had not seen Miss Lynn that morning; I believed her.

I couldn't try all Lynn's friends. I packed up my things, locked the safe, returned a couple of files to Registry and left the Embassy. I hadn't managed to do much work.

And when I got back to the apartment, it didn't welcome me. It was too hot and too neat and tidy and too empty. I turned down the thermostat; Lynn had left it at seventy-five, her favourite indoor temperature in the winter. I changed into some comfortable clothes and, from force of habit, hung up my suit. Irritably I threw the *Washington Post* on the floor. Then I put on a record, collected some books and poured myself a glass of sherry. The place looked quite habitable.

I eyed Bruno's bear which once more menaced me from his shelf, but decided to take no action. About the emptiness I also did nothing because there was nothing I could do.

The afternoon stretched before me. I thought of ways of occupying it. I could watch the telly, sports highlights, a hockey game, old movies: no, thank you. I could listen to the radio. On Saturday afternoons I often listened to the opera broadcast from the New York Met. Today I couldn't face it.

So, I could read, play records, go to a movie – or back to the office. I could ring up a friend. I promptly thought of the Minister and wondered why. Perhaps I was stuffy and preferred the company of people older than myself. But what about Lynn herself and Virginia?

Suddenly I made up my mind. I couldn't take part in this great march but I could go and watch it.

There were the remains of a chicken in the refrigerator, bread, butter, cheese. With a tin of soup it made a good meal. I ate it from a tray in the living-room. The radio was tuned to a local station and between recorded music an announcer gave a running commentary on news and events. I listened idly, thinking of Lynn.

The marchers, he said, had assembled in the favourite place for protesters, by the Lincoln Memorial. There were fewer than had been forecast considering how bitter the American people were feeling. And who could blame them? It was clear by now that the Vietnam war would not be over and that the boys would not be home for Christmas as the President had hopefully opined in his

44

last State of the Union address. Instead the war had hotted up again and the bombing had been resumed. So maybe other groups would be joining in on the way or planned to meet at the White House – if the marchers ever got to the White House. It was rumoured that the police, reinforced by riot squads, would try to break up the marching column before it reached the Ellipse and, if this were true, there might be big trouble.

The announcer stopped to play a recording of the latest top of the pops and I went into the kitchen. While the coffee was dripping I rinsed the few bits of crockery I had used and stacked them on top of the dishwasher. By the time I went back into the living-room the music was over and the announcer was saying:

' – more shopping days till Christmas. And in downtown Washington the temperature is 32°. There's a biting wind from the north, the sky is overcast, and the weatherman says there'll be snow later in the afternoon. So, folks, if you're thinking of going on this Peace March or going to watch it, I suggest you all bundle up in nice warm clothing.'

I took his advice. I put on corduroy trousers, woollen jumper, jacket, padded car coat with a fur collar which protected my ears and face, and a cap. The taxi dropped me at the corner of 14th and Pennsylvania, which was not what I had intended. The other streets were blocked, and the police had thrown a cordon around a rectangle bounded by Pennsylvania and Constitution Avenues to north and south and by 15th and 17th Streets to east and west. The White House was in a state of siege. The President, incidentally, was far away in San Clemente, California.

My taxi-driver said: 'If I was you, bud, I'd go home. These marches ain't nothing but trouble.'

A cop, confronted by my English accent, said the same thing. I ignored them both.

I walked south as far as 15th and Constitution, where there were more police than ever and more sightseers. A couple of Black Marias and an ambulance were trying not to look conspicuous; I guessed that further reinforcements were being kept out of sight. Clearly this was to be the point of confrontation, the so far but no further for the marchers that the radio announcer had predicted.

It was not a good place to hang around in. The last thing I wanted was to get involved in even the smallest scuffle.

While I hesitated, huddling into the warmth of my coat, the odd snowflake began to flutter to the ground. The sky had darkened appreciably and the wind seemed more piercing. As if the snow were a signal the police suddenly lost their air of watchful indolence and came to attention. Something was about to happen.

First there was the sound of a band. Then, in the distance, the head of the marching column appeared. I began to make my way towards it, keeping to the back of the pavement where there was no obstruction from police or pedestrians and I could move quickly. When I drew level with the leading drum major I pushed myself to the front of the sightseers where I proposed to wait until the Peace March had gone by. I had no other intention than to catch a glimpse of Lynn.

This wasn't an impossible ambition. The marchers were proceeding in a pretty orderly fashion, some twelve or so abreast, closely shepherded by police on motor-cycles. They were of all ages and some had small children. They were interspersed with bands which, oddly enough, played extremely martial music. Sometimes there were shouts of 'Peace! Peace! We want peace!' Sometimes they sang the favourite protest song, 'We shall overcome.' They represented a mixed collection of aspirations, to judge from the placards they carried, demanding everything from a united Ireland to freedom for all political prisoners everywhere. But the main demand was for an end to the war in Vietnam, no more bombing and the return of the POWs.

The People for Peace and Freedom carried a huge banner announcing who they were and what they wanted. Luckily for me they were not a very large or important contingent so it wasn't difficult to spot Lynn. She was marching on my side of the road and she was waving a flag. She wasn't the only one with a flag. Virginia was carrying the Stars and Stripes and there were a lot of other American flags scattered throughout the parade. What distinguished Lynn, however, was the fact that she was waving the Union Jack.

In ordinary circumstances I don't feel strongly about my

country's flag. I wasn't brought up to reverence it as are all American school-children, who pay daily homage to the Stars and Stripes. I associate it with British Embassies abroad and state occasions in the UK. I don't in the least mind seeing it on shopping bags in Oxford Street or on sweat shirts in the Champs Elysées. But when I saw Lynn Almourn carrying it on this march I minded like hell.

'Pardon me,' a nasal voice said and I was elbowed aside so that the owner of the voice could get a better view. His cine-camera whirred. By now Lynn was almost level with us and he was getting some excellent footage of her and the Union Jack. This was too much. My earlier anger against her flared up once more.

I thrust past the photographer and out into the road among the marchers. I had to push my way through a couple of ranks before I could reach Lynn. I stood in front of her. At close quarters she looked unhappy, pale and strained, but I didn't care. I seized the Union Jack from her, broke its stick across my knee and shoved the rest of the flag into one of my pockets.

'Damn you!' I said. 'Damn you!'

Lynn had stopped dead when I confronted her. Automatically Virginia stopped too. And the marching line behind broke around us. I'm not sure what happened next except that order became disorder. There was some shouting, blows were exchanged, the police weighed in, a few of the marchers sat down and refused to move, an onlooker began throwing stones – the Americans make it sound worse by calling them rocks – and a minor riot began.

Why I am so vague about it is that almost immediately somebody kicked me behind the knees and I fell down. Everything took place above me while I grovelled on the road among a collection of boots, most of them trying to do me damage. That they didn't have better success was due solely to the protective padding of my clothes. I am not an unathletic type. I ride well, play a fair game of golf and tennis and am an adequate swimmer; but rugger has never been my line. I managed to clamber to my feet only when the bodies over my head thinned.

And at the precise moment that I staggered upwards a stone –

this time it really must have been a rock – whistled through the air and struck me on the temple.

I came to in what was an ambulance though I didn't take in that fact at first. Two faces floated above me, one white, one black.

'He's comin' round,' the white face said. 'Better cuff him.'

'No need to cuff him,' the black face said. 'He ain't goin' nowhere.' I tried to sit up and he pushed me back gently. 'Lie still, man. You'll be okay.'

'I'm goin' to cuff him,' the white face said again.

There was a clink of metal. Somebody was pulling my arms sideways, sliding something cold over my wrists and I could no longer move my arms except fractionally. I realized that I had been handcuffed to the stretcher on which I was lying. It was most uncomfortable. I forced my eyes to open.

'British Embassy,' I said. 'Telephone. My name's Almourn.'

'Okay, man. Later. Right now you're goin' to the hospital.'

'British Embassy. Diplomat,' I persisted.

Or thought I persisted. I doubt if my words were emerging. My eyelids drooped and I was sliding. I wanted to be sick. I was going to be sick. Somebody thrust a tin bowl under my chin and supported my head. I vomited.

'He's just throwing up,' a voice said.

It was different from the voices of white face and black face. This was a loud, cheerful, female voice. And the scene was different. I was no longer in an ambulance but in the ward of a hospital. I could hear coughs and groans and shuffling and somebody else 'throwing up'. I couldn't see anybody because of the screen around my bed. There was a strong smell of antiseptic mingled with body odours. Somebody began to scream. It was a steady, high, ghastly sound – it stopped, at the very moment I could bear it no longer.

I lay back among the grey blankets – there were no sheets or pillowcases on the bed – and the plastic covering of the mattress crackled. I was feeling considerably better. I could see my coat and cap on the chair beside me and I was still wearing my other clothes, a fact which cheered me enormously. What is more, after a tentative exploration of my anatomy, I discovered that, apart

48

from a splitting headache and a stiff, sore side to my face, there was nothing much wrong with me.

The nurse poked her head around the screen. 'Hi!' she said. 'The fuzz have gone.'

'What?'

'The fuzz – the cops, the police! They brought you to the hospital. But you kept on muttering about being some British diplomat so they went through your pockets and they sure must have found your credentials because they called your Embassy and then they beat it.'

'I see.'

It was all coming back to me now, the march, People for Peace and Freedom, Lynn, the Union Jack and – I didn't actually remember the fuzz except as two floating faces. Lynn! Where was Lynn? By now she might well be in gaol. I half suppressed a groan.

'You got nothing to worry about. Your friends from the Embassy are on their way and Doc says you can discharge yourself as soon as they get here.'

'Thank you.'

She came around the corner of the screen and looked at me curiously. 'Say, are you really a diplomat?'

'Yes, I am.'

'Well, isn't that something! I've been four years in Washington and I've never met a diplomat before, leastways not to know. A British diplomat!' She shook her head in amazement.

I made an effort to smile at her. I wished I could share her enthusiasm for my status. It seemed to me not impossible that it might soon be my ex-status. Christ! If only I knew what had happened to Lynn.

The nurse disappeared and, after a long ten minutes, I heard another voice. I sighed with relief. I was about to be rescued, and by a friend as well as a colleague.

'Thank you very much, Doctor. Thank you very much. And thank you too, Nurse. But I don't see him. Where have you put him?' The screen around my bed toppled towards me. 'So sorry. Ah, Derek, there you are then.'

'Hullo, Dickie,' I said weakly. 'I'm very pleased to see you.'

'I'm sure you are, dear boy.' He looked at my immediate surroundings and wrinkled his nose. 'Not the sort of setting in which
one expects to find the Hon. Derek, is it?'

'Then take me out of it, for God's sake.'

'Yours to command, dear boy. I'm grateful to you for relieving
the tedium of a weekend on duty.'

He found my shoes, helped me on with my coat and put my cap
gently on my head. It hurt. I stood, swaying a little and searching
in my pockets for gloves. I pulled out one glove and dropped the
other and what looked like a dirty rag wound on a stick. Dickie
picked them up. The dirty rag was what had once been a Union
Jack. Dickie regarded it with feigned awe before pushing it back
in my pocket.

'Let's go,' he said. 'I'm filled with curiosity. You're going to
have to tell uncle all.'

And on the way home I told him all – well, almost all – and he
promised to say nothing about the damned flag. I wanted to keep
Lynn out of it as much as possible.

She wasn't in the apartment when we got back and there was no
answer to Virginia's phone. I couldn't think of anything else to do
about her. And Dickie, in spite of my protests, insisted on stuffing
me with pain-killer and putting me to bed. He promised to wait
until Lynn returned or we had some news of her and I had to be
content with that. I lay in bed, feeling unutterably miserable and
hoping he wouldn't still be there in the morning. Eventually I
went to sleep.

I must have slept for four or five hours. It was after nine when I
woke and Dickie had gone. Lynn was home. I could hear her – and
Virginia – in the living-room. She had left the bedroom door open
and I would have called to her at once if it hadn't been for Virginia.
As it was I lay, enjoying the comfort of my own bed which smelt
faintly of Lynn's favourite scent, and listened to them talking.
Perhaps I dozed.

'. . . Derek's own fault, Lynn. You mustn't blame yourself – or
Bruno.'

'But I do. I know I would have marched anyway. Derek had no

right to stop me. But I oughtn't to have carried his flag. Why did Bruno insist? I don't understand why . . .'

Bruno? Bruno, the bear. Lynn said she would have marched anyway but he had made her carry the Union Jack. No, I must be wrong. I must have misheard. Their voices weren't loud and I hadn't been listening very carefully. Now I propped myself up on my elbow and tried to eavesdrop but they had lowered their voices again. And I couldn't concentrate. The pain-killer had made me dopey. I caught only snatches of conversation.

'. . . I warned you but you said it was worth it. Lynn, it's too late to regret – '

'I don't, Virginia. I love Lloyd and I'd do anything for him . . . Surely I've proved . . . Bruno must understand . . . I love Lloyd . . . Derek . . . Bruno . . .'

The three names went round and round, my eyes shut, my head fell back upon the pillow. My head hurt. I slept and dreamed, horrid dreams in which Lynn and Virginia and Lloyd were all muddled up and everybody was menaced by a great brown bear called Bruno. The next day I couldn't remember what had been dream and what had been for real.

Lynn swore that it was all dream and that she and Virginia had never had any sort of conversation about Bruno. She was very contrite about the march and very concerned for me and I wanted to believe her. In the end I said I did but it wasn't really true. I knew she was lying.

Chapter Four

'Peace with honour' was what President Nixon called it.

Other people called it other things. At any rate the beginning of 1973 saw the United States withdraw the last of her troops from Vietnam. And the prisoners of war, including Lieutenant Lloyd Charlton, came safely back. There was very little public celebration – no great victory had been won – but a lot of private rejoicing as husbands and fathers and sons and lovers were welcomed home.

Senator and Mrs Charlton had planned a succession of parties to celebrate Lloyd's return to Washington. They and Lynn had flown out to the Philippines to meet him but that had been something very personal. Now they wanted, as they said, to reintroduce him to his old friends – and introduce him to some new ones, including me. They expected it to be a time of unadulterated happiness.

The week began with a small dinner party. There were ten of us around the table. Apart from the immediate family the ten included Lloyd's aunt (Mrs Charlton's sister) and her husband, who was a doctor, Lloyd's godmother and her husband who was another Senator, Virginia Urse and myself. This was the first time I had met Lloyd.

He was, of course, the centre of attention at dinner and dominated the conversation. But he did his best to include everybody and refused to take either himself or his experiences too seriously. Nor would he be or let anybody else be over-emotional. I was beginning to like him.

'I never want to leave the old USA again,' he said lightly. 'When we landed at Clark Field and I came down those steps I could have kissed the ground.'

'You looked wonderful,' Lynn said, radiating happiness, 'and very calm.'

'I didn't feel it. You know, Derek –' Lloyd leaned forward so

52

that he could speak to me across Virginia – 'I can't understand you diplomats. You choose to spend most of your lives outside your own country. I could never do that.'

'If I hadn't been posted to Washington,' I said, 'I should never have met your sister. There are prizes to be won.'

'So it seems.' Lloyd laughed. 'Well, I hope you're not planning to take her away from me immediately.'

I shook my head. 'We should be in Washington for another couple of years.'

'And after that?' He seemed really interested. 'Another foreign posting?'

'Probably.'

'Any idea where?'

'No. None.'

I thought he was going to press the point but he didn't. Somebody asked him what he himself intended to do and he said that he expected to go back to school, finish his doctorate and, eventually, follow in his father's political footsteps. There was room in high places, he said, for those who had seen communism in action. Then, in case he had been too pompous, he touched the scar which ran down his right cheek and added with a grin:

'Alas, since I've lost my beauty I've had to give up my long-cherished ambition to become a film star.'

There was a murmur of sympathy and some laughter. Lloyd's doctor uncle said he had heard that acting ability came in very useful in politics. Nobody asked Lloyd how he had acquired the scar. We all knew. And indeed, in a day or two, the whole of America was to know since Lloyd was himself to discuss the incident in a television interview and the media were to make something of a minor hero of him.

The scar was a result of what he had said and tried to say to the American people last July from his POW camp in Hanoi. As the Senator had feared, there had been repercussions. Lloyd had been badly beaten up, thrown back into solitary confinement and given no food at all for eight days. Apart from the scar, however, he showed no signs of the treatment he had received; he looked very well and fit. And, for that matter, the scar had made a handsome,

53

rather expressionless face far more interesting. I didn't believe the experience had damaged him, mentally or physically.

Because I was so sure of this, when we were having coffee, I mentioned the tapes he and the other POWs had made. I said that most of what we had been allowed to see had stunk of communist propaganda and that I had been not only surprised but very impressed when he had spoken out.

'Thanks, Derek. Good of you to say so. A lot of others have said the same. But I expect the majority took those films at their face value.'

'Oh no,' I said, 'surely not. They were too incredibly bad. They might as well have been labelled 'propaganda'. Nobody can have been expected to take them seriously.'

Scar or no scar, a shutter seemed to come down over Lloyd's face. For an appreciable moment he didn't answer. I didn't know whether to apologize or to talk hurriedly about something else.

Then he said: 'You're very observant, Derek, but you don't know the communists as I do. They don't play games, I can assure you.'

It was not a friendly remark and he hadn't meant it to be. I could feel his sudden hostility though I couldn't understand it. I had to assume that inadvertently I had touched a nerve and, God knows, after four and a bit years in a POW camp in Hanoi my brother-in-law was entitled to some nerves. Nevertheless, I was glad for once when Virginia joined us – though not for long.

'Are you talking about your POW camp, Lloyd? You know, I've always thought that one of the worst things about being incommunicado for ages as you were is catching up on what has happened in the interval.'

'Yes.'

'At least your friends can help you there. Derek, you should tell Lloyd about John Day-Brune.'

'John Day-Brune? Who's he?'

'A traitor – or so the British say. It was one of last year's great scandals. Day-Brune's an Englishman – friend of your father's

54

wasn't he, Derek? – but there were all sorts of international ramifications.'

Virginia smiled at me maliciously and I hesitated. Lloyd was looking politely interested. His tension had eased. And I didn't want to make myself unpleasant. I excused myself, saying that Day-Brune was someone whom I preferred to forget and that I really had to go and speak to Lynn. I was conscious as I left them that they both watched me walk across the room – unless, of course, I imagined their eyes on my back. I felt as if I were being watched.

Virginia was to annoy me again in the course of the evening. Having decided it was high time to go home I went to look for Lynn who seemed to have disappeared for the moment. Tomorrow was going to be a bad day for me; I had meetings from eleven onwards and a speech to write for the Minister. I didn't want to be too late getting to bed.

There were voices coming from the TV room, Lynn's and Virginia's. The door was open and it didn't occur to me that they might be having a private conversation or that they could be so absorbed in it as not to notice me when I walked into the room. In all innocence I stood and listened.

'But why not, Lynn? He's intelligent, hard-working, attractive, sensible, everything your father could ask for.'

'My father's not asking for anything.'

'No, but a Senator can always make room for the right sort of ambitious young man in his office, can't he?'

'The right sort of young man?'

'Yes. Surely in the circumstances it's not too much –'

'Virginia, my father's a United States Senator. He holds a position of trust and you want me to introduce to him a – a –'

'Why, Derek! Hullo!' Virginia interrupted her.

'Hullo, Virginia,' I said. 'Lynn. We ought to be going, darling.'

'Yes, okay, Derek.' Lynn gave me a small, tight smile. 'Virginia. I'm sorry.'

'I'll call you tomorrow first thing. It'll give you time to think it over.'

'I don't need to think it over.'

55

'Lynn, please. You could regret it, sweetie.'

'No, Virginia. I'm sorry but the answer's "no". I've made up my mind. Good night.'

In the car, on the way back to our apartment, I asked Lynn what it was all about and I wouldn't be put off with it being 'nothing important'. Virginia had been trying to force Lynn to do something she didn't want to do and to me that was important. I always resented Virginia's influence. I blamed her, perhaps unfairly, for the disastrous consequences of that Peace March last Christmas. And I was not going to let her involve Lynn in some other dubious project. Lloyd was safely home now and Lynn must have paid any imagined debt she thought she owed to the People for Peace and Freedom. The sooner she severed all connections with them the better I would be pleased; it was too much to hope that she would do the same with Virginia.

'Who is this peacenik anyway?'

'What peacenik?'

'Lynn, this chap Virginia wants you to introduce to your father. Isn't he one of your People for Peace and Freedom?'

'No. He's nothing to do with them. Not as far as I know. He's a – a cousin of Virginia's. He – he comes from the Middle West. He wants to go into politics and he hasn't any influence. If he could get into Dad's office it would be a big help to him.'

'But you don't like him?'

'I've never met him.'

'Then why –' I swallowed my exasperation. 'Darling, let me get this straight. Virginia, to whom you're always vowing gratitude for helping you over the bad bit when Lloyd was missing, has asked you as a special favour to introduce her cousin to your father and you've refused. Is that right?'

'Yes.'

'It doesn't seem to me very much to ask. Half an hour of your father's time. If he doesn't like the chap –'

'Virginia thinks if I persuaded Dad he would take him on. And I won't do it.'

I flicked the car lights at a maniac in the on-coming lane who was trying to blind me. I was tired and I didn't want to argue with

Lynn. Besides it was absurd that I should find myself on Virginia's side against Lynn. I didn't care a damn about Virginia or her politically ambitious cousin and if some scruple stopped Lynn from helping him it was her business. Virginia had no right to bully her.

'Darling,' I said, 'nobody's going to make you do what you don't want to. So cheer up! Remember you've a big brother to look after you now as well as a husband. Tell Virginia to go to hell.'

'It's not Virginia, Derek. She wouldn't – '

But I was no longer listening. I had run the Jaguar on to the ramp which leads down to the doors of the underground garage beneath our apartment block and, in theory, I should have put my hand out of the window and turned my key in the lock which operated the doors. Stupidly, however, I had stopped too far away and I couldn't reach the key-post. To insert the key I had either to get out of the car or go through the business of reversing. I got out of the car. It was easier. But when I got back in Lynn read me a lecture, insisting that in Washington, especially late at night, this was one of the ways people got themselves mugged. She even made me promise to be more careful in future.

The subject of Virginia's cousin was forgotten.

It wasn't until the Thursday evening that I saw Virginia or any of the Charltons again. For that matter, except in bed, I had scarcely seen Lynn. She had become her brother's shadow, a situation which I had rather expected and which I didn't resent unduly. Anyway I had no cause to complain. I had spent most of the last two days in meetings at the Pentagon, followed by receptions which could equally well have counted as work. Now Lynn had had to go alone to a party at Rock Creek Park and I was hopelessly late.

At least this meant there was some parking space. I slipped my Jaguar into the slot left by the great, boat-like automobile of a departing guest and went up to the house. The party was far from over. The drawing-room was still full of people coming and going and Lloyd was busy shaking hands and receiving congratulations on his broadcast. When it came to my turn, he said:

'What are you doing in the line-up, Derek? You're one of the family.'

'It was the simplest way of saying hullo to you and apologizing for not having watched you on the box yesterday.'

He laughed. He didn't look too well. The scar down his cheek was taut and he seemed over-bright, almost feverish. I hoped he wasn't going to crack under the weight of the hero's welcome he was receiving.

'Lynn has been looking for you,' he said. 'So has Virginia.' He obviously found this amusing. He grinned at me. 'Better see what they want.'

Lynn didn't want anything except to reassure herself that I had arrived so I took advantage of her wifely concern to plead hunger. I had had no dinner. She said the kitchen was full of hired help and we wouldn't be welcome but she would bring me something on a plate if I waited in the TV room.

Virginia did want something. She found me eating cold game pie and salad and drinking coffee; Lynn had done me proud. Two or three of the guests who had wandered into the room had had the decency to leave again when they saw I was having a meal, but Virginia had no such scruples. She was glad to have cornered me.

She sat herself down beside me on the sofa and gave me a bright smile. The light from the lamp was shining on her face. I could see that she was more heavily made-up than usual, but the make-up failed to mask her blood-shot eyes and the deep callipers between nose and mouth. She looked old and tired and rather as if she was suffering from the aftermath of a crying jag. I felt quite sorry for her for a moment. And I must have shown it because she deliberately moved the lamp so that her face was in shadow.

'Derek, I want to ask you something but it's a little embarrassing.'

I hastily swallowed some pickle. 'Embarrassing?'

'Yes. You remember when we were in here Monday evening. Lynn and I were talking about a young man –'

'I'm sorry, Virginia, but Lynn has told you that the answer's "no". Your cousin will have to find some other means of furthering his career.'

'My cousin?' Virginia had interrupted in mid-sentence.

'Isn't he your cousin, this young man you want Senator Charlton to employ?'

'Grant, you mean? Sure, he's my cousin but many times removed. That's not what's important. His mother has been very good to me. I owe her a lot. If I can help Grant, I must.'

Virginia had made a quick recovery but one thing was certain. This Grant character was not a relation of hers. I suppose she had lied on the assumption that Lynn would be more ready to put herself out for a relative than for a mere friend. I concentrated on finishing my game pie and said nothing.

'Derek, I know you and I don't get on too well but please try to be sympathetic about Grant.'

'Why?'

'Because – because you must persuade Lynn. It's essential he should get this job.'

'Then I suggest you ask Senator Charlton yourself.'

'I have done. God help me, I have done.'

I was surprised by her vehemence. 'And he refused?'

'He said there wasn't any vacancy just now. But if Lynn – '

'That's too bad!'

'Yes!'

Virginia stood up. She was a tall woman and she appeared to tower over me. For one absurd instant I thought she was going to hit me. I am damn sure she would have liked to.

'You god-damned fool!' she said. 'You god-damned fool!'

I sighed. It seemed to me that I had spent the entire day dealing with irrational, illogical people. I had had enough.

I finished my coffee, took the tray into the kitchen and joined the dregs of the party. Virginia, I noticed, had already left. For a while I made myself sociable. Then I collected Lynn and said good night and thank you to the Senator and Mrs Charlton. Lloyd insisted on seeing us out to the car. I thought he was a bit high. He kissed Lynn twice and patted me fondly on the back. I yearned for home and bed and Lynn.

Just as on the Monday evening, we talked about Virginia; Lynn was obviously annoyed by her persistence. And just as on the

Monday evening when we got back to the apartment block I placed the car badly on the entrance ramp and couldn't reach the key-post from my seat. But this time, mindful of Lynn's warning about muggers, I didn't get out. Instead I backed, turned and came up on to the ramp again. As I did I saw in my rear mirror a dark-coloured car, possibly a Chevrolet, parked on the same side of the road but some fifty feet behind us. I hadn't noticed it when we drove up.

Now I paid no attention to it. I inserted the key in the lock, waited while the heavy metal doors came slowly up and drove down into the garage. Nobody followed us.

The garage is a huge, cavernous place stretching over more than half the ground taken up by the actual apartment building. The floor is concrete and drained. The walls, ceiling and supporting pillars are white-washed. It always appears very clean, fresh and bright because it is air-conditioned and the lights are kept on twenty-four hours a day.

There are several doors leading from the garage to other parts of the basement such as the furnace room, the storage bins and the elevators. These are kept locked and the keys are not the same as that required to open the outer doors. In spite of such precautions, however, the garage has been burgled twice in the last twelve months; once three expensive, almost new cars were stolen and on the second occasion about thirty cars were ransacked. When the night watchman interrupted the first lot of thieves he was coshed; only the fact that he had a particularly hard skull saved his life.

All in all, then, the garage is not somewhere that one lingers.

It was about half past eleven, not really late, when I parked the Jaguar in its slot between a Cadillac and a big American Ford. Because by American standards the Jag isn't a large car there was comfortable space around it. Lynn got out on her side and I on mine and I reached back to collect my briefcase. I was conscious of darkening shadows.

'Derek!'

'What is –'

Even if I had understood her warning and reacted at once it would still have been too late. We didn't have a hope.

There were four of them. Three of them were about five foot ten, give or take an inch, because that's my height and they measured up to me, but they were of heavier build. The fourth one was shorter but he was a broad powerful man. They wore sneakers, jump suits, stocking masks over their heads and cotton gloves. At least three of them were white men, though I've no idea why I was so sure of this. And they were armed with knives and coshes, silent weapons. Indeed one of the horrors of the whole business was the almost total silence in which it took place.

The other horror was that except in the beginning I didn't know what was happening to Lynn.

The beginning, strange as it may seem, was not too bad. The short, strong man carried Lynn under his arm around the bonnet of the car to where the other three stood over me. She was kicking and struggling and as he set her on her feet she bit his hand which was covering her mouth. He clouted her across the head and she collapsed, gasping with shock. I struggled up towards him. Somebody kicked me in the groin, for the second time. The pain was agonizing but I managed to say to Lynn:

'Don't struggle, darling. Let them have what they want.'

It was probably wasted advice. I doubt that Lynn could have done anything else at that moment anyway and I was in no position to help her. But the classic rule if you are mugged is to hand over your money with a grin.

A pad of sticky tape was slapped across my mouth and while I choked on it someone felt for my wallet and gave it to the short man. He extracted the notes, riffled through my credit cards and took a long look at my Embassy passes. Then he threw wallet, cards and passes back at me; the contents of Lynn's evening bag were already scattered on the ground. Altogether they must have netted about forty dollars. It didn't seem worth the risk.

That was the beginning and, as I said, the beginning was not too bad.

So far it had been a simple mugging, the sort of thing you don't believe will ever happen to you, not even in Washington where it is an everyday occurrence.

I expected that they would tie us up now or cosh us, and leave us to be found by the watchman on his rounds. But it was to be much worse than that.

The short man hauled Lynn to her feet and held her up with one hand. With the other he gagged her. Then he nodded at the smallest of his henchmen, who produced a knife and slit her long dress from neck to hem. Under it she was wearing the flimsiest of bra and briefs; she might as well have been naked.

Lynn began to struggle again in a sort of frenzy. But the short man could easily contain her. Her wrists and ankles taped, he tucked her under his arm as if she had been a doll and carried her to the other side of the Jaguar. The man with the knife followed, making an unmistakable and obscene gesture.

And what did I do? What had I done? What could I hope to do? Damn all! My mind was a long, piercing scream, first for Lynn and then, I am ashamed to say, for myself alone as the two remaining thugs systematically worked me over. If I had had any secrets that they had wanted I would have vomited them all up gladly but they weren't interested in secrets and I had no means of buying immunity. So I concentrated on surviving.

I have suffered physical violence before. At the age of twelve I was beaten regularly by a sadistic prefect until my House Master discovered what was going on and put a stop to it. I was once thrown and rolled on by a horse. On another occasion I wrapped my car around a tree. And it was only a few months ago that I was knocked down, trodden upon and finally concussed by the Double PF. Each time I had felt fear but it was nothing to what I experienced in that garage.

This was not only different in degree it was different in kind. The prefect had loved me after his perverted fashion. The horse and the car incident had been acceptable risks and anyhow hadn't involved other people. The fracas with the peaceniks had been almost accidental. This was indescribable, a deliberate attempt not to kill me – they had torn the tape from my mouth so that I didn't choke to death on my own vomit – but to strip me of my humanity.

When I regained consciousness they had gone. But I wasn't alone. There was somebody near me, somebody whimpering. I was horrified to discover that the disgusting little noises were coming from me. I bit my lip until I could taste the blood. The lip didn't hurt. I had no feeling in it. And I had stopped whimpering.

I knew where I was and what had happened. I thought of Lynn. They had left me with my head half under the Jaguar and by turning it very slowly and very carefully I was able to see on the other side of the car what had to be Lynn. I tried to call to her but only a croak came from my throat. Somehow I had to get to her. Somehow I had to get help.

God knows how long it took me to crawl around to her. The thugs, surprisingly, had removed the tape from my wrists and ankles but I was incapable of standing upright. As it was, every movement was an agony. My whole body was a mass of bruises. My face I couldn't feel, though one eye was shut, and I dared not think of my genitals. I could hear my broken ribs scrape together. And my left hand was smashed where a cosh had descended on it so that I had to propel myself on my elbow. It made for slow going.

But I got there at last. Lynn was lying on her back, her breathing was regular and there were no visible signs of violence except that one side of her face was slightly bruised. Dreading what I might see, I forced myself to open the front of her slit dress. Nobody had touched her. For the first time that evening I wept.

Then I began to crawl again, setting out to reach the fire alarm, which was on the other side of the garage. But our luck had to change some time. I was almost half-way there, lying face downwards in a patch of oil, when the garage doors went up and a car swept down the ramp. It stopped within a foot of me and a man whom I knew slightly got out and bent over me.

'Lynn! My wife!' I said, trying to point with my broken hand. And once more I lost consciousness. My last thought was of Lloyd and how the Charltons' home-coming welcome for him would now be ruined.

Chapter Five

It was better than the last time I was in hospital. In fact there was no comparison. I am referring, of course, to my surroundings.

I lay in bed with whiter than white linen, in a room that was a cross between a clinical laboratory and a home from home. There were pictures on the wall, two comfortable armchairs, a small desk, and a gigantic colour television set. Kind friends had provided books, flowers, fruit, candy and get-well cards. If I needed anything else I pressed a bell and a disembodied voice asked me what I wanted. A television eye monitored the room twenty-four hours a day, which made me yearn to pick my nose or do something else unseemly, and both oxygen and iced water were piped in. The general atmosphere was antiseptic.

My physical shape was much worse. I had three broken ribs, a badly fractured hand, two missing teeth and a body that was a mass of bruises and contusions. However, I had been lucky. There were no internal injuries. Eventually, the doctors assured me, I would be as good as new.

Meanwhile I could enjoy the peculiar isolation from reality that hospital life ensures. I had nothing to do and nothing to worry about. Lynn was in a room similar to mine along the corridor. She was physically unharmed but she had been threatened with heaven knows what and thoroughly terrorized. The psychiatrist said the experience would probably have a more lasting effect on her than on me. Nevertheless, she was recovering and Mrs Charlton hoped to take her home tomorrow. I didn't need to worry about her. I could relax. I shut my eyes and dozed.

When I next woke there was a man sitting in one of the armchairs. He was a neat grey man in a neat grey suit, medium height, medium build, medium age. As soon as he saw I was awake he got up and stood beside the bed. He showed me his identity card. He was from the Federal Bureau of Investigation, the FBI.

'Good morning, Mr Almourn.'

'Good morning, Inspector. You don't look a bit like Ephraim Zimbalist Jr, if you don't mind my saying so.'

'I am for real, Mr Almourn.'

He did mind. 'I'm sorry, truly sorry, Inspector. One of these days there'll be a famous television diplomat and everybody'll say to me: "You don't look a bit like whatsisname" and I'll hate it too.'

'Mr Almourn, are you with me?'

'If I concentrate.'

He smiled at last and it was a very charming smile, as charming as Mr Zimbalist's. I didn't tell him so. As he had said, he was for real, though what the FBI could want was beyond my imagination. I asked him.

'Why the FBI? I assume it's about this mugging.'

'And mugging isn't FBI territory as you've learned from your TV viewing?'

'*Touché.*' He deserved to score that point.

'Mr Almourn, we're not sure it was an ordinary mugging. Conceivably, it could tie in with something else in which we're interested.'

I knew better than to ask him what he meant by that. I said: 'Of course I'll help if I can. You've seen the police report, I suppose?'

'Thank you. And yes, I have seen the police report. But if you would tell me in your own words –'

So I went through the whole thing again. He listened without interrupting. Then he began to ask questions.

'Have you ever been mugged before, Mr Almourn?'

'No-o.' But I had hesitated too long. I had to tell him about the time I was on my way to my first date with Lynn – it must have been May of last year – and I had felt myself threatened by two young punks. 'It hardly seems relevant,' I said.

'I'm interested in your reactions, Mr Almourn. Were they the same on each occasion?'

'In the beginning, yes, superficially. But that first attempt – if it was an attempt – was so – so casual, so amateurish.'

'Most muggings are, Mr Almourn.'

'Not that one in the garage.'

'Why do you say that?'

'The fact that they were all dressed alike and for the job,' I said, arranging my thoughts. 'Then they were organized. There was one man in command and, I think, they had a car and driver waiting for them. I don't believe that Chevrolet just happened to be there. Besides, they seemed professional. They were business-like and horribly efficient.'

'And they netted forty bucks! They didn't bother to take your watch or your wife's rings or her mink jacket. But they beat you up systematically. Mr Almourn, do you have any enemies?'

I had seen how the inspector's mind was working, how he was making my mind work. His conclusion was absurd. I didn't number even among my acquaintances the sort of people who would know how to get hold of such thugs. I would have laughed at him but laughing hurt my broken ribs.

'Inspector, are you suggesting that those bastards were waiting for me personally?'

'Yes. Somebody, alone, drove his Mercedes into that garage five minutes before you did. He saw the Chevrolet, though it was further along the street than you described it. Nobody touched him. Then you arrived in your Jaguar, the Chevy moved up and those bastards as you called them were waiting by your parking space. That's not the pattern of a simple mugging, Mr Almourn.'

The inspector had shaken me; I hadn't known about the man in the Mercedes. His next question shook me much more.

'Mr Almourn,' he said, 'what are your connections with People for Peace and Freedom?'

'I don't have any,' I said slowly.

'Come now, Mr Almourn. What about that March for Peace before Christmas? You landed in hospital then too, didn't you?'

'That was an accident. Nobody knew I was going to be there. I went to watch the march and on impulse I decided to join my wife, who – who was marching. Her brother, Lloyd Charlton, was a POW in Hanoi and she felt strongly that the Vietnam war should be ended.'

66

'Yes. I see. I know about Mrs Almourn's affiliation with People for Peace and Freedom. Did you join her on other occasions?'

'I went to one meeting once, merely because Lynn was going. I was interested in her, Inspector, not in the peaceniks. I'm apolitical by profession and by nature. Anyway – what can the Double PF possibly have to do with my being beaten up?'

'I don't know, Mr Almourn. Probably nothing. But your association with them is the only unexpected thing in what could be described as an otherwise exemplary life. Therefore it's interesting.'

I gave him a sharp look. I thought he might be pulling my leg but his face was unsmiling and he was busy studying his nails. He was beginning to irritate me a little. And my hand was hurting.

I was glad when the nurse came in with my pain-killer. I hoped the inspector would go but he sat and watched while she took my temperature and my blood pressure, felt my pulse, asked euphemistic questions about the workings of my bowels and finally allowed me to take my beautiful pills. He continued to sit after she had gone. And I lay, waiting for the pain to ease and wondering what the FBI had expected to learn from me. Nothing seemed to make very much sense.

'Feeling better now?'

'You're very observant, Inspector.'

He gave his charming smile. 'Mr Almourn, has it occurred to you that those thugs treated your wife in a very odd fashion? Why did they bring her around to your side of the car? Was it so that she could see what was happening to you? But then why take her back again? Why did they slash her dress, threaten her with a knife but never violate her? Indeed she was untouched, except for the slap on the face you mentioned.'

'I think they intended to rape her but they were interrupted. Another car drove into the garage.'

'There was more than enough time while you were being beaten up. And no car interrupted them.'

'But Lynn said –'

'She was mistaken, Mr Almourn. We checked very carefully. It so happened there were not many cars out that night and the next

67

to come in after you was the gentleman whose attention you managed to attract. They had plenty of opportunity for rape if that was what they were after.' He paused. 'Very odd, isn't it?'

I said nothing. Lynn had given me a somewhat incoherent account of what she had endured. She hadn't wanted to talk about it. If pressed she wept and there was an end to it. But she had been explicit about the rumble of the garage doors, the hiss of tyres on the ramp, the sound of voices at the other end of the basement, all of which had filled her with a hope that had been justified. The thugs had left as soon as it was safe for them and she had fallen into a state of sleep-like shock.

This was Lynn's story and I had never doubted it before. Now I didn't know what to think. The inspector had been positive. The FBI had checked and they didn't make those sort of gaffes. So Lynn had imagined the whole thing, or she was lying. The inspector seemed to have accepted that she had been mistaken but it was difficult to know what he really did believe. Anyway, why the hell were he and the FBI concerning themselves with the mugging at all? That was the real mystery.

'I understand Mrs Almourn's going home tomorrow.'

'Yes. She's going to stay with her parents.'

'I would very much like a little talk with her. There are one or two things she might be able to clear up for me.'

'She's in a – a very nervous state still. I don't think –'

'I appreciate that, Mr Almourn. And I was wondering if you felt up to walking as far as her room with me. I'm certain your presence would be reassuring for her.'

'How very thoughtful of you, Inspector.' He was going to interview her whether I agreed or not, which made me determined to be there. 'If you don't mind taking it slowly along the corridor I should be delighted to introduce you to my wife.'

I pushed the bedclothes back, gently and quietly urged my legs over the edge of the bed, slid my feet into some slippers and stood upright. My battered body responded well. The inspector was already beside me, holding up my dressing-gown. I manoeuvred my arms into the sleeves, taking care of my broken hand, and he kindly tied the belt. I was ready.

68

The progression from my room to Lynn's was the equivalent of Mao's Long March. I had made it every day, except for the first, since we had been in hospital and only recently had it begun to seem shorter. Lynn never visited me, although she was capable of doing so without any effort. She refused to leave her room.

I began the slow progress with the inspector by my side. He didn't try to hurry me. Nor did he talk. He allowed me to go at my own pace and to concentrate on not causing myself pain. Because the early journeys along the corridor had been such hell I had divided the distance into ten with a recognizable mark for the end of each. We had reached the fire hydrant, or mark four, when a nurse came out of a washroom and went into Lynn's room. She was carrying a vase of red roses and I wondered idly which of the Charltons' rich friends had belatedly heard that Lynn was in hospital.

We were at mark seven, a wall telephone into which as usual a doctor was busy muttering, when the altercation began. Angry voices floated from Lynn's room and the inspector lengthened his stride automatically. He was almost level with her door when the vase bounced through it, shattering on the second bounce. Water and roses sprayed across the corridor and over the inspector's trouser legs.

'Mrs Almourn! Mrs Almourn, you did that on purpose.'

'I told you to take them away.'

'Those lovely flowers. And you've broken the vase. You did it deliberately. Mrs Almourn, you'll have to pay for that vase. It'll be on your account.'

The doctor went on murmuring into the telephone. The inspector mopped his trousers with his handkerchief and carefully removed a rose that somehow was hanging by a thread from the sleeve of his jacket. He swore as he pricked his finger on the thorn. In desperate haste I limped past him into Lynn's room.

Lynn was sitting in an armchair. The nurse stood over her. Lynn looked pale and frightened, her eyes enormous. The nurse had dark spots of anger in her cheeks; she was fighting to control herself.

'You've no right to behave that way, Mrs Almourn. No right at all. To throw those flowers out! To break the vase! Look at the mess you've made!'

'I told you I didn't want them in here. I don't have to have them if I don't want them.' Lynn saw me and began to cry. 'Oh Derek! Derek!' She sounded hysterical.

'It's all right, darling.' I hated to see her in this state.

I started to kneel beside her but those bastards had kicked me where it hurt most and I couldn't make it. The inspector, always considerate, pushed up a chair. I sat down gratefully and tried my best to console her. The nurse stood glaring at us all.

The inspector bent and picked up a card that was half hidden under Lynn's chair. It was the sort of card that florists provide for their customers. Presumably it had arrived with the roses which Lynn had treated so disrespectfully. The inspector smoothed it out and placed it on the bedside-table.

'Who is Bruno?' he asked.

Lynn's head was buried in my shoulder. I stroked her hair and hoped the inspector wouldn't notice that her whole body had gone rigid. I wondered what reaction to his question I myself had shown.

'Bruno,' the inspector mused. 'It's an unusual name, isn't it?'

We were saved, temporarily, by the disembodied voice, which now took charge of the situation. 'Nurse Wantage, please go at once to the Nurses' Room. I'll send an aide to clear up the mess Mrs Almourn has made. Mr Almourn, please go back to your own room and take your friend with you. And Mrs Almourn, please lie on the bed and try to relax. A nurse will bring you a sedative in a moment.'

We did what we were told, more or less. Nurse Wantage disappeared. A jolly black woman swept up the glass and the roses with equal indifference and mopped the floor. Lynn lay on the bed. The inspector rearranged the furniture so that I could sit beside her and hold her hand. We did not leave.

Another nurse arrived with two capsules, which she watched Lynn swallow. Then she drew the curtains, darkening the room, unplugged the telephone and moved it so that it was beyond Lynn's reach. She asked us to go. We went. There was no point in arguing. Lynn, her eyes shut, her breathing regular, was already half asleep.

We set out on the journey back. I say 'we' advisedly because the inspector didn't desert me. He saw me through the ten stations – the distance between them seemed to have increased since the journey out – to my room. He helped me off with my dressing-gown and watched solicitously as I manoeuvred my body gingerly into bed. I felt exhausted.

'Okay now?'

'Thank you, Inspector. Yes. You've been very kind.'

He gave me a pleasant nod. 'That's fine. I must be off then. But first do tell me about this Bruno. It's such an intriguing name, isn't it?'

'Yes, I suppose it is.' I had been expecting this question and I had had plenty of time to think up an answer. 'I always assumed he was nicknamed Bruno because his surname was Brown, but I could be wrong.'

'He's not a close friend of yours then?'

'No. An acquaintance really. You know what Washington's like, Inspector. We've got a host of casual friends.'

'We move in different circles, Mr Almourn, but I can imagine. Mrs Almourn hates Bruno, does she?'

'Good heavens, no. Why should you think that?'

'Because he sends her expensive roses and she throws them away, vase and all.'

'That must have been an accident. I mean, that it was Bruno's flowers which received such treatment. He sent us a porcelain figure for a wedding present and Lynn takes great care of that, I assure you.' I gave him my blandest smile. 'Inspector, I don't understand why you're so interested in Bruno.'

'Casual curiosity, Mr Almourn. You must forgive me. And now I am going. Goodbye and thank you for your help.'

'Goodbye, Inspector.'

He was almost out of the door when he turned back. He hesitated, looking at me with his head on one side. Like a sitting duck I waited for the *coup de grâce*.

'Mr Almourn, may I give you a word of advice? If the British

Government will allow you, arrange to be posted someplace else. After this shocking business I'm sure it would be best for you and Mrs Almourn to get out of Washington for a while.'

'But, Inspector, why –'

'That's good advice, Mr Almourn. Take it if you can.'

And he was gone, leaving me with a mass of unanswerable questions. Not least of these was why, almost in spite of myself, I had done my utmost to mislead him about Bruno.

I suppose I had acted more or less instinctively. The truth is, I didn't believe Lynn hated Bruno. I believed she was afraid of him, though I had no real reason for this belief. Lynn had always stuck to her story that Bruno was no more than a fellow-member of People for Peace and Freedom and Virginia had backed her up, not that in the circumstances Mrs Urse's backing was worth anything.

As for the other problems the inspector had set me, they were insoluble. I puzzled over them throughout lunch and was as thankful as any child on his first day at kindergarten when it was time for my rest period. The curtains drawn, the telephone unplugged, I closed my eyes. Soon I slept. I seemed to have an infinite capacity for sleep in this place.

When I awoke Senator Charlton was sitting in what I found myself thinking of as the inspector's chair. Lloyd was sprawling in the other one. I pushed aside layers of sleep and grinned at them.

'Hullo.'

'Hullo, my boy.'

'Hi, Derek.'

They regarded me benignly. The Charltons had been exceedingly good to me since the mugging. One, if not all three of them, had visited me each day and I had only to mention a book, a magazine, anything, for it to be brought to me. They couldn't have been kinder if they had been my own family.

'How are you?'

'And what have you been doing with yourself all day?'

These were stock questions to which I usually gave stock answers but for once I could contribute something interesting. I told them about the visit from the FBI and Lloyd at any rate was duly impressed. The Senator seemed to think that the inspector's interest might be due to his own position, that it was because his daughter and son-in-law had been involved that the mugging was considered more than a routine affair. I didn't disillusion him but the same idea had occurred to me and I had dismissed it. The inspector had not been paying a social call.

Incidentally I didn't mention anything about Bruno to the Charltons. I merely said that Lynn had had an argument with one of the nurses, that a vase had been broken, and Lynn had been very upset. I don't know why I was so reticent but I am fairly sure that Lynn never mentioned Bruno either.

I did tell them about the inspector's parting advice. I expected them to brush it aside, to argue that Washington was home to Lynn and that she was best off among her family and friends. However, to my surprise, they both gave it serious consideration.

The Senator was doubtful. 'I don't know what her mother would have to say about it – or Lynn herself. Have you asked her?'

'No.'

Lloyd was enthusiastic. 'I think it's a swell scheme if you can swing it, Derek. After what you and Lynn have been through you're bound to see muggers in every shadow here. A change of scene would make a hell of a lot of difference. Help you to get back to normal. I don't really mean you, Derek. I mean Lynn. I sure am worried about her.'

'So am I,' I said, 'but it isn't all that simple, unfortunately.'

'You mean your Foreign Office would cut up rough if you asked to be posted?'

'Not exactly cut up rough, but – '

'Well, that's tough. But what about Lynn?'

'Lloyd, Derek's got to consider his career.'

'Sure, but Lynn's got to come first, hasn't she?'

'Of course,' I said. 'I'll talk to her about it. If she wants to leave Washington I'll fix it somehow. I promise.'

I didn't think Lynn would buy it or I mightn't have promised so glibly. I was wrong.

Later in the afternoon I once again made the Long March to Lynn's room. She was sitting up in an armchair and chatting to her mother. She looked much better. She greeted me with en-

73

thusiasm and immediately swept the carpet from under my feet.

'Derek, is it true that you could get another posting, that we could leave Washington?'

'Possibly. But there's no guarantee where we would be sent.'

'I don't care. Anyplace else but Washington. I used to love this city but after that –'

'Lynn, honey, it'll pass.'

'Perhaps, Mum. I hope so. God, how I hope so! But at the moment – Derek, please, fix it so that we can go away. Please! Lloyd said you could. He said you promised.'

'Yes.'

'Are you sure it's what you want, honey?'

'Positive. It's only anticipating what's going to happen in a year or two anyway. We'll have to go then. Why not now? Oh Derek, please fix it!'

I sighed. Suddenly I felt very tired. An inspector from the FBI, for some mysterious reason that I didn't understand, had given me advice. Lloyd had seized on the idea and had fired Lynn with his enthusiasm. Senator and Mrs Charlton wanted only what their daughter wanted. Nobody asked me what I wanted.

I wanted to stay in Washington. And why not? The chance that we would be mugged again was no greater than that we would be knocked down twice by a car. On the other hand, if the inspector was right and we had been subjected to an act of personal terrorism, which I could not bring myself to believe, it was not likely to be repeated either. I could understand Lynn's fear, even feel it myself, but I didn't think it was rational. And I didn't think we would get over it any faster by running away.

But the big thing for me was the job. I don't particularly care for Washington as a city; the hot, humid summers are oppressive, the social life is frantic, and the very fact that Washington is not New York makes it of necessity a provincial place. Nevertheless it is the most important political capital in the Western World and for any ambitious young diplomat probably the most interesting of posts. As a Political Secretary, close to the Minister whom I briefed daily, I read all the important telegrams, sat in on top-secret meetings and knew more about what was going on at an international level than I could hope to in any other equivalent posting. For me, whatever the Charltons' concept of it might be, this job was a plum. I would be a fool to give it up.

I was a fool.

When it was obvious that Lynn had really set her heart on getting away from Washington I applied for a posting on compassionate grounds. The Minister who, as I have said before, was a good friend of my father's and to some extent considered himself *in loco parentis*, tried to talk me out of it, but, when I refused to be dissuaded, he promised to use his influence on my behalf.

And, since the Office is on the whole a benevolent concern and the Minister carried a lot of influence, my cross-posting came through very rapidly. I was to go as First Secretary to our Embassy in Oslo. Lynn was delighted. I wish I could have said the same for myself.

Part Two

OSLO AND BORIS GLEB

Chapter One

It was, thank God, the end of the week, the end of a long week of travail. With a sigh of relief I turned the nose of my car out of the British Compound and pointed it towards home. There was a reception at the Canadian Embassy at six-thirty – unusual for a Friday but they had visiting firemen – and after that I could look forward to a nice peaceful weekend. I was so glad I had refused the invitation of our Military Attaché and his wife to visit their *hutte*. I didn't want to be sociable. I wanted to be alone with Lynn, perhaps do some mild sight-seeing around Oslo, perhaps to go for a walk in Frogner Park, near our house, and look at the extraordinarily sexy Vigeland sculptures, perhaps just to lie in a hammock in the garden and read.

With the last thought in mind I decided to go home by way of the public library where the British Council houses its collection and see if I could get some novels or a new biography. I was lucky and was running down the library steps, clutching my acquisitions, when I bumped into a man coming in the other direction.

'*Unskyld*,' I said politely.

'My fault. I am sorry,' he said with equal politeness and picked up the book I had dropped.

It was then I noticed that one of the papers he was carrying was *The Times*. Abandoning any attempt at Norwegian, I said: 'May I ask where you got your English newspaper?'

'On the aeroplane. Today it is very late. There is a – not a strike, a slow-go at your Heathrow. And not much better at Fornebu. It will be an hour before they are in the town.'

'Thank you.' I wasn't going to drive all those miles out to the airport to buy a newspaper, not when I had already read the international edition of the *Herald Tribune*.

But he had seen my disappointment. 'Please, you have this one. I don't need it any more.'

In spite of my half-hearted protest he tucked the paper under my arm, gave me a quick bow and ran up the stairs. '*Takk takk,*' I called after him and he waved a hand in acknowledgement.

Inordinately cheered by this encounter I remembered where I had left my Ford Capri – I was always catching myself looking for the Jaguar which, in fact, I had sold to Lloyd before leaving Washington – and threw the books and the paper on to the front seat. *The Times* slid down on to the floor, unfolded itself and revealed the headline: Gaol break by Traitor Day-Brune.

For a moment I gaped at it. Then I dashed around to the other side of the car, threw myself into the driving seat and reached for the paper. I read the twenty-line column avidly.

The headline was somewhat misleading. Day-Brune had not broken out of gaol. Indeed he had got no further than the hospital wing of the prison, to which he had been admitted over a month ago because of a suspected heart condition, probably faked. He was now safely back in his cell where he was being treated as a high security risk; there was no possibility of his escaping in future. Nevertheless, the Home Secretary stated, a definite plot to free Day-Brune had been discovered and, if it had not been for the quick thinking of one of the prison guards, could have succeeded. The Home Secretary refused to disclose the plot or say anything about it, except that it was old history.

I thought of the Minister in Washington and of my father in London; both of them had called John Day-Brune their friend. I gritted my teeth. There was so much going on at the moment, the Watergate affair, the Lonrho affair, the Lambton affair; there was no end to the political, financial and sexual scandals of the day, not to mention such supposedly fascinating events as the cod war with Iceland and Princess Anne's romance. And here was I in Oslo, cut off from all my contacts and hearing of all these things second-hand or third, fourth or fifth hand from the newspapers.

All my frustrations since leaving Washington suddenly came to a head. Why hadn't anybody at the Embassy mentioned that there had been an attempt to spring Day-Brune? Why hadn't I seen some reference to it in the telegrams? Why hadn't my father written or my mother told me in her last letter? They must have known. At the realization that I had gone so far as to blame my mother, who was a wonderful correspondent, common-sense reasserted itself.

There was no point in being peevish because nobody had seen fit to tell me about Day-Brune. After all it wasn't my business; I had no need to know how near to success a plot to free him had come or who had engineered it.

I decided to forget Day-Brune and lost passports and stranded British subjects (at the moment I was a sort of acting consul at the Embassy) and most of the things that cluttered my mind. I started the Ford and set off for Smestad.

Smestad meant home and Lynn. Having been a bachelor for so long I had thought, when we arrived in Oslo, in terms of a flat close to the British Compound. But Lynn had wanted a house and a garden and, thanks to some of the wives at the American Embassy, she had got what she wanted – a typical Norwegian house in a pleasant suburb with a big, rough garden, a flag pole and an apple orchard. It was extraordinarily pleasant. And the important thing was that Lynn was happy here. I couldn't remember her being so happy even when we were first engaged. How could I, in the circumstances, have regrets for Washington?

The Ford roared up the steep driveway and parked beside the house. Lynn, who had been sitting on the verandah, came running to greet me. She kissed me hard on the mouth and I held her to me.

'Hullo, darling.'

'Hi, honey. You're late.'

'I went to the library. But there's plenty of time. We don't have to leave before six.'

'Leave – for what?'

'For the Canadian reception. Had you forgotten? You haven't changed yet.'

'No. I mean, yes. I had forgotten.'

'You do want to come?'

'Yes, I suppose so.' She wasn't enthusiastic. 'Where is it – the party?'

'At Bygdøy, near where we went to see the Viking ships and the Kon-Tiki last Saturday. It'll take us about half an hour to get there.'

'Okay.'

'Lynn – ' I hesitated. I took her face in my hands and looked at her. She smiled, a small tight smile, and pulled away from me. 'Darling, is something the matter?'

'No, Why do you ask?'

'You seem a bit – down somehow.'

'I'm fine, Derek.' Her voice was sharp.

It wasn't until we had reached Bygdøy that Lynn mentioned she had had some letters 'from home', and I diagnosed her slight edginess as home sickness. In fact, my diagnosis was poor but, because of it, I felt the more loving towards her and, when she said that one of the letters was from Virginia Urse and that Virginia had invited herself to stay with us for a few days, I made a big effort to appear pleased about it.

'Good,' I said. 'You'll enjoy having her, won't you?'

'Sure. It's super.'

I didn't think Lynn sounded quite as delighted as she might have been, though I could have misjudged her. And I wondered why she hadn't told me the great news as soon as I got in.

'When is she coming?'

'About the twentieth. She's flying to Copenhagen from New York. She said she would call me from there.'

'Did she – er – say how long she would be staying with us?'

Lynn laughed. 'Honey, I know you wouldn't have chosen Virginia as our first house guest but you must be nice to her. She really is a very good friend to me.'

'I promise. I'll be on my best behaviour, darling.'

'She's going to London so I guess she won't be with us too long. She said she's been feeling a bit grotty lately so she's decided to take a vacation. But I don't know for how long.'

I made a non-committal noise. We had just reached the Canadian Residence, which is situated on a ribbon of a road that makes parking difficult, but this was only my excuse. I didn't want to talk about Virginia any more. She reminded me of too much about

Washington that I wanted to forget and that I wanted Lynn to forget.

We walked back from the car to the Residence in silence, both of us busy with our thoughts, and followed the trickle of guests. We were greeted first by the Defence Attaché, whom I remembered with pleasure from NATO meetings in Washington. Then we signed the Book and passed on with a brief welcome from the Ambassador and his lady into a rather pleasant double drawing-room. The French windows were open and already one or two couples were drinking on the stone terrace which runs along this side of the house. I hoped to have a chance later of seeing the grounds; they were reputed to be lovely.

The party began like any other diplomatic 'do', though I noticed that there was less English being spoken than I was used to; it was very much a multi-national gathering and, I judged, pretty high-powered. But if I didn't have the rank I certainly had the most beautiful wife; as always, there was no shortage of men eager to listen to Lynn's American.

I was happy enough to be led away by a young Canadian, whose job it obviously was to help mix the guests, and for the next forty minutes I did my duty. At one point I found myself discussing the trials of my job with a Norwegian and an American. The American was sympathetic.

'I know just how it is,' he said, grinning at me. 'When I go in of a morning there's a positive queue of kids on my doorstep. They're mostly very scruffy and very polite and they've all lost their passports and they haven't any bread and they wanna go home.'

'I'm new to this consular game,' I said. 'It gets me down.'

'You mustn't let it do that. The other day I asked a kid, very casual like, how much he had gotten for his passport and he told me before he realized what he was saying.'

I laughed. 'I hope he did well,' I said. 'The UK passports seem to be losing their value. Some of my chaps are getting pretty aggressive.'

'You mean, they threaten to write to their Congressman – that sort of thing.'

'That sort of thing.'

I had had a boy this very morning, who had claimed to be the son of an MP and had as good as told me that if I didn't play along with him my days in the Foreign Service were numbered. I don't like blackmailers. I pointed to the little wooden block that sat on my desk and gave my name. I suggested he should refer his father to my father.

It made, I thought, rather a nice story but not one I was prepared to tell to the present company. Instead I listened while the Norwegian explained why Oslo was a particularly bad city for 'distressed nationals'. According to him it was the end of a route. The kids set out through Southern Europe or North Africa for Turkey and points east and came back via Russia, Finland, Sweden and Norway.

'But here they can go no further or they fall into a fjord. So – home.' The Norwegian gave an expressive shrug.

'Having stopped over at their Embassy,' the American said. 'They are all tax-payers, of course.'

'Ja! They know every soft touch. I am told there's even a list of houses that they pass from one to the next, where they can perhaps spend a night or get a free meal. It is very – organized.'

Another Norwegian and a Danish couple joined us. I took the American over to Lynn; I thought she would like him. She was holding a glass a quarter full of ice-cubes, around which swirled a crimson-coloured liquid and various pieces of fruit. She saw my glance.

'Cranberry juice, honey. Strictly non-alcoholic.'

'Good. Then I can have another whisky.'

My consideration of what Lynn was drinking had been more than casual. The dictum that 'if you drink you do not drive' was applied to the letter in Norway. Prison sentences could be stiff. And there was no question of diplomatic immunity; this had been impressed on me at my very first briefing. As a result most missions followed the practice of putting any of their members, who as much as came under suspicion, on the next flight home, which was not a prospect to be treated lightly.

On this occasion, however, Lynn was to drive us so I could

indulge my moderate appetite. I went in search of my second whisky and had a chat with my host who, I discovered, had been at various times both at Canada House in London and in Washington. We found we had a lot of mutual friends and acquaintances and we talked for some while.

Guests were beginning to leave and I was thinking it was time that Lynn and I went too, when there was a crash of breaking glass on the terrace. Those who were not already outside stared through the French windows; conversation sighed almost to a halt and slowly gathered momentum again; a servant appeared with a dustpan and brush; and the incident was over. Lynn, whose glass had been smashed, continued to sit on the balustrade swinging her legs.

Then, to my horror, as I made my way towards her, she swung herself in a forty-five-degree arc and disappeared over the edge. Nobody paid any attention. Not more than half-a-dozen people had seen what had happened and they did nothing about it. Lynn had gone so quietly and so neatly that she was not worth more than a smiling comment. I myself could scarcely believe what I had seen.

But I ran, along the terrace, down the steps and back to where I expected to find Lynn in a crumpled heap among the bushes. It was an appreciable drop from the top of the balustrade and she couldn't have fallen lightly. Nevertheless, she was standing on her feet, smoothing her dress and appeared completely unruffled – and unaware that she had done anything out of the ordinary.

I caught her by the shoulders. In my anger and my relief it was an effort not to shake her. A near-by couple, who had been walking in the garden, stared at us curiously.

'What the hell do you think you are doing?'

'I can fly. I can fly. It's super great!'

'Lynn, are you drunk?'

'No, don't be silly, Derek. I've got to drive us home. You've been drinking so you can't.'

I bent down and smelt her breath. She blew at me, laughing. Her breath was clean and sweet, untainted by alcohol. She was certainly not drunk. She was articulate and rational. But she had just done an extremely stupid, even dangerous thing. And she was a responsible, sensible girl. I shook my head. I didn't understand.

'They do have a lot of birds here, don't they?' she said, chattily. 'And are they ever beautiful. Look at that yellow one with the long red tail, Derek, and that blue one with white and mauve wings.'

Lynn went on pointing at the flowering shrubs and describing the great, multi-coloured non-existent birds. She wasn't joking. When I said acidly that all I could see were a few sparrows and what might be a couple of wagtails, she became very angry. She stamped her foot and said I was jealous because she could fly like the birds and I couldn't.

Then suddenly, without warning, she took off and ran, waving her arms up and down. Presumably she thought that she was flying. I paused only long enough to pick up and stuff into my pocket the cocktail bag that she had dropped, before I ran after her.

When I caught up with her she was draped, arms and legs spread wide, over a bush. It was difficult to get her down. I set her on her feet, and inspected her, keeping a tight hold on her wrist so that she couldn't dash off again. She was a pretty awful sight. Her white dress was now far from clean, her tights torn, and her face scratched; there were leaves and a broken flower in her hair. She was pale and sweating. She began to talk about the birds. She seemed quite happy.

I stood there, holding her wrist and wondering what on earth I was going to do. At least we were out of sight of the terrace and the ground-floor windows of the Residence. With luck Lynn's worst eccentricities had been unobserved. I had a minute to think. But it didn't get me anywhere.

The situation was bizarre. The fact that I now knew – perhaps I should say guessed – what was wrong with Lynn, that she was not drunk but drugged, didn't help very much. On the contrary it made the possibility of leaving her alone for even the shortest time absolutely impractical. I wished I knew what she had taken, how long the effects would last and how important it was that she should see a doctor.

I tried to consider objectively the courses of action open to me. As I saw it there were three. I could take Lynn back into the house, say our goodbyes and thank-yous, and we could leave like any ordinary couple. But apart from Lynn's appearance, her behaviour at the moment was completely unpredictable. I couldn't risk some ghastly scene. So that was out.

For much the same reasons I dismissed the second possibility. I couldn't wait in the grounds until all the guests had gone and then throw myself on the Canadians' mercy, saying that Lynn had been taken ill. She was patently not 'ill'; she had blown her mind. But neither could I tell them the truth which was that my wife thought she was a bird and could fly because, so I believed, she had been fed some pep pills or other at their party. It sounded too much like an accusation. The Ambassador had been extraordinarily pleasant to me but he was an Ambassador and I, a mere First Secretary, had not met him before this evening. Commonwealth relations aside, I had no right to expect that he would have any sympathy with my crazy, unsubstantiated story.

Besides, most importantly, I had no idea how long we might have to wait and I wanted Lynn to be seen by a doctor as soon as possible.

There was, therefore, no choice.

Without returning to the house – it was unlikely that anyone would notice that we had not made our farewells – I had to get Lynn out of the grounds – there had to be a side door somewhere – and back to the car. Then, in spite of the whisky I had drunk, I would have to drive us home and send for the Norwegian doctor accredited to the Embassy. If I could achieve all this, the whole wretched episode might conceivably be forgotten. But I was going to need the devil's own luck.

It took us twenty minutes to reach the road. Five minutes of these were spent hiding from a cat. It was a real cat. Otherwise Lynn was amenable. This doesn't mean we progressed normally. Because I was holding her wrist Lynn had decided that she had a broken wing and couldn't fly, but she was still a bird. Part of the time she walked but part of the time she hopped and suddenly she

87

would jump into the air and pretend to flutter. It was nerve-racking, but nobody saw us.

Once in the road it was a different matter. At the moment few guests seemed to be leaving the Residence but, in order to get to the Ford, we had to pass the front of the building where a clutch of chauffeurs, belonging to the cars of the high-paid help, were chatting. I could not bring myself to let Lynn hop past.

'Come on!' I said fiercely. 'Run!'

Startled by an order barked at her like a military command, Lynn ran. Panting and breathless we arrived at the Ford. But the chauffeurs had scarcely turned their heads; another obstacle had been overcome. I thrust Lynn into the front seat and did up her safety belt. By the time I had got myself behind the wheel, however, she had undone it and was opening her door. There was still a long way to go.

I fixed Lynn's safety belt again. I was getting more and more worried about her. Her face had a greenish pallor and sweat glistened on her skin. I was horribly afraid that when I started the car she might try to throw herself out. I bound her hands in front of her with my handkerchief. She began to kick. So I looked for something to bind her ankles; her own handkerchief was too small. In the end I tore the belt off her dress and tied her up with that. She swore at me and went on swearing at me, calling me Derek and Lloyd and Bruno indiscriminately, but she didn't scream.

I started the car and drove off towards Smestad at a steady thirty miles an hour. What with the state Lynn was in and the whisky I had drunk we were done anyway, if the police stopped us. But there was no need to ask for trouble.

And our luck held. Somehow we got home safely. I carried Lynn into the house and laid her on the bed. She complained about the light which I had switched on; she said it hurt her eyes. She said she wanted to vomit. She clung to me. She called me Lloyd continuously. She seemed to have forgotten about birds and flying.

After an agonizing hour the doctor came.

I told him what I believed to be the truth and he confirmed it. Somebody had given Lynn LSD. He said there was no doubt. She had all the classic symptoms, high blood-pressure, sweating, nausea, trembling, eyes sensitive to light, exotic visual illusions. But no harm had been done. She would sleep now and tomorrow she would be fine.

'I don't understand,' I said.

He shrugged. 'It's very easy. What did she eat at this party? What did she drink?'

'She didn't eat anything. She never eats tit-bits. She says they make her fat. She did have a drink but it was non-alcoholic – cranberry juice on ice with bits of fruit in it.'

'That will be your answer, I suspect. It's easy to put LSD on a sugar lump and slip it in a sweet drink.'

'But why?'

'Perhaps a joke. Perhaps it wasn't intended for your wife particularly. She may just have been unlucky.'

'I suppose that's possible.'

'But you don't think it's the explanation? You believe it was deliberate. Perhaps you are right. I wouldn't know. Do you have enemies, Mr Almourn?'

The last person who had asked me that had been the FBI inspector in Washington. Then I had ridiculed the idea. Now I was beginning to wonder. But it was absurd. If I had had an enemy in the States he couldn't have followed me to Norway. This LSD business must have been a bad joke, as the doctor had suggested – and best forgotten. I told him so.

'*Ja!*' He nodded understandingly. 'However, take care. You and your wife don't want to become accident-prone, do you?'

Accident-prone. It was a chilling concept. I thought about it later, after he had gone and I had made myself a scratch meal and checked that all was well with Lynn. I felt that I needed some air but I didn't want to go far from the house, so I wandered around the garden among the apple trees. The inhabitants of Smestad seemed prone to apple orchards – just as Lynn and I were becoming prone to accidents.

Feeling despondent I strolled back towards the house. A piece of the Oslo newspaper, *Dagbladet*, had blown on to the drive. Being tidy-minded I picked it up to throw in the dustbin.

The rubbish collection here is very efficient. The tall standardized containers are lined with plastic bags. When the collection is made the plastic bag currently in use is removed and another substituted for it. Today we had had a new bag and, as I threw the paper away, I couldn't fail to see lying in it one of those neat, round bouquets that bridesmaids sometimes carry.

I fished it out. It was made of pink rosebuds, fern and something that looked to me like travellers' joy. It was very pretty. But Lynn hadn't even bothered to remove it from its cellophane cover. She had, however, opened the attached envelope which was addressed to Mrs Derek Almourn. The enclosed card with its Interflora symbol, that she had torn into small pieces, lay scattered at the bottom of the container.

It took me a certain amount of time to collect the bits but because of the system they were perfectly clean. When I was sure that I had them all, I took them into the house and assembled them. I left the flowers where Lynn had thrown them.

The card read: Don't forget me. The signature, which I could have guessed long before was: Bruno.

It did nothing to cheer me up.

Chapter Two

The following week Virginia Urse came to stay with us.

The first intimation I had of her arrival was when I got home on Tuesday evening and saw the Stars and Stripes flying from our flag-pole. I regarded it with exasperation. The drizzle, which had started earlier in the afternoon, was now thickening into rain and the last thing I wanted to do was to plough through long grass and struggle with a flag. But it had to be done.

I put my briefcase in the hall, shouted to Lynn that I was home and went into the garden. I had never previously had occasion to raise or lower a flag but I assumed it would be easy. It wasn't. There was a sort of pulley affair, which refused to work and then worked too well. Several square feet of heavy, damp material descended suddenly, enshrouding my head and shoulders.

Cursing, I struggled free. I hadn't bothered to put on a mackintosh when I left the Embassy, so now not only were my shoes and the bottoms of my trouser legs soaking but my jacket and my shirt and my tie were wet. I heaved an angry sigh and plodded back to the house. What on earth, I asked myself, had made Lynn decide to fly her flag today and where had she got it.

The answer to both these questions was, of course, Virginia.

Lynn and Virginia were in the living-room. They hadn't heard me before, when I came into the hall to dump my briefcase and call to Lynn that I was home. They didn't hear me now either. They were too absorbed in their conversation.

For my part, at the sound of voices, I abandoned the idea of a storming protest against the Stars and Stripes. Leaving the American flag in a heap by the stairs, I picked up my briefcase and approached the living-room with some circumspection.

'Tell Bruno not to send me any more flowers, ever.'

'Lynn, sweetie, you know I can't do that.'

'Why not? I don't want to have anything more to do with him, not ever again.'

'Lynn, you must be sensible.'

'Tell him. Please, Virginia. I paid my debt before I left Washington. I don't owe –'

'Why, Derek! How grand to see you again!'

Interrupting Lynn, Virginia was effusive in her greeting. She came towards me with both hands outstretched and kissed me on the cheek. I returned her kiss.

'But, Derek, sweetie, what have you been doing to yourself? You're soaked.'

'I've been pulling down the American flag, Virginia. I didn't realize Lynn had put it up in your honour.'

'You've pulled down Old Glory?' Virginia laughed. 'There you are, Lynn. I told you he would be mad if we flew it.'

'I'm not mad,' I protested. 'But as a member of the British Embassy staff here I really cannot fly an alien flag.'

'Well, it's my flag. And I think it was a nice idea. Oh, Derek! Virginia brings us a present and you – you –'

'It's lying in the hall,' I said, wondering at Virginia's constant ability to put me in the wrong. 'I brought it in. I didn't throw it in the dustbin, Lynn, as you did poor old Bruno's flowers.'

There was a short, startled pause. Lynn looked as if I had slapped her in the face. She hadn't known I had found the bouquet that Bruno had sent her. Although she had recovered from her LSD trip by the next day, as the doctor had predicted, she had been very upset by the whole incident and I hadn't wanted to add to her unhappiness by discussing Bruno and his flowers. Then I had forgotten about them. I wished I could have forgotten about them altogether.

'Darling, I'm sorry,' I said. 'I should hate it if you loved his bloody flowers, but I don't understand why you – sort of spurn them so madly.'

'I want to be free of him, free of – all that.'

'All what? You make it sound as if Bruno had some kind of hold over you.'

'Oh no, he hasn't! He hasn't any hold over me, Derek. Has he Virginia?'

'It's really very simple,' Virginia said slowly. 'Bruno's an odd man. He doesn't like losing touch with people. He believes that once somebody undertakes to work for a cause, as Lynn did through People for Peace and Freedom, they ought not to abandon it. Therefore, since he has plenty of money he sends Lynn flowers to remind her she must go on working for – for peace and freedom. The way he looks at it, she can't do otherwise.'

'What utter rot!' I said. 'He must be round the bend. Darling, forget him. We're in Oslo now. You pour us all some drinks while I get out of these wet things. I won't be five minutes. And I'll put a bottle of champagne in the refrigerator for us to celebrate Virginia's arrival.'

In the bedroom, while I changed my clothes, I thought about Virginia's unexpected explanation of Bruno. I suppose it was logical, given that he was nuts. But it didn't explain why Lynn reacted so violently to his gifts or why she was afraid of him, as I was sure she was. Still, as I had said, we were in Oslo now, and there could be nothing to fear from long-distance flowers.

Determined to make the evening as pleasant as possible I went back into the living-room. For a moment Lynn and I were alone; we made the most of it. Then Virginia came back, bringing us what she called her 'real house-guest presents'. The Stars and Stripes, she said, with a conciliatory smile at me, had only been a joke. Responding, I promised to fly it on July 4th.

Neither Lynn nor I had any cause to complain about Virginia's 'real presents'. She had brought Lynn a shoulder-bag and me a book. The bag was beautiful, made of the softest leather and expertly crafted. It made me think of those splendid Gucci products that my younger sister always hankers after but which, her husband says, are too atrociously expensive to buy. But there was no label inside. I was curious enough to ask about it.

Virginia seemed startled by my questions. 'It was hand-made,' she said. 'Somebody told me about a little man, a paraplegic actually, who accepts special orders. He doesn't make enough to set up a real business so I suppose he wouldn't have name labels.'

'It's absolutely super! Thank you, Virginia. Thank you. I've never had such a beautiful bag.'

'And it's just what you want?'

'Yes. Yes, it is.'

Virginia's last remark had struck almost a sour note, although Lynn's pleasure in what she had been given couldn't have been more genuine. She was obviously delighted by the bag.

'I hope your gift is just what you want too, Derek.' Virginia said.

I smiled at her brightly. 'I'm sure it will be.'

'Open it, honey. I'm longing to know what it is.'

I already knew. Through the wrapping I could feel the hard edge of the cover and the spine. Virginia had bought me a book. In one way she couldn't have made a better choice. I like books the way Lynn likes clothes and bags and other pretty things. But people always seem to give me the book that they want to read and never the one that I want to read. I solved the problem long ago with my family by always providing a list before Christmas and birthdays. Friends are more difficult – and as for Virginia, well, whatever she had thought fit to buy me, I was going to be pleased about it, for Lynn's sake.

I tore off the wrapping, the muscles of my face taut as I waited for the blow. But I had been a pessimist. Virginia hadn't been good. She had been brilliant. She had brought me the one book that I would have chosen – just what I did want, in fact – the new biography of John Day-Brune, which had been written by two journalists and was said to be the definitive work. My reaction was as genuine as Lynn's.

'Virginia, how terribly kind of you and how clever. Thank you very much. I had heard of this book but I didn't know it was published yet, and certainly not in the States.' I was leafing through the pages. 'But this is an English edition. How on earth did you get hold of it?'

'I – er – got it at the airport.'

'At Fornebu?'

'No, not Fornebu. When I was leaving Copenhagen. I hope it interests you?'

'Very much. I was intending to order it from Hatchards. Thank you again.'

'You are welcome.'

It just crossed my mind that by choosing a book about Day-Brune Virginia was getting at me. I remembered the Stars and Stripes that she had also brought. But I told myself that I was being fanciful. Virginia had taken great pains to bring Lynn and me presents that we would enjoy. It was uncharitable to suspect her motives.

I got up to pour us all a second drink. Lynn said that she must go and cook and went into the kitchen. I rather expected that Virginia would follow her but she didn't. I was obviously in for a *tête-à-tête* and, deciding on a safe neutral subject, I began to talk about our life in Oslo.

'It's very pleasant here,' I said. 'Quiet, of course, after Washington, but I hope it'll turn out to be a good post.'

'Lynn seems to like it.'

'Yes. She particularly likes this house. I think that's because it's wooden. It reminds her of the Charltons' place at Rehoboth. Not that there's a great deal of resemblance otherwise.'

'Derek!' Virginia hadn't been listening to my chatter. 'How is Lynn? Has she completely recovered from the shock of that dreadful mugging?'

'I hope so. I think leaving Washington was on the whole a good idea. She's happy – '

'You do, do you?'

'Yes.'

I wondered what Virginia was getting at. It wasn't my imagination; half the things she said seemed to have a double meaning.

'Tell me about this LSD trip. Was it bad for her?'

I hesitated. Lynn and I had agreed not to talk about last Friday to anyone. However, Virginia was presumably privileged.

'In retrospect the incident has its funny side,' I said.

'I dare say. But I want to know what effect it had on Lynn. She doesn't remember very clearly. Derek, please tell me. I'm not just asking out of curiosity. I – I'm very fond of Lynn.'

Virginia was leaning forward in her chair, her gaze fixed on my

95

face. And I noticed that the hand with which she held her glass was unsteady. She was very much in earnest.

For the first time since I had seen her in Washington, I took a critical look at her. She had lost weight, which meant that the poor bone-structure of her face was more apparent. Her mouth, large but not generous, turned down. Her eyes, which were her best feature, were dark-circled. She looked as if she had problems.

'Not to worry. Lynn's all right,' I said, in an effort to reassure her.

The look that Virginia gave me in return was one of utter contempt. I was glad when Lynn came back and said that dinner was ready. And later I was gladder still when Virginia, pleading tiredness, went to bed early. I regretted it but I couldn't share Lynn's enthusiasm for our first house-guest.

The following evening, when I got home, Virginia was by herself on the verandah. She said that she and Lynn had been sightseeing in Oslo most of the day and Lynn had a headache, so she had made her take some aspirin and lie down.

I hurried into the bedroom. Lynn was not lying down. She was sitting at the desk, writing in her diary. I went across and kissed her, relieved that she wasn't sick. Immediately she shut the book and folded her hands on it. I laughed. Lynn's diary had become something of a joke between us.

'Darling, are you all right? Virginia said you had a headache.'

'It's better. It never was much. An excuse. I – I wanted to be alone for a while.'

'You're sure? You don't look terribly cheerful.'

'Quite sure, honey. I'm fine.'

'You haven't been crying, have you, Lynn?'

'No, I've not been crying. And please don't nag, Derek.'

'Sorry, darling, but you really don't look –'

'Derek! I'm okay. Please, honey. I asked you – don't nag!'

She said precisely the same to Virginia when we joined her on the verandah, but with more asperity. Virginia took it well. She offered to cook the dinner for us. Lynn, however, spurned the offer, saying that we were going to have cold meats and salad, and that we must eat early because she had asked some people to come in for drinks later. She herself felt like a party – her headache had completely gone – and she hoped that Virginia and I both felt like a party too. Doubtfully we acquiesced.

To change the subject, I supposed, Virginia asked me about my work.

'Rather boring after Washington,' I said. 'I'm a sort of odd-job boy at the moment. But I spend most of my time on consular work.'

'What does that mean?'

'Dealing with one's nationals. For example, today I've been trying to arrange the shipment of a Scottish corpse to Glasgow. The chap had the temerity to get drowned in the lake at Lille-hammer, which is a sports resort, and his family insists that the body be flown home and buried in the ancestral grave. You would think that would be comparatively simple to organize, but I can assure you it isn't. For one thing the amount of paper work involved is colossal.'

'That's not the kind of thing you did in Washington, is it?'

'No, I was on the NATO desk there. But HMG expects her foreign servants to be versatile.'

'Don't you do any NATO work here, Derek?'

'Not so far I haven't, though H.E. out of the kindness of his heart has asked me to write him a paper on the Northern Flank.'

'That means we won't be going on this visitation to Lapland then?'

This was the first remark that Lynn had made for at least five minutes. She had been eating nuts and sipping sherry and taking no part in the conversation at all. Her question surprised me.

The invitation, issued by the Government of the USSR to the Norwegian Government to bring a party of diplomats from countries belonging to the NATO alliance and their wives to visit the Soviet side of the border with Norway, was still under advise-ment; it had come as something of a shock to Norway and her allies, since the border had been closed for some years. And if the invitation wasn't top secret at least it was confidential. I hadn't mentioned it to Lynn.

'How on earth did you hear about that?'

97

'Oh – one of the wives from the American Embassy. I don't remember what her name is. We met her by chance in the Munch Museum.'

'And she made a casual reference to it?'

'She asked me if I was going.'

'How you women gossip.'

'It is true then?' Lynn persisted.

'It's true the Russians have issued an invitation. But it hasn't been decided yet if we, or anybody, will accept.'

'But you must surely,' Virginia said. 'Isn't it a fabulous chance to inspect the border from the Soviet side? The Brits couldn't be stupid enough to pass that up.'

'You should advise His Excellency,' I said coldly. 'Anyway, it's no concern of mine. He won't ask me to accompany him. I'll be left to my passports and corpses and distressed nationals.'

'But you must want to go. Couldn't you pull some strings, Derek?'

'No, Virginia, I couldn't. If the thing's on, H.E. will take Martin Gatling, one of the Counsellors, and his wife or the Political Secretary or the Military Attaché. I envy them but I can't do anything about it. And, incidentally, when these people come for drinks tonight, please don't mention the visitation. It's not meant to be public knowledge yet.'

When Lynn had said that she had asked in some people I had envisaged three or possibly four couples. I hadn't appreciated that we were giving a full-scale party in Virginia's honour. But, as I was to discover, when Virginia had telephoned from Copenhagen to confirm her expected arrival, Lynn in her turn had immediately telephoned all our Oslo acquaintances; I hadn't realized that in three and a bit weeks we had acquired so many. At one time I could have counted twenty-five guests in our living-room.

I wouldn't have minded if it had been a good party but it wasn't. Lynn seemed to have lost interest in the middle of organizing it. Luckily my monthly supply of diplomatic liquor had arrived but we ran out of soft drinks, which meant that I had to dash off in the car to get some. And the food we were offering our guests was awful, potato crisps and nuts. And there was no help, so that I found myself the solitary waiter. And the guests themselves were about sixty per cent North American, and thirty per cent British, which was an insult to the solitary Norwegian couple who represented the host country. Because these people were not personal friends of ours; they were diplomatic and government service colleagues and their wives. We were new arrivals to their Oslo circle and they had come to visit us, in part out of duty. They didn't expect a shambles.

Of course it could have been worse. I have exaggerated. And it was, from my point of view, much worse.

Lynn had asked the Ambassador – the British Ambassador – and his wife and they were kind enough to look in on their way to a dinner party. I was livid when, in spite of my earlier request not to mention the Russian invitation to anybody, I heard Virginia and Lynn discussing it with H.E.

'Lynn and I were saying how much we would adore to go to Lapland. It sounds a fascinating place.'

'There's nothing to stop Mrs Almourn from going or you, Mrs Urse. Tourists are very welcome in north Norway.'

'But tourists aren't allowed across the border into Russia. That's what would be so interesting, wouldn't it, Lynn?'

'Yes. It – it would be a super experience.'

And when H.E. came to say goodbye and I was showing him to his car, he said:

'Your women have been getting at me, Derek. But I'm afraid it's not much use.'

'Sir?'

'This trip to the north. Incidentally we've decided to take up the invitation. I can understand you wanting to come but seats on the plane are going to be at a premium. The best I can do is to short-list you.'

'Sir, I apologize. Lynn should never have spoken to you about it. I assure you I had no idea she was going to.'

'That's all right. She's very young – and very charming. Don't be angry with her. By the way, she made it crystal clear that she hadn't learned about the visitation from you.'

I wasn't angry with Lynn. I was angry with Virginia who, from what I had heard of the conversation, had first brought up the subject. But it was no use being angry. The damage, if any, was done and, in the event, H.E. had been extremely understanding. He must have known anyway that I would give my eye-teeth to be included in his party. Nevertheless, I wouldn't have wanted him to think that I had got Lynn to plead a cause I didn't have. I hoped he had believed me.

I turned to go back into the house. There were heavy steps on the gravel of the drive and, thinking that yet more guests were arriving, I waited.

Two young men came around the corner. They were very similar in appearance, both tall and ash-blond and bearded, typically Scandinavian-looking. They wore jeans and T-shirts, which were decorated with the American flag and USA. They carried enormous rucksacks, bowing their backs. For no explicable reason I felt, somehow, apprehensive.

'Hi!'

'Hi!'

'Hullo. What can I do for you?'

'We just want to park our tent for the night and some drinking water maybe.'

'Mind you, we wouldn't say no to a bite to eat. We're a bit short on bread and we've not had a square meal today.'

'I'm sorry. But – why should you have come here? You're Americans, aren't you?'

'Sure we're American but, man, what difference does that make? You're a house, aren't you?'

'A house? What do you mean?'

'You know, you're on the list. Someplace the kids can spend the night, have a wash and a meal maybe.'

One of them produced a grubby piece of paper and passed it to me. He was right. Our address was the last on the list. And I remembered what the Norwegian commander, whom I had met last Friday at the Canadian reception, had said about the travelling hippies. This was verification of the list of which he had spoken and not a try-on. Nevertheless, I didn't want these boys and possibly a long line of their successors camping in my garden.

'I'm sorry,' I said again. 'But you can't stay here. The house has changed hands and shouldn't be on your list any more. Goodbye.'

'Not so fast, man!'

'Once on the list, always on the list. We'll put up our tent in the apple orchard, shall we? That way we won't interfere with your cocktail party none.'

'Unless, of course, you would like to invite us too. We might enjoy that, mightn't we, Chuck? The last party we went to turned out to be a load of fun – at any rate for us.'

'It sure did, Hank. Wow-ee!'

I swallowed. There had been menace behind their words. Unless I played they would make it their business to break up the party and, because everybody would be so surprised, they would probably succeed in getting away with it. People could get hurt. I looked at them and they grinned at me. They meant what they had said – and hadn't said.

It was not so long since I had believed myself threatened by a couple of black kids in a quiet street in Washington and even less time since I had been systematically beaten up in that garage under my own apartment block. I knew a threat when I met one. My skin crawled and I took a step backwards into the hall.

Hank and his pal were pressing me now. They thought themselves in control of the situation and I suppose they were. But I was damned if I was going to collapse as they expected and tell them to make free of the apple orchard. I wasn't that much of a coward.

'Show me your passports,' I said authoritatively, startling them both.

'Why?'

'Because if you are what you say you are, *bona fide* American travellers, your passports will prove it. Please.' I held out my hand. 'I want to see them.'

'No,' Chuck said. 'You've no right to see them.'

'Shall I fetch the American consul? He happens to be a guest at my party. Or would you prefer the Norwegian police?'

'Now look, man. We've not done you any harm. There's no need for the fuzz. Is there, Hank?'

'No. We don't want trouble. We'll go quietly, mister.'

I had won a moral victory – but not for long.

Crowding into the hall behind me came Lynn, three of our departing guests and Virginia. They had no intention of being but, in fact, they were an American contingent to the rescue of their fellow countrymen. Chuck was quick to size up the new situation.

'Well, if you say no, that's that, sir.' He hadn't called me 'sir' before. 'But we wouldn't cause you any trouble. All we want is someplace to pitch our tent for the night and maybe some drinking water. You see, this is the last day of our vacation in Europe. We fly back to the States tomorrow. And we don't have money for a hotel.'

Immediately I was a minority of one, a prejudiced, unchristian Limey who wouldn't give even a glass of water to two fine American boys. I'm not blaming Lynn or our guests; in their place I would have responded in exactly the same way. As it was I tasted black bile and gave in as gracefully as possible.

'All right,' I said. 'Take your gear down to the orchard. Somebody'll bring you some beer and some food later.'

But it wasn't going to be Lynn or me; I was determined on that. Luckily Virginia volunteered at once so that problem solved itself.

And I went back to the party.

I sought out the very attractive wife of the American Naval Attaché, thanks to whom we had been able to rent our house. (I had abandoned my butling; people were helping themselves to drinks and, as a result, the party was improving.) She and her husband had been in Oslo for two and a half years. She knew all about the list of houses shared among students and hippy travellers. She assured me that our house was not and never had been on that list. The Norwegians who owned it, and who themselves had been posted to Warsaw, had lived there for the previous six years. They were close friends of hers and she would certainly have known. I didn't doubt her.

Nevertheless, I told myself in the middle of the night when I couldn't sleep, there were two young men in a tent in my garden;

two young men whom I didn't in the least trust. Because I had not imagined it; they had threatened me, and in the most unlikely circumstances. This was out of character. Whatever one might think of the itinerant student he didn't go out of his way to be physically aggressive. What's more I wasn't at all sure that their claim to be Americans was valid. I have a very good ear and, apart from the Hank and Chuck routine, which was ripe corn, something about their intonation had jarred on me.

I must have dozed. About a quarter to four by my watch I woke up, my heart thumping and my pyjamas damp with sweat. I had dreamed myself back to that underground garage in Washington. But a more immediate noise had awakened me.

I slid out of bed, taking care not to disturb Lynn, who herself had been tossing and turning most of the night. I put on slippers and a dressing-gown and went downstairs. Through the living-room window I saw two figures, weighed down by heavy ruck-sacks, tiptoeing down the drive.

My two unwelcome visitors were leaving and, as they had promised, they had caused no trouble. I don't know why I felt even more disconcerted than before.

Chapter Three

Midsummer's day is an occasion for celebration in Norway. If the weather has not been so dry as to make them a fire hazard, beacons are lit all the way up the coast. Parties are given and there is general rejoicing. This year midsummer happened to fall on the Sunday of Virginia's first weekend with us and we were planning to celebrate with an evening picnic at Holmenkollen, to which we had been invited by Martin and Lorna Gatling.

I was sprawled in a deckchair on the verandah when Martin arrived to fetch us, and I was still unfolding myself from it after he had parked on the drive and come across the lawn to me. I say 'lawn' advisedly because I had spent the better part of yesterday afternoon mowing the grass immediately around the house.

'You've been working, I see, Derek.'

'Yes. I thought if I didn't do something soon the outdoors would start encroaching on the indoors. Thank you for noticing.'

'I hope Lorna doesn't notice or she'll be getting at me. I wish she weren't so keen on my taking exercise. I'm always telling her that, once a man reaches forty, he has quite enough exercise walking in the funeral processions of his more athletic friends, but she won't believe me.'

I laughed. I liked Martin Gatling. He was a tall, lean, elegant man, slightly foppish in behaviour but with a quick, incisive mind. He had been my boss in London for a period and we got on well together. Since our arrival in Oslo both he and Lorna had gone out of their way to be kind and helpful to us. But Lynn, for some reason – she said they were patronizing – didn't like them, which was a pity.

'I'll go and see if Lynn and Virginia are ready,' I said.

'Right.'

Martin lowered himself into my deckchair and stretched out a desultory hand for the book that I had been reading. It was the biography of John Day-Brune that Virginia had given me.

'Derek!'

'Yes?' I was halfway through the French windows when Martin halted me. 'What is it?'

'This book about Day-Brune, where did you get it?'

'Somebody gave it to me. Why?'

'You lucky devil! I suppose you realize it's pre-publication?'

'Are you sure?'

'Positive. I was talking to Sam last night. I asked him to send me a copy and we discussed it.'

Sam was Martin's father who, having retired from the army as a half colonel, had achieved his life's ambition to run a bookshop on the south coast. I had met him a couple of times and had been very impressed. He was a real bookman. If he said that this particular biography of Day-Brune was still pre-publication, there was no question about it.

Therefore, there was no question but that Virginia had lied to me. She hadn't bought the book at some airport, as she had said. She had had to make a special effort to acquire a pre-publication copy, which wasn't terribly difficult – but why had she bothered? To have a bag made especially for Lynn was one thing; but she didn't care a damn about me.

I pondered the problem idly as Martin drove us out to Holmenkollen but, once we got there, I forgot all about it. The sight of the famous ski-jump, which dominates Oslo from the north-west, is awesome at close quarters. The idea of human beings screaming out over that white void to land far below on what in winter is a bed of frozen snow but, this warm midsummer evening was a lake in which people were actually swimming, was frightening and exhilarating. I was fascinated by it.

I followed the rest of the Gatlings' party reluctantly into the Ski Museum, which is housed in the building under the ski-jump. I could find little to interest me there. Luckily, however, Martin shared my boredom and suggested that we should take the lift to to the top of the tower and admire the view.

From over one hundred and sixty feet up the view was superb.

I was content to stand and stare. It must have been a minute before I realized that instead of looking down over the beautiful reaches of Oslo Fjord as I was doing, Martin was gazing speculatively at me.

'Can you keep a secret, Derek?'

'You mean – scouts' honour?'

'I never was a boy scout. My mother thought they were too rough. But cross your heart and hope to die.'

I grinned at him. 'Yes. What is it?'

'H.E.'s trying to arrange for you to come on this northern lark with us.'

'What?' I couldn't believe it; this was nothing to jolly about.

'He thinks it would be good for you – and for us. After all you were becoming something of a Northern Flank expert, weren't you? You must find passports pretty dull.'

'Look, Martin, there's nothing I'd like better. But what about Peter and Iain?' Peter was Political Secretary and Iain Military Attaché. 'H.E. can't pass them over.'

'No. He wouldn't dream of it. But it seems Iain will be on leave and Peter will have to help mind the shop. Which means that, if the Russians do let us have another place, you'll be going – though not Lynn, I'm afraid.'

'When shall I know?'

'It'll have to be next week, won't it? But H.E. suggested I warn you now in case they agreed at the last minute – so that you could "make your domestic arrangements", as he put it.'

'That was very kind of him.'

'I hope it comes off. In the meantime, remember, top secret. Remove that anticipatory gleam from your eye.'

I did my best to follow his instructions but it wasn't easy. I didn't believe that H.E. would have allowed Martin to mention the possibility if the Norwegians had expressed the slightest doubt about the Russians' acceptance. No, I should be going on this NATO jaunt and, needless to say, I was terribly pleased at the prospect.

My only regret was that I wouldn't be able to take Lynn. It was hard when H.E. and Martin would be taking their wives. She would be disappointed, although for her it was just a sightseeing tour. In the three years that we expected to be in Norway she would have plenty of opportunity to visit Lapland; except on the Russian side, tourists were very much encouraged and, later on, I might even be able to wangle a semi-official trip. What I really minded about was leaving her alone in Smestad for the three nights I expected to be away. I wondered if Virginia could be persuaded to stay on. For that matter I had no idea when Virginia planned to leave.

If I had not been so self-absorbed as we came down from the tower I mightn't have reacted to Hank as I did; in which case I wouldn't have been sure that it was Hank. What happened was this.

When Martin and I got out of the lift I found myself confronted by somebody whom instinctively I took to be Hank. He was the same height and build. He had the same eyes, nose, complexion. I recognized him at once. However, he had shaved off his beard, he was no longer wearing a T-shirt advertising his Americanism and on his head was the red-tasselled, black-peaked cap of the Norwegian student.

'Hullo, Hank,' I said. 'What are you doing here? I thought you were back in the States by now.'

It was not the ideal place to come on someone you know. People were pressing from behind to get out of the lift and pressing from in front to ensure that they retained their pecking order to get into the lift. Martin, Hank and I were in everybody's way. Inevitably we were being jostled and I put a hand on Hank's arm so that we shouldn't get separated. He shook me off roughly and let flow a flood of Norwegian.

'He asks what you want of him,' Martin said. 'He has never seen you before and he knows nobody called Hank. He says he speaks no English. There was some more but I didn't get it.'

'Tell him he's a liar,' I said cheerfully.

'What?'

'He spent most of last Wednesday night in my apple orchard, he and the other half of the comic turn of Hank and Chuck.'

I had been watching his face carefully while I spoke to Martin. It was wooden and expressionless which, in the circumstances, was not the response one would have expected from a genuine Norwegian student. Besides there was a small pale mole beside his eyebrow. This was Hank, without doubt. I turned away.

'*God aften*, Hank,' I said.

'*Pass deg!*' he answered, scowling at me.

Martin wanted to know what it was all about and I told him, except that I omitted my certainty that Chuck and Hank had threatened to break up our party the other evening. He wouldn't have believed me anyway. He would have thought that I was still over-nervous because of that mugging I had received in Washington, and we would both have been embarrassed.

'Are you sure it was the same character?'

'Positive.'

'Don't be so fierce. I believe you, Derek. But you must agree that it's very odd.'

I shrugged. 'Please don't mention it to Lynn.'

'If you say not. Incidentally, do you know what *pass deg* means?'

'What?'

'That's what your pal Hank said when you bade him good evening. It means "take care" – not a usual salutation exactly.'

To me it sounded like another threat but I was too proud to admit that I could be so easily made apprehensive. I laughed. I had decided to pass the whole thing off as a joke. Whatever it was about I didn't want to involve Martin.

The encounter with Hank had worried me and taken much of the shine off Martin's good news that I would most likely be included in H.E.'s party to the north. It had also made me determined that Lynn wouldn't stay in our house at Smestad, either with or without Virginia, while I was away. I could too easily imagine Hank and Chuck turning up on the doorstep and making themselves at home. My imagination was overly vivid. I could still picture that garage in Washington and the thug holding Lynn up with one arm while the other bastard slit her dress down the front. Nothing remotely like that, I swore, must ever happen to her again.

Such gloomy thoughts tended at first to spoil this midsummer evening for me but it was too beautiful to waste. By half past ten the museum and tower were shut, the last visitors had left the cafeteria under the lip of the jump and, apart from a large group of students on the far side of the lake, we had the place almost to ourselves. From time to time the students sang and one of them played a concertina. Occasionally somebody plopped into the lake and swam around. Otherwise everything was very quiet and very peaceful.

I lay on my back on the grass. If I opened my eyes I could see the rising moon and the setting sun both high in the sky, both giving light. If I turned my head I could see the dark shadow of the ski-jump towering above us and dominating the scene. Closer I could see Lynn and a Norwegian girl, called Ilse, helping Lorna to unpack the picnic. The rest of the Gatlings' party lay or sat on the grass, drinking beer and chatting; a couple of them were swimming; another had gone to dress. It was very warm. I could have gone to sleep.

'Food in about five minutes,' Lorna said, 'so if any of you want a last swim before we eat, now's your chance.'

Half reluctantly I stood up. If I hadn't felt so sleepy I would probably have stayed where I was but I thought a quick dip would wake me up and make me enjoy the picnic more. I went to the edge of the bank and slid quickly into the water. Martin did the same, shying away as Virginia's shallow dive splashed him. We swam slowly, side by side, towards the middle of the lake. Then I turned over and floated for perhaps sixty seconds, staring up in awe at the ski-jump above me.

Suddenly I shivered. The air was warm but the water was cold. I had had enough. I kick-rolled on to my front. And a hand gripped my ankle. I had the time and the presence of mind to take a great gulp of air before I was pulled below the surface. For a moment I thought it was Martin, though he was scarcely given to playing jokes; he had been nearest to me and I didn't know that he was swimming back to the edge of the lake. I let myself go, conserving my breath, and felt myself being drawn along under water.

Then, when I became aware that this was not Martin and no joke, I panicked. I began to struggle. Inevitably this brought me into contact with my enemy's body. It was a big, powerful, young body with a lot of blond hair on the chest. Seizing a handful of hair I pulled it with all my strength. I saw his teeth bared in sudden pain and he let me go. I thrust myself upwards and, as my head cleared the water, gulped air.

But I sensed that he was coming after me again. I turned and tried to kick him. It was a feeble effort. He seized me by the leg and, using me as a counter-weight, propelled himself to the surface at the same time as he thrust me down. Our faces passed within an inch of each other. My eyes were open. Because things are distorted under water and because I saw his face only briefly and because I was in no fit state to recognize anybody, I wouldn't have sworn to it. However, in my own mind I was convinced that my enemy was Hank.

If he had wanted to drown me he could have. He was bigger and stronger and a far better swimmer. Yet when I surfaced again he was gone. Only the wake of a powerful crawl stroke moving rapidly towards the singing students indicated where he was. Somebody in the familiar red-tasselled and black-peaked cap came to the lake-edge and gave him a hand up the bank; from his build this could have been Chuck.

I dog-paddled and enjoyed breathing. My chest hurt. I wondered what I should do. There were still swimmers in the lake and I could shout for help; someone would hear me. I could make for what had become the nearer bank where the students were and where, I had no doubt, I should be quite safe; Hank and Chuck – if it had been them – would have disappeared long before I got there. Or I could try to get back to Lynn and my friends which would cause the least fuss and the least embarrassment. My inclination was to opt for the last but I wasn't sure that I could make it. Hank, or whoever had half-drowned me, had dragged me away from them and inadvertently I had been paddling in the same direction as he had taken me, so that now our picnic appeared an enormous distance away.

In the event I didn't have to make up my mind. I was aware of a flurry of excitement among the Gatlings' party on the far bank. Then Virginia came churning across the lake towards me. She was a very powerful swimmer and I remember thinking that Hank would have had more difficulty drowning her than me, when she reached me and promptly pushed my head under water. I came up choking and retching.

'Okay, Derek. You're okay. Don't struggle. I've got you.'

She had most certainly got me. She turned me on my back and proceeded to tow me back to safety but, either on purpose or from intent, she continued to dunk me so that the cure was almost worse than the complaint. I gave up trying to help her by kicking with my feet and concentrated on getting an adequate amount of air into my lungs. It could have been my imagination but I thought that when the Norwegian colonel and the chap from Allied Forces, Northern Europe, the NATO Headquarters near Oslo, swam out to meet us I received somewhat better treatment.

Martin Gatling, being a mediocre swimmer such as I was, had wisely stayed on the bank, ready to help us out of the water. Still coughing and spitting, but in no need of artificial respiration, I was lifted up and laid on the grass. Martin began to towel me down. Lorna had brought hot coffee in vacuum flasks for the picnic and Lynn, white-faced, knelt beside me and held a cup to my lips. The coffee burned my throat but it stopped me shivering, my panting eased and I was able to speak.

'So sorry,' I said. 'Didn't mean to cause all this trouble.'

Everyone laughed as if I had said something tremendously funny. Somebody asked what had happened and, before I could stop her, Virginia had given her version. It was as near the truth as I could have provided, perhaps nearer. She claimed to have seen the whole thing and made impossible any hope of pretending that I had merely had a touch of cramp. But she went on to blow up the incident, repeating that if she hadn't noticed what was happening I would certainly have drowned. This was not true. Once Hank had left me I was in no real danger. However, if she wanted to make a heroine of herself I was the last person to object.

'Thank you for saving me, Virginia,' I said. 'Very much. I should hate to have found a watery grave at the foot of a ski-jump, even such a famous one as the Holmenkollen.'

'No need to thank me, Derek,' she said sharply. 'I – I did nothing. You should take more care.'

She swept aside the others' praise for herself with the same brusqueness. So I was wrong. I had misjudged her. She didn't want to be a heroine. But, in that case why hadn't she made light of it all instead of upsetting Lynn more than was necessary? I sighed. Life seemed full of unanswerable questions these days.

I said as much to Martin as, having dressed, we trudged up the hill to where he had parked his car. I had insisted, in spite of Lorna's anxiety and Lynn's unhappy silence, that we must have our picnic, that I did not want to go home, that I was none the worse for my semi-drowning. In fact I felt rather shaky and the walk up-hill was an effort.

'Such as?' he said.

'Why the team of Hank and Chuck picked on my house. Why Hank is one day an American and the next a Norwegian, a student who doesn't know a word of English, although English is compulsory in all the schools here.'

'Why he says *pass deg* and an hour or so later you're nearly drowned. Derek, was it Hank?'

'Yes. I'm pretty sure it was Hank. But he didn't mean to drown me. Virginia embroidered somewhat. I think he meant to give me a bad fright. I might add that he succeeded.'

Martin grunted but made no comment. We had reached the car. He went to the boot, unlocked it and produced a dilapidated box with a red cross on it, which contained a miscellany of first aid stuff, including a battered pewter flask. He passed it to me.

'Here you are. Have a good swig. You look as if you need it.'

'Thanks, Martin. What about you?'

'Better not. I'll smoke and you drink.'

We leaned against the bumper of his car and he lit one of those small, dark cheroots that he affected. I sipped his brandy; it was typical of Martin that it was a particularly fine brandy. If the coffee had been good this was wonderful. I began to feel my old self.

Suddenly he said: 'I suppose you wouldn't consider telling our Security chaps about Hank and Chuck?'

'No.'

I had spoken more sharply than I intended. He looked at me over the top of imaginary spectacles and waited for me to amplify the bold negative. I plumped for a half-truth.

'They'd laugh at me. Say that, because of Washington, I was getting a persecution mania.'

'And are you?'

I didn't answer. It wasn't really an open question; Martin expected me to say 'no'. But I wasn't so sure. It seemed to me that Lynn and I were becoming too accident-prone for me to pretend, even to myself, that it was chance. Yet none of the accidents appeared to bear any relation to each other.

'I would advise it, Derek.'

'Are you saying that if I don't, you will?'

'No. I accept that you're my guest and that what I've learned from you this evening is – privileged. But I do advise it.'

'I'm sorry, Martin.'

'All right. If you've finished that brandy, let's go. I'm yearning for some food.'

We strolled back to the lake. We talked about the Northern Flank and Russia's surprising decision to open her border with Norway for a NATO visitation. I promised to lend him my copy of Day-Brune's biography, if I had finished it before his father sent him a copy. He said that he hoped I was looking forward to seeing a reindeer in its natural habitat and I said that what I yearned for was to stand on the soil of Mother Russia. We both knew that what I really wanted was to stop acting as a consul and get back to work that I enjoyed.

It was an awful pity that Martin Gatling was such a civilized character. Perhaps, if he had insisted that the Security people should be told, things might have turned out differently.

Chapter Four

It was Wednesday and not, thank God, a day on which I had to meet the public. I sat in a small room furnished with the minimum of chair, desk, typewriter, filing cabinet. Wasting the tax-payers' money, I brooded; I should have been writing a report. There was plenty to brood about. Things were not going well at home or at the office.

Primarily I was worried about Lynn. She was tense and on edge, see-sawing between depression and an unnatural gaiety. She made love as willingly as ever but with a sort of frantic intensity that took most of the pleasure out of it for me, and last night had reduced her to tears. Yet she stone-walled all my questions, saying that nothing was the matter, that she was perfectly healthy, that she had no problems, that she was not unhappy and she loved me very much. We were back to the worst of Washington.

Virginia was kind and helpful and understanding, at any rate to Lynn who seemed to rely on her more and more. To me she was pleasant enough too, even admitting that Lynn was very moody, but somehow I felt excluded, perhaps because Virginia tended to compliment Lynn's moods. Again, as in Washington, I tried not to be jealous.

And my main feeling this morning at breakfast, when Virginia had announced that she would be leaving us the following Tuesday – the day before the NATO party was due to fly to Kirkenes – had been one of dismay. Lynn was so obviously unhappy about it. Twice she said, as if to console herself, that London wasn't really very far from Oslo and twice Virginia said how sorry she was but that was the way it had to be. None of this prepared me for Lynn's announcement that she proposed to give a supper party for Virginia the evening before she was to go. Personally I thought we had done enough entertaining for the moment as we ourselves were such new arrivals, and I suggested taking Virginia out to dinner. But Lynn would have none of this and, to my annoyance, said that she had already asked the Gatlings. In something of a huff, I left her and Virginia sitting at the breakfast table discussing our other guests-to-be, and went off to the Embassy.

By chance I arrived on the Ambassador's tail. He greeted me affably and said that he had been seeing off his son at Fornebu – which explained what he was doing out of the Compound so early – and that he had been very impressed by the speech my father had made last week at the Royal College of Defence Studies. But he did not say anything about the NATO trip to the north. I was beginning to think that Martin had unintentionally misled me and that I was not going to be asked which, I thought resignedly, would at least solve the problem of leaving Lynn by herself.

Thinking of Martin reminded me that I had brought to the office my biography of John Day-Brune, which I had promised to lend him. I got it out of my briefcase and hesitated. He would probably be busy now, either reading telegrams or closeted in some meeting. But I wanted a change of scenery. I could always leave the book with Janet, his secretary.

I met her in the corridor. She was pinch-nosed, thin-lipped and had a patch of red colour in each cheek. She carried a large vase of steaming hot water which was beginning to burn her hands. I held open the door of her room and, as she passed, she leaned towards me and hissed:

'Please follow me, Mr Almourn. Please! And make him see a doctor, whatever he says.'

After that nothing would have stopped me. I pressed on her heels and found Martin in his shirt and underpants. He skipped behind his desk as we came in but relaxed when he saw it was me.

'Good, some water.'

'But no towel, Mr Gatling. They're all fixed on those metal things, and – '

'To stop us stealing them, yes. All right, Janet. I expect Mr

Almourn has a handkerchief. You go and telephone Lorna and tell her to bring me a suit and a clean shirt as soon as possible. Say I spilt something on myself. Don't worry her.'

'No, I won't. But you ought to see a doc – '

'Out! And keep everybody else out too.'

'Do you want me to go?'

'No, you stay, Derek. You can help. There's a bit of me around here that I can't see but that hurts like hell. And it hurts if I try to twist myself.'

'Not surprising. You're grazed right down one side – and bruised, I expect. What happened?'

'Let's get me cleaned up first.'

It took about ten minutes to wash the grazing and deal with some places where the skin was broken. Luckily most of the damage was on the surface, but Martin was going to be stiff tomorrow. And he was in more pain now than he liked to admit. He saved his lamentations for his suit, which was beyond repair.

'Maybe the chap who knocked me down will buy me a new one. He jolly well ought to.'

'You haven't told me yet what happened.'

'There's nothing much to tell.' Martin paused to light a cheroot. 'Lorna's mother, who lives in Ireland, is planning to come and visit us and I decided to go to the SAS offices in Russeløkkveien to make some enquiries before coming to the Chancery this morning. I was walking back to where I had parked the car when a motor-bike mounted the pavement and hit me.'

'Just like that?'

'Yes. The driver said he wasn't very experienced and he had lost control. He admitted it was completely his fault. I was lucky he wasn't going fast or I might have been badly hurt.'

'You've been hurt enough – apart from your suit. What's he doing about it? What did the police say?'

'We didn't call the police.'

'Why not?'

'For God's sake, Derek! Look, I was pretty shaken and so was he. I didn't want a fuss. He gave me his card and told me to contact him when I knew what the damage was, which is fair enough, though I must say he didn't look as if he could afford my tailor.'

'Well – as you like. Incidentally, I came to bring you this.' I gave him the Day-Brune. 'You'll enjoy it, I think. It's well written and researched, though it doesn't really explain him.'

'Thanks a lot. If I can catch up with my work I've a free evening tonight. I'll look forward to reading it.'

It was a gentle dismissal but a dismissal nevertheless. I went. My other reason for seeking him out, my real reason – the book had been an excuse – had not been so much as mentioned. It hadn't been necessary. If Martin had had anything to tell me about the trip to the north he would have told me. At least I knew that the Russians hadn't yet refused me. Notwithstanding, I returned to my office slightly more depressed than when I left it.

I didn't see Martin again until the next day, Thursday, when he sent for me. I had spent the last hour with the brother of the man who had drowned in the lake at Lillehammer. He was not content with the fact that the corpse was at last being flown home. He wanted to know what had happened to the gold watch, a family heirloom according to him, that his brother wore constantly. I refrained from saying that the corpse, when found, had been wearing only swimming trunks or that I had a very nice gold watch of my own, thank you, and had not needed to pinch his brother's. I said I would make further enquiries. I said that I was aware that he was a tax-payer but he could not see the Ambassador; if he had a complaint he should make it in writing.

And he probably would too, I thought bitterly, as I went along to Martin's office. Martin waved me to a chair while he finished dictating a telegram to Janet. He was looking as elegant as usual but a bit black under the eye, as if he hadn't slept well.

'How are you?' I asked, after Janet had gone back to her type-writer.

'Damned stiff, if you must know. I could scarcely move when I got up this morning. And I've pulled a muscle in my leg. Otherwise all right.'

'Good.'

'It could be better,' he said morosely. 'That chap who knocked me down was a phoney. I telephoned him last night to – to put his mind at rest. I thought he might be scared of getting an enormous claim from me. And the sod doesn't exist.'

'Doesn't exist? You mean there was no such number? What about the card he gave you?'

'The telephone number exists, the house exists, the man whose name was on the card exists. He's a dentist. He had just flown in from a holiday in England. He does not own a motor-bike. He has a son but the son is only four and rides a tricycle. If I would care to visit him he would be pleased to give me proof of this. But what's the point? You were right, Derek. I should have got the police.'

'You don't remember the number on his licence plate?'

'No. Anyway that was probably phoney too. Or he had "borrowed" the bike. I must say he showed enormous presence of mind in producing that dentist's card.'

'You could describe him to the police.'

'My dear Derek, I would be wasting their time and mine. He was a big, tall, exceedingly fair Norwegian. He could have been your friend Hank or a hundred like him.'

'You mean he looked like Hank? He – he could have been Chuck. They do look awfully like each other. Martin, you don't think – '

'Or a hundred other students. For God's sake, Derek, you're getting manic about those two. Do you think Hank and Chuck are working their way through a list of the Embassy staff and we ought to warn H.E.? If they are, they haven't done very well to date, have they? You're no worse for being half-drowned and all I've got to show from my little accident are a few bruises. So shall we forget the whole thing?'

'Sorry,' I said stiffly. I didn't remind him that it was he who had advised me to tell the Security people about Hank and Chuck, advice I had refused to take. I cheered myself with the thought that Lynn and I weren't the only ones to whom odd things happened. 'You wanted to see me about something?'

'Yes. Yes, I did.' Martin shook his head. 'Sorry I was so – so sharpish just now. I seem to be a little fraught at the moment.'

I grinned at him. 'I sympathize.'

He sighed. 'And I've some bad news for you. The Russians have flatly refused to let H.E. include you in his party on this NATO lark. I hope I didn't raise your hopes too high? Everybody, including the Norwegians, were sure they would agree but – *niet*.'

'Did they give any reason?'

'Only what one could have guessed. If the British bring an extra bod the other countries will want to do the same. And they wouldn't buy you taking Lorna's place. H.E. tried that. They said it would upset their arrangements. They're expecting so many diplomats and so many wives and that's how it's to be. Of course the Norwegians would be happy for you to come but you can go up to their side of the border any time.'

'Yes.' I was disappointed. It was no use pretending otherwise; but it was no use spitting in the wind either. 'Well, thank you for trying to fix it, Martin – and especially thank Lorna for offering me her place.'

Martin laughed. 'Lorna knows nothing about it. And best keep it that way. Not that she would have complained. I tell myself that one of these days I must make ambassador merely because she deserves to be an ambassador's wife.'

'I'm still grateful.'

I nearly added that I was glad not to have to leave Lynn behind, but I didn't want to get on to the subject of Hank and Chuck again. It was altogether another depressing day.

Because of our last somewhat feeble effort at entertaining I had decided to keep an eye on the supper party we were giving for Virginia and, on the following Monday, came home from the office early. But I need not have bothered. Everything was under control. Virginia had spent the penultimate day of her visit with us in the kitchen and the result was magnificent. Lynn is quite a good cook – much better than my sisters were when they were first married – but she couldn't have produced the cheese-flavoured straws and puffs, the glazed salmon, the prawns in aspic, the spiced tarts, and various other delectables with Virginia's professionalism. It was a chef's banquet.

I had already seen to the liquor, the wine and the soft drinks. Lynn had arranged the flowers and put out cigarettes. The china and silver were gleaming, the glasses were polished, the house had never looked more attractive and in the kitchen, ready to serve us, was a capable American girl and her Norwegian husband. Whatever could be done to ensure the success of a party had been done. We awaited our guests.

Meanwhile the three of us were meant to be having a quiet, relaxed drink on the verandah before anybody came. But Lynn kept on popping up and down to do something or fetch something and each time Virginia seemed to follow her. They were making me as jittery as they were and without cause. Everything was fine.

There was the sound of a car growling up our steep drive. The first guests were about to arrive. Lynn jumped nervously to her feet and sent the martini jug flying across the verandah. The telephone emitted that disturbing whistle to which Scandinavian phones are prone. The American girl came to say that she had cut her hand on a can and did we have a Band-aid.

The party had begun as it was to end.

I sent Lynn to deal with the cut, asked Virginia to sweep up the mess and myself answered the telephone. I did know the Norwegian for 'wrong number' but I couldn't remember what it was, so I used the English phrase firmly and put down the receiver. Then I dashed to the front door as the bell rang again.

'We thought we had come on the wrong day,' Lorna Gatling said.

'Sorry I was so slow but we had a slight crisis.'

'All over now?'

'If we can find another martini jug.'

Martin laughed. Lorna said how pretty the flowers were as we went through the house – we had planned to have drinks in the garden but to eat indoors – and how nice everything was looking. Lynn, who had appeared to greet them, ignored the compliments. She led the way on to the verandah, where Virginia, I was glad to see, had got rid of the broken glass and was far more welcoming to the Gatlings than Lynn had been.

However, as more guests arrived, Lynn cheered up. A Swedish couple, who were visiting our house for the first time, brought her flowers – a charming Scandinavian custom. And some American friends, not to be outdone, arrived with one of those glorious cream-filled cakes that are so popular in Norway.

'Which reminds me,' Martin said. 'I too have come bearing gifts but I left them in the car.'

When he rejoined us he gave me two books, the biography of Day-Brune that I had lent him and another called *What Now, Day-Brune?* which was a proof copy.

'I had a parcel from Sam over the weekend so I now have my own biography. But many thanks for lending me yours. Incidentally the book's being published next week. And this other may interest you. It deals with Day-Brune's future as opposed to his past.'

'Does he have a future – outside of prison?'

'That's the question. The author maintains that he could still be of immense value to the Russians and that they'll try either to spring him – this book was actually at the printers when Day-Brune failed to escape – or to swop him for the next import-export businessman whom they manage to catch on their side of the Iron Curtain. It makes fascinating reading.'

'Would you Brits be prepared to swop him for some business man?'

I was startled. I hadn't realized that Virginia was standing at my elbow and offering a plate of cheese straws.

'That would be up to the politicians.'

'Yes, but your Foreign Office would advise them. Martin, you're a Counsellor, a senior official, what advice would you give?'

Martin shook his head at the cheese straws and took out a cheroot. 'I can't see our lords and masters asking me. However, I would say that he would have to be a very important businessman indeed.'

'Yes, that's what I would have said too.'

Virginia carried off her cheese straws and Martin looked at me quizzically. 'Strange woman,' he murmured. 'You know, I think I'm rather frightened of her.'

We were joined by the American Military Attaché before I could think of an adequate response.

'I heard you discussing John Day-Brune,' he said, 'and there's one thing I can tell you for sure. If you Brits did try swopping him, even for quite a big fish, you would be hearing from the United States Government in no uncertain terms.'

'And from all our other NATO allies,' I said.

'Oh for God's sake, Derek, can't you ever talk about anything except your work?'

There was an awkward silence amongst our guests. It was not what Lynn had said but how she had said it. Her voice had been high and piercing and full of savage anger that was difficult to ignore. But we were a well-trained bunch.

The American said: 'That's just what my wife's always saying to me, aren't you, honey?'

'Yes,' his wife said. 'And you don't pay the least attention, sweetie.'

'Men are all alike,' Lorna Gatling volunteered and, encouraged by a small chorus, added: 'Whatever they may say they're much more devoted to their jobs than to their wives.'

'I, of course, am the exception that proves the rule,' Martin said with supreme complacency.

'Of course,' Lorna said and smiled at him lovingly.

For a split second I envied Martin Gatling. Lorna must have been forty; they had been married almost twenty years. She was neither beautiful nor particularly clever and, after a succession of miscarriages, remained childless. But there was a *rapport* between her and Martin which I didn't believe Lynn and I would ever achieve. Certainly we couldn't have been further from it at the moment.

Lynn, with a muttered apology about food, disappeared towards the kitchen and I set myself to being a good host. Virginia went tactfully after Lynn. They reappeared together to announce that supper was ready some short while after.

As we went into the house I managed to get beside Lynn. 'Are you all right, darling?' I held her by the arm.

'I'm fine, honey.'

'No headache?'

'No. I'm fine, Derek.'

Trying not to be impatient she gave me a bright smile aimed in the direction of my left ear. I let her go. She did not look fine and, I noticed later, she ate almost nothing. But she drank a great deal of wine.

I must have drunk a lot too, because I woke next morning with a hangover headache. I don't really remember. And anyway there were other reasons for that headache.

The supper itself was a success. The women praised the *cuisine* and the men had second helpings. The couple serving us were pleasant and efficient. Everything went smoothly. Our guests were enjoying themselves. On the surface it was a good party. Only Lynn and I seemed to be out of tune – and maybe Virginia, who appeared to me to be working over hard at her dual role of guest-of-honour and friend-of-the-family. But then I was always misjudging Virginia. We took our coffee and liqueurs into the garden.

Martin was standing on the verandah when he became ill. I was close to him and saw exactly what happened. It was very sudden. He was talking amiably to our Swedish guest in her own language when he stopped in mid-sentence, thrust his coffee cup and saucer towards her, and, as they fell, turned away and vomited prodigiously into a wild clump of daisies. Then he staggered off the verandah and fell flat on the grass, where he lay breathing stertorously. The smell of vomit was revolting.

There was the dead moment of shock.

After that we responded. The women tended to withdraw, the men to come forward. Lorna knew. Although she was walking in the apple orchard with the American Attaché she knew at once that it was Martin who was in trouble; she came running. My first thought was that he had had a heart attack.

I helped to turn him on his back, loosened his collar and tie, made sure his tongue was not obstructing his breathing. I shouted to Colin Kirkham, a First Secretary at the Embassy who has excellent Norwegian, to telephone our doctor; Lynn would show him where the telephone was and, if there was any difficulty, he could deal with the situation. Somebody suggested that Martin should be taken indoors, so we carried him into a small room on the ground floor where there was a couch and propped him up with pillows. Somebody else suggested that he should be kept warm, so I sent Virginia to fetch blankets. I turned everyone out of the room, except Lorna.

Lorna and I waited together. Virginia came back with some brandy which I made Lorna drink, although, as I would have expected, she was quite calm. She sat on the floor beside Martin, propping herself against the couch, and held his hand. Occasionally she wiped the sweat from his face with her handkerchief. She said that Martin had never had any such sort of attack before, that in spite of his somewhat frail appearance and his refusal to take exercise he was very strong, that he was almost never ill or caught things like colds or flu as other people did. I suppose she talked to reassure herself.

Eventually the doctor came, then the ambulance. Lorna wouldn't let me go to the hospital with her. She said there was no need for anyone to go with her but, when I insisted, she agreed that Colin and his wife could follow her on their way home. She kissed me good night. She even apologized on Martin's behalf for spoiling our party.

By now it was late. As soon as the ambulance had driven away the rest of our guests began to go. I shook hands and said goodbye automatically. My thoughts were concerned with Martin but it was Lorna's face, like a well-kept grave, that I couldn't forget.

When everybody had gone Lynn went off to bed, saying that it had been a horrible evening and she was going to take a sleeping pill. I told Virginia to go too. Our helpers had left everything very tidy and there was nothing to do. I would have to wait up until Colin telephoned from the hospital but I didn't need or want any company.

I hosed down the verandah and the daisies where Martin had been sick. I went round the house, making sure that everything was locked up for the night. I tried to read *What Now, Day-Brune?*

I made myself a cup of tea and walked up and down the drawing-room. I willed the telephone to whistle.

I had to wait until ten minutes to two. Then I was across the room and had picked up the receiver before the second note had ended. I cut short Colin's greetings.

'How is he?'

'He's in a coma. It's serious, I'm afraid. Lorna doesn't know, but he could just – just slip away without regaining consciousness.'

'Oh God!'

'The doc persuaded Lorna to lie down. He gave her a sedative. I think it must have been pretty strong because she's asleep.'

'She'll never forgive herself if Martin dies while she's sleeping.'

'But he could be in a coma for days, I gather.'

'I see. Well, Colin, you and Catherine had better push off home. I'll go along to the hospital myself first thing in the morning. And thank you both.'

'There's no need to thank us. Catherine and I would do more than that for Martin and Lor – Oh Christ, Derek!'

'It'll be all right, Colin.' Suddenly I felt very old. I shouldn't have let him go to the hospital. He was too young, too junior. I should have gone. Lynn and I should have gone. And what bloody difference would that have made? Martin was dying. 'Lorna said he was very tough. He's never had a heart attack before. He'll pull through.'

'But it wasn't a heart attack, Derek. The doctors – they won't commit themselves – but they think Martin was poisoned.'

'Poisoned!'

'Yes. They think he may have eaten something or – or drunk something at your party that he was particularly susceptible to. They say that if he hadn't vomited he might be – be dead by now.'

Poisoned. First Martin gets knocked down by some maniac on a motor-bike and then . . . It had to be coincidence. A minute ago I felt very old. Now I felt very young and very helpless and very afraid.

Chapter Five

It was a short night. I fought my way through wads of cotton-wool to consciousness and turned off the alarm. My head ached. My mouth was dry and had a nasty, hangover taste. Even the sight of Lynn, her corn-coloured hair spread out over the pillow, couldn't excite me. I shut my eyes. I didn't want to face the day.

But, slowly and reluctantly, I slid from the bed. I washed, shaved, dressed. I made some coffee and forced myself to eat some toast and marmalade. I wrote Lynn a note explaining that I was going to the hospital and from there to the Embassy; I said that I would telephone later. I propped the note against her dressing-table mirror so that she couldn't miss it. I thought of knocking on Virginia's door to say goodbye but it seemed a pity to disturb her; instead, I added a postscript to Lynn's note wishing Virginia *bon voyage*. I kissed Lynn on the cheek, very gently, so as not to wake her, and left the house.

At the bottom of the drive I swung the car to the left with its nose pointing up the hill. Then I braked sharply, got out and waited for the figure in the green trouser-suit to come up to me. When I had looked to my right to make sure that the road was clear I had had the impression that, on seeing the car turn out of the driveway, she had stopped; but there was no cosy place to hide and she had had to continue towards me. I was certain that she had been walking very fast in spite of the steepness of the hill. Now she was approaching at a leisurely pace.

'Good morning, Derek,' she called.

'Good morning, Virginia. You're up early.'

'I couldn't sleep any longer. I'm not used to these light nights and the birds seemed particularly noisy this morning, so I went for a stroll.'

'Did you go far?'

'No, just along by Smestad Pond. The ducks are up already. And where are you off to? Is there an emergency at your Embassy?'

'I'm going to the hospital.'

'Oh yes – of course. How is Martin?'

'He's seriously ill. He's in a coma.'

'I'm very sorry.' Virginia frowned. 'He was a nice man. It's most unfortunate.'

I thought that 'most unfortunate' was an inadequate phrase to describe the situation but I didn't comment. It wasn't worrying about Martin that had kept Virginia from sleep – she had clearly forgotten about him – but, now reminded, she really was concerned.

'Most unfortunate,' she said again. 'I am sorry. Will you give Lorna my – my sympathy.'

'Yes, of course,' I said. 'And I must go. I'm glad I caught you.'

'Caught me?' Her voice was sharp.

'To say goodbye and all best wishes for the rest of your holiday,' I said blandly. 'I'm going straight from the hospital to the Embassy. I didn't expect to have a chance to bid you farewell today in person.'

'Goodbye, Derek, and thank you.'

'Goodbye, Virginia.'

We shook hands and our cheeks touched as we kissed the conventional air. Virginia started up the drive. I got into the car and drove off, racking my brains as to what Virginia had been doing. It could be true that she hadn't been able to sleep but it wasn't true that she had been for 'a stroll'. When I first saw her she was striding up the hill at a rate of knots. What's more the alarm had woken me at six o'clock and by then Virginia was already out of the house or I should have heard her. Forty minutes to walk at a leisurely pace to Smestad Pond and back were more than ample. I couldn't believe that she had spent another twenty minutes contemplating the ducks. And I was assuming she had left the house just before the alarm went off. She could have been gone much longer.

But where had she been and what had she been doing? Virginia was always creating these small, maddening, senseless mysteries. And too often she seemed to involve Lynn.

I drove very fast. There was almost no traffic and I was able to park close to the hospital. I said, in English, that I was from the British Embassy and wanted to enquire after Mr Gatling. Martin's name worked magic. A nurse, who spoke excellent English, was produced and led me to a small but comfortable waiting-room, where Lorna and tea for both of us arrived simultaneously. I had already learned that there was no change in Martin's condition; he was still in a coma. I asked Lorna if she was satisfied with the care Martin was getting and she said that it was splendid and everybody had been very kind.

She had telephoned Sam, Martin's father, and he would be arriving later in the day. Her mother's visit she would postpone; her mother was over seventy and needed looking after herself. There was nobody else. They were, as she said, a sparse family.

She had given Colin the key of their house and Catherine would bring her some fresh clothes. Catherine would also take the stray cat that had adopted them. She herself would stay at the hospital until – She left the sentence unfinished.

'Isn't there anything I can do?'

'I don't think so, Derek. Except pray for him – if you know how.'

'I know how,' I said gently, 'and I will pray for him.'

'I – I'm sorry. I didn't mean – '

Tears filled her eyes and wetted her cheeks. She put her head on the table, her face buried in her arms, and sobbed. I would have given anything in the world to have been able to tell her truthfully that Martin would live.

I left the hospital and drove to the Embassy. I have rarely felt more helpless or more angry. I had to do something.

I made a list of the couples who had had supper with us – it seemed much longer ago than yesterday evening – and asked one of the girls to contact each of them for me. Making the excuse that I wanted to tell them how Martin was, I discovered that nobody else had had any ill effects from the party. Although I hadn't expected otherwise, this was a relief. But I still felt responsible for Martin.

I asked the girl to make a person-to-person call for me to Lord Almourn.

To my embarrassment the call came through as I arrived in the Ambassador's office. There was some initial confusion because H.E. thought my father wanted to speak to him. Then, when this had been straightened out and he had told me to be his guest, I pushed the wrong switch so that my father's voice boomed through the squawk box.

'For God's sake, Derek, they're a dozey lot at your Embassy. I've been hanging on this line ten minutes while they tried to find you. And my time's worth something. I'm not in the Diplomatic Service.'

'Francis!' I said desperately; I have called my father by his first name as long as I can remember.

The Ambassador gave me a sour smile and, leaning across his desk, reversed the switches so that instead of a loud boom from the squawk box there was only a small torrent from the telephone receiver. I cradled it in my hand until that ceased. H.E. had buried himself in his papers but he had not left me alone; it was not going to be a private call.

'Francis, listen. I need your help.'

'All right, Derek. What can I do?'

I told him. I wanted him to get the best possible specialist and fly him out to Oslo to examine Martin Gatling. I gave him all the details of Martin's illness that I could. He said that he would do his best which I knew would be good enough. He said that the family was flourishing as usual and asked after Lynn and me and I said that we were fine. I cut the conversation as short as possible.

I apologized to H.E. and he waved my apology aside. He was affable again, prepared to forget my father's insult if Francis in his turn was prepared to help Martin. We discussed Martin and he said:

'You realize that this means I shall want you and your wife to come with us tomorrow.'

Tomorrow. It took five seconds for the penny to drop. He was telling me that I was to accompany him on the formal visitation to the Russo-Norwegian border and I ought to have been delighted.

In other circumstances I would have been. Now I was merely surprised that the probability had never once occurred to me after Martin had become ill. And yet I was the obvious choice.

'I think you know,' H.E. continued, 'that I tried to take you as an extra or in Lorna Gatling's place, but the Russians wouldn't accept either proposition. And it did occur to me that they might have something against you personally.'

'Why on earth should they, sir?'

'Why indeed? Maybe because you're Lord Almourn's son.' He couldn't resist the dig. 'They don't have to be logical. Anyway I thought it worth checking and I was wrong. I spoke to the Russian Ambassador myself. He assures me they'll be pleased to welcome you and – er – Lynn.'

'Well – thank you, sir.'

'There'll be a full briefing at two o'clock this afternoon. If possible I would like – er – Lynn to come. The Security Officer wants to have a little chat with the ladies.'

'I'll see she's there, sir.'

But I didn't. As soon as I got back to my own office I telephoned the house but there was no answer. I coudn't remember which flight Virginia was catching but I presumed that Lynn was either at Fornebu, seeing her off, or on her way to or from the airport.

And then we had a consular crisis. Some bloody British business-man had been arrested for drunken driving and had spent the night in gaol. He was now awake and roaring for his Ambassador. He wasn't going to get him but somebody had to cope. I tried to persuade the Trade Secretary that it was his job but he had his hands full with a delegation and I had to go.

By the time I had escorted Big Business to his hotel and arranged for him to catch the next plane to London, it was after twelve. I telephoned Lynn from the hotel lobby. There was still no answer. I couldn't pretend that Smestad was on the way from Stortingsgaten to the Embassy but it was the way I decided to go.

It was a wasted effort. The house was locked up and there was no sign of Lynn. I made myself a scratch lunch from the remains of last night's party and waited as long as I could, but she didn't appear and I had to go back to the Embassy by myself, suspecting that, although it wasn't my fault or Lynn's, H.E. would take a dim view of her not attending the briefing. He didn't disappoint me.

The following day H.E.'s party set off for Fornebu airport and points north.

And we set off in style. The ambassadorial car, its pennant flying, contained His Excellency seated between his lady and mine, and the Press Attaché and myself sitting opposite them on the tip seats. Behind us came the Embassy estate car with the Admin Officer, the Security Officer and our luggage.

We were not the largest contingent to arrive at Fornebu. Both the Dutch and the Belgians had brought two extra bods to wave goodbye and the Americans, although numerically the same as us, had come in a third car. We were greeted by a bevy of Norwegians from their Ministry of Defence and a couple of po-faced characters from the Russian Embassy.

As usually happens on such occasions there was a scene of utter confusion, which gradually sorted itself out. The actual party was to be twenty-two in number and, in spite of all the fuss and blow accorded our departure, we were to travel on the ordinary commercial flight as far as Bodø, just north of the Arctic Circle. Our flight number had been called and the unfortunate Norwegian colonel, who was to be in charge of us, was beginning to make noises when Lynn seized me by the arm.

'Derek, I've lost my bag!'

'What?'

'My bag! My shoulder bag – the one Virginia gave me. You know! Derek, I can't go without it!'

'Darling, don't panic. When did you have it last?'

'I – can't remember.'

'Think. You had it in the car. H.E. commented on it. Did you bring it into the lounge?'

'Yes. Yes, I did. One of the girls said how fantastic it was. But it was slung over my shoulder. I didn't put it down anywhere. And even if I had, it's not there now. I've looked – on all the tables and under the seats. Derek, it's gone. Oh God, what am I going to do?'

'Darling, it's not the end of the world. What did you have in it?

Your passport? Money, keys, cosmetics – anything else? Lynn, was there anything else, anything valuable?'

'Oh – no! Nothing valuable. But there was a letter from Lloyd that came just before we left and that I haven't had time to read yet.'

'Well, that's not irreplaceable.' I didn't mean to sound unsympathetic but H.E. was signalling to me and I couldn't go on ignoring him. The party was moving out of the lounge. 'Listen, Lynn, I'll tell the Security Officer. He'll see there's a proper search made for it. And not to worry. It'll turn up, darling, I'm sure no one has pinched it. You must have put it down somewhere and forgotten.'

'No, Derek! You don't understand. I can't go without it. I won't. I'll pretend to faint. Make a big scene. Perhaps if they believe I'm really ill –'

'Are you mad? Lynn, if you do anything like that, I'll go without you. I swear I will. Don't you understand? This isn't a – a package tour, whatever it may look like. I'm here on duty.'

'Duty!'

She spat the word at me and we stood, glaring at each other. I had a sense of *déjà-vu*. I could have predicted how the argument would continue – and end.

'Derek!' The Ambassador had a commanding voice.

'Coming, sir.'

'The loo. The loo!' Lynn said and dropped her coat.

She ran. I waited. I wasn't sure what she had meant. Was she pretending to be sick as she had threatened or had she remembered where she had left Virginia's damned bag? The Ambassador had come back and so had the Norwegian colonel. They bore down on me together.

'There's something the matter, *ja*?'

'What on earth's going on, Derek? Don't you realize you're keeping everyone waiting?'

'Sir. I – I'm terribly sorry.'

But Lynn was flying towards me, the found bag over her shoulder and anchored to her side by one hand. She came to a halt in front of us. She was wearing some sort of mauve outfit, very plain, very well-cut, very expensive. Her straight, corn-coloured hair hung down to her waist. Her violet eyes were enormous. She looked young, vulnerable, appealing.

She said: 'Am I ever sorry. But I had to –' She gestured towards the ladies' room. She didn't look at me.

The two middle-aged men escorted her from the lounge. I followed, carrying her coat and trying not to grin. The crisis was over.

In ten minutes, after a lot of hand-shaking and well-wishing in a variety of languages, we were all emplaned and in another ten we were air-borne.

Lynn and I sat side by side in companionable silence, our flash of tempers forgiven. I studied my Norwegian Grammar and Lynn read her letter from Lloyd. He wrote to her regularly, with what I considered extraordinary devotion for a brother, and usually she was delighted to hear from him. But today, for some reason, what he had written seemed to annoy her. She thrust the letter into her bag and stared out of the window.

'Derek.'

'H-mm.'

'I love you.'

'I love you too, darling. *Gjennom tykt og tynt,* which is Norwegian for "through thick and thin". You know, given some German this isn't a difficult language.'

'Derek, please.' She slid her hand into mine. 'Please, honey, let's be very close for – for the next day or two.'

'Yes, of course, darling.'

I smiled at her and squeezed her hand, wanting to comfort her. I told myself for the umpteenth time that I had to be more sympathetic, that I had to remember how cut off from her family and her friends she must feel and how dependent she was on me.

'We'll be very close, I promise,' I said.

And odd as it may seem in retrospect, for the next day or two we were very close and I at least was very happy – in my fool's paradise.

Our SAS DC-9 landed at Bodø after an uneventful flight and we were greeted by the Mayor, gallons of coffee and tea and the inevitable open sandwiches. While we lunched, the Norwegian colonel explained that our party would be transferring to a couple of Twin Otters, which would enable us to fly low up the coast to Narvik over a beautiful stretch of fjords backed by mountains and lakes, then inland, keeping close to the border of Finland, to Kautokeino (where we would land) and Karasjok – the two main Lapp gathering places on the Finnmark plain – and on to our destination, Kirkenes, near the Soviet border. He sounded like a travel agent, as Lynn whispered to me.

Nevertheless, at least the male half of his audience appreciated that they were not making the trip to admire the scenery. We were here to 'recce' the terrain and Norway's vulnerability if an enemy should ever again attack from the north, a vulnerability about which we, as diplomatic representatives of NATO countries, would be expected to advise our governments, since it was their responsibility to safeguard the Northern Flank. But this wasn't something that would interest Lynn.

Still I didn't see why husband and wife should have monocular vision. I was glad that she should enjoy herself and at any level this trip was fascinating. It was as if Finnmark, this northernmost province of Norway, had laid itself out to please us. The scenery was awe-inspiring and, although we had been warned that in summer all the herds were driven to the islands, there was no shortage today around Kautokeino either of Lapps in their picturesque blue and red suits and jester caps or of their reindeer.

What pleased Lynn more than anything, however, was the silver, fashioned after traditional Lapp designs, which was on sale at a kind of jewellery-manufacturing commune in Kautokeino. She let me buy her a pendant and then herself bought a necklace, earrings, cufflinks, a bracelet. Because I thought they would prefer them I bought brooches of modern design for my mother and sisters and, on the spur of the moment, added another for Lorna Gatling.

Neither Martin nor Lorna had been far from my thoughts all day. Indeed I wouldn't have been able to enjoy myself so much if the news hadn't at last been hopeful. Martin had regained consciousness yesterday afternoon, not long before the Harley Street consultant had flown in. My father had produced one of the top people from University College Hospital and he had confirmed the Norwegian doctors' diagnosis. Martin had consumed something – there were one or two suggestions – which could have been expected to upset his stomach for a few days, rather as an intestinal bug does but, because of some quirk in his metabolism, he had become seriously affected and, if he had not vomited, would probably have died. However, now that he had come out of the coma, his prospects were good. I was enormously relieved.

I hoped that Lorna would like the brooch. Lynn was certainly delighted with her buys. From the time our Twin Otters took off from the grass strip which served Kautokeino for a runway, to the time we landed at Kirkenes about an hour later, she brooded lovingly over them. She wasn't the only one – everybody had bought lavishly; the commune must have wished there was a diplomatic visitation every day – but she was the only one who listed her loot. Not that it was fair to call it loot, since against each piece she wrote the name of the person for whom it was intended. It wasn't like Lynn to be so methodical and I teased her about it.

'You look as if you were making a will, darling.'

'Don't say that! Oh Derek, what a horrible thing to say.'

'You shouldn't take things so literally,' I said. 'It's a North American failing.'

'I didn't get anything for you,' she said. 'You're with me and – and I didn't think you would want any sort of memento.'

'Not – not particularly,' I said, though I had noticed that there was nothing for me or for anybody else, for that matter, outside of her family and, of course, Virginia. 'Forget your baubles now. We'll be coming in to land in a few minutes. And tonight, darling, do you realize, we should see the midnight sun.'

As far as I could make out not only we but the entire population of Kirkenes over the age of four was eager to see the midnight sun. Perhaps because the hours of darkness are so long and there are so many months of winter in this part of the world the local inhabitants have to make the most of the brief summer light. At any rate during the three nights I spent there it was my impression that nobody except the very young and the very old ever went to bed.

Because we had been travelling for most of the day and some of the diplomats were not in the first flush of youth it had been decided that there would be no formal entertainment that evening; but there was plenty to do. Kirkenes positively throbbed with vitality. In the attractive hotel in which our party was staying – built of wood but a shower to every room and all mod cons – there was a night-club and a formal dance.

I never did know what the dance was in aid of, but a word in our Norwegian colonel's ear and, although we were foreigners and not properly dressed for the occasion, Lynn and I were made welcome. I think the colonel had got the impression that we were only just married, because he was especially kind to us.

'*God fornøyelse!*' he said, beaming at us both.

'*Takk takk,*' I said. 'We will.'

And we did; we had a wonderful time, not missing a dance until the band finally abandoned their instruments. Then bed and love and the minimum of sleep.

The next day was entertaining. After breakfast, at which with care it was possible to avoid cold fish, we were met and briefed by the Border Commissioner, a retired Norwegian admiral, and then driven along beside the Pasvik River, whose waters form part of the border with the Soviet Union. From Svanvik on the Norwegian side we stared through high-powered glasses across the river to the mining town of Nikel, the nearest we should ever be allowed to it. We had lunch at one of the many wooden guest houses, were shown the chapel dedicated to Oscar II at the mouth of the Jakobs River and were driven back to Kirkenes.

In the evening the Mayor of Kirkenes gave a banquet for us at which there were so many *skols* that it was easy to predict a lot of thick heads in the morning. Then again for Lynn and me there was bed and love and the minimum of sleep. It was not unlike our honeymoon.

Chapter Six

And so we came to Friday, the day we were to visit Boris Gleb on the Russian side of a border which had been closed for over seven years.

At ten o'clock our party assembled in the bar, presumably because it was the most convenient room, and was given coffee. I found myself drinking quickly, refusing a second cup. Others were doing the same, I noticed. Somehow there was a general air of suppressed excitement that had been missing at the start of yesterday's expedition. When the Norwegian colonel knocked on a table for attention there was an almost immediate silence.

'Ladies and gentlemen,' he said, 'buses are waiting for us outside the hotel and when you are ready we shall go. But there are a couple of points I must make.

'First I have to tell you that today it is forbidden to take cameras.' There was a murmur of disappointment. 'I'm sorry, but our Soviet hosts insist. So, please, no cameras, not even very small ones.' He grinned but there was no doubt that he meant what he said. 'I am told we shall all be given picture postcards of Boris Gleb and permitted to buy anything we like at the souvenir shop.

'Secondly I must ask you all to stay together. Please, nobody is to wander off by themselves. We do not want anyone to get lost.'

'Or kidnapped!'

Everybody turned and looked at the unfortunate American girl who had made the remark; she had intended it for her husband alone but her voice had bombed. Now the freckles on her long, horsey face were drowned in blushes.

'That, madam, is such a remote possibility as to be unthinkable,' the colonel said severely. 'If coffee is finished may I suggest that we meet outside the hotel in five minutes. Thank you very much.'

I collected Lynn's camera and offered to take H.E.'s but he

wanted to go up to his room. It was the Ambassadress who suggested I should take Lynn's coat.

'You won't need it, my dear. We shall be back quite early and it's going to be a lovely day – warmer than yesterday.'

'I – want to take it.'

'But why? Either you'll have to leave it in the bus or it'll be an awful nuisance.'

'I want to take it. I was cold yesterday – on the drive.'

'Darling, you were – All right.'

I had been about to say that she was talking nonsense; yesterday she had complained that she was too hot. But I stopped myself. What the hell? If she wanted to take her coat, why not? She was wearing the mauve outfit that she had travelled in to Kirkenes and, although she looked rather tired, she was still going to be the most beautiful thing around.

Besides, she hated to be carped at. That's why I hadn't commented earlier when she had pinned on her lapel the gold brooch that Lloyd had given her before we left Washington. This was the first time I had seen her wear it. Either she didn't like it or she objected to the fact that it was a British bulldog and so implied, as Lloyd had joked, that she was British now herself. Anyway, I hoped that neither H.E. nor his lady would make a crack about it.

In the bus we sat dutifully behind them and, under cover of the offending coat, held hands. I was sorry it was such a short journey to the border but here, through a quirk of history, a peninsula or salient of land jutting into Norwegian territory does in fact belong to the Soviet Union. It was this well-wooded peninsula that we hoped to visit, with the compound on the west side of the Pasvik River that used to be freely open to foreign tourists until the local Norwegian authorities began to worry about imports of duty-free vodka, the village of Borisoglebsk – as the Russians call it – to the east of the river, the various power stations, some built by the Norwegians for the Russians, and of course anything else the Russians chose to show us.

We came on the actual border crossing in what seemed the middle of nowhere. Our buses slowed and groaned to a halt in front of the barricade. There was a pill-box on either side of the narrow road, soldiers standing to attention. Slowly the barricade was raised. A gentleman in resplendant uniform, who turned out to be the Russian Border Commissioner, stepped forward so that the toes of his highly polished boots just grazed the line where the barricade would fall and saluted. He was accompanied by three aides and a character in a badly-fitting brown suit, who must have been KGB but who was to be introduced to us as Comrade Igor Vetski, in charge of security.

It was all very formal and very smart, even though the impression given was that everything had been laid on for our benefit and that tomorrow soldiers, pill-boxes, barricade and welcoming committee would have been replaced by the barbed wire fence which was the normal method of demarcation along this part of the border. By this time, however, we had spilled from our buses and the road was covered with members of the *corps diplomatique*, some of them quite senior, all of them trying to appear as unruffled and at ease as if they were in their own drawing-rooms. Military precision was ruined.

None of our party, not even our Norwegian colonel, was in uniform but this didn't appear to disconcert him. He shook hands with the Commissioner and replied to his fluent Norwegian in fluent Russian. They both laughed; they would speak English which was after all today's universal language. Everybody would then understand.

'Lucky our French colleagues aren't with us,' H.E. murmured in my ear.

'The Belgian Ambassador's not looking too pleased,' I said.

'Must be indigestion,' H.E. said. 'I can't believe he'd consider the use of English an insult to either his country or himself. He's Flemish born.'

I grinned. We were moving across the border now and into Russian buses. As we boarded our respective vehicles the Norwegian colonel presented each of us to the Russian Border Commissioner, his aides and Comrade Vetski. It was the oddest reception line that I have ever passed along.

Indeed the whole scene could have been lifted from the theatre of the absurd and I was so entertained by the anomalies that it was not until I had been sitting beside Lynn in our new transport for over a minute that I realized she was shivering. I put out my hand and touched her face. Her cheek was warm. And the inside of the bus was hot and airless. I stared at her.

'Why are you shivering? Darling, are you feeling ill?'

'N – no.'

'What's the matter then?'

She made a big effort, taking several deep breaths and, sure enough, the shivering stopped. 'Sorry, Derek. I'm okay now.'

'But what is it?'

'Nothing really. Nerves, maybe. Don't make a fuss – please. I told you. I'm okay now. I just haven't been getting enough sleep.' She gave me her small, secret smile. 'You're to blame, you know, honey.'

I laughed, half relieved and ready to accept her explanation, half still anxious. 'It's not altogether my fault,' I said.

'Well, don't worry about me so much. There's no need. Derek, I know I sometimes seem to you sort of – sort of unreliable, but I'm not. And I'm tough. I can look after myself.'

'But you don't have to, darling. That's my job.'

She didn't answer. We were arriving at the tourist compound. The buses were drawing up in front of a medium-sized wooden building whose only interesting feature was a display of all our flags. The Union Jack was upside down.

Here, after a speech of welcome from the Border Commissioner, we were given an excellent stand-up luncheon. Much of it, including the imposing mounds of caviar, must have been flown in for the occasion. The Russians who had met us at the border, their number supplemented by two more officers and some Intourist hostesses, moved amongst us making themselves agreeable. There was little exchange of hard information but it was a good party.

Nevertheless, it wasn't exactly what we had come for. When the offering of coffee and liqueurs dragged on the Commissioner must have sensed that his guests were becoming restless. He asked for our attention and told us what had been planned.

Our party was to be divided into two. The diplomats would be given a briefing on the work of the Border Commission, and would then be driven to visit the power stations on the Pasvik River and the village of Borisoglebsk. The ladies would not leave the tourist compound but would be taken to the old church with its bell-tower and twin-balled turrets and to the souvenir shop; afterwards, as there was nothing else of interest in the area, they would be shown a film on the Soviet Union. We would all meet for tea back where we started. It sounded most efficient, if not exactly inspiring.

'I'm afraid you're going to be bored,' I said to Lynn.

'No. I shan't be bored.'

'Are you all right?'

'Yes.' She sighed. 'You never listen, do you, honey? I told you when we were in the bus. You mustn't worry about me. I'm fine.'

'You don't look –'

'Derek!'

'Sorry, darling. Well, I hope you enjoy your afternoon. Goodbye for now.'

'Goodbye.'

I enjoyed my afternoon. The Russian Border Commissioner had gone to great trouble to make the briefing interesting. He began with a short history of the northlands through which the Lapps had roamed at will for centuries and through which they still roamed, regardless of which part was called Norway or Finland or the Soviet Union. He brought the history up to date, touching lightly on the events of World War II. Then he discussed the work of the Border Commission – that unique but little-known joint Norwegian-Soviet arrangement which controlled this sensitive Arctic border between East and West. He showed us maps, slides, charts. He even answered some questions.

Then we were loaded into some Russian jeeps and driven down river by the power house and the dam to the village of Borisoglebsk on the other side of the Pasvik, where the workers for the power station lived, and north again to the border through woods that were interlaced with paths. The essence of the Commission was said to be its mobility; in the summer the Russians patrolled the border in jeeps and in the winter on snowmobiles. There was no sign of gun emplacements or any kind of defence – not that we were permitted to see at any rate. As H.E. murmured in my ear, it was 'all good clean fun but scarcely worth NATO's price of admission'.

I began to look forward to my tea. I thought of Lynn and wondered what she was doing. I hoped she hadn't abandoned the company of the Ambassadress for that of the more congenial Americans. I was glad when we got back to the hall where we had had lunch and where it was clear from the plates of sandwiches and little iced cakes that we were to have tea.

We waited. The Russian Commissioner had been called away as soon as we arrived back. We had been shepherded through the cloakroom and into the hall by his aides, who had then left us. It wasn't until one of the older ambassadors, who had a weak bladder or an irritated bowel, decided that he needed to pay another visit to the lavatory that we had any reason to suspect something was wrong.

He came storming over to our Norwegian colonel. 'There's a soldier outside the door,' he said, 'and the fellow won't let me pass. I told him I needed to go to the washroom but all he'll say is *niet, niet*. And I must go.'

'He must have misunderstood, Your Excellency.'

'Couldn't you just ignore him?'

'Was he armed? Did he threaten you?'

'What are they doing anyway, putting us under guard?'

But apart from the ambassador whose need, to judge by the redness of his face and the way he shuffled from one foot to the other, was great, none of us was taking the matter seriously. The colonel went to the door and argued with the soldier. Somebody suggested that, if the Russians didn't return soon, we should help ourselves to tea. Somebody else wondered where our wives were. Nobody was really anxious.

A whistle sounded outside the door. Heavy feet clumped along the corridor. The ambassador went to perform his natural functions, under escort. The colonel also went away, demanding to see the Russian Border Commissioner. The conversation in the hall became muted, uneasy. The ambassador returned. The colonel did not return. Time passed.

'I think there's trouble, Derek,' H.E. said.

'What sort of trouble, sir?'

'We-ell, it has occurred to me that, in spite of the warning we were given before we left Kirkenes, one of those blasted women may have smuggled in a camera. That would be more than enough to upset our Russian friends.'

'One couldn't blame them either.'

'No, one couldn't blame them at all. And pity the poor husband when we get back to Oslo. His fellow diplomats will not be nice about it.'

'No, I suppose not, sir.'

'However, we must stick together now and, I think, start throwing our weight around.'

I never knew what H.E. had in mind because there was more tramping of feet and the Russian contingent entered. It consisted of Comrade Igor Vetski, who spoke only through his interpreter, the Border Commissioner, two aides and a woman. With them was our Norwegian colonel. He looked stunned.

'Gentlemen, please be seated,' the Commissioner said.

There were chairs scattered around the room and hurriedly the aides pushed a dozen together. We sat, forming an audience. The Norwegian colonel sat too; he was one of us. But somehow he seemed to disassociate himself.

The Russians stood, grouped in a semi-circle, their faces blank. To the front of them, his interpreter at his elbow, was Igor Vetski. Obviously he was the king-pin. He stared at us accusingly while we sheltered behind the diplomatic carapace. But I was fascinated. Never for a single moment did it occur to me that Lynn might be involved. At this point I was still thinking in terms of what H.E. had said and I knew Lynn hadn't taken her camera.

The Border Commissioner took one step forward.

'Gentlemen, may I present to you Comrade Igor Vetski. You have already met him, I know, but you should now be aware that he is a very important person connected with the security of the Soviet Union. He wishes to speak to you on a matter of grave importance.'

The Commissioner stepped back. Comrade Vetski spoke and his interpreter produced almost simultaneous translation; they were a team, which meant that Vetski really was a VIP. My Russian is fairly fluent – it's one of the languages I read at Oxford – but I found it easier to follow the interpreter. I listened avidly. I was wildly interested but detached. The Comrade took a long time getting to the point.

'. . . invited to Borisoglebsk in good faith and you have shamefully abused our hospitality. You would have known that – because of the nature of your visitation – none of you would be searched either entering or leaving the country. For our part we assumed that you could be trusted. We, alas, have been proved wrong. And that our trust should have been so misplaced is hurtful.'

It was a typical Russian speech, melodramatic, emotional, full of barbed insults; but this was not the United Nations. The audience did not intend to remain docile. They shuffled their feet, murmured to each other and finally made a signal to H.E., who was the doyen of the ambassadors present. He rose and interrupted the interpreter.

'Kindly inform Monsieur Vetski that we are tired. We wish to rejoin our wives and return across the border to Norway, the country to which we are all accredited diplomats. Perhaps the Border Commissioner would be good enough to arrange this – at once.'

'Certainly it will be arranged, Your Excellency. There's no question of keeping any of you or your wives against your will – except of course for the one who has engaged in subversive activity. She must stay. Charges will be preferred.'

'Nobody will stay,' H.E. said firmly. 'I don't care what charges may have been trumped up. Our party has diplomatic immunity and unless Monsieur Vetski wishes to create an international incident he will do well to remember that fact.'

'Comrade Vetski says that an international incident has already been created, Your Excellency. And there are some things which diplomatic immunity do not cover – such as acts of subversion.'

'Acts of subversion! What is he talking about? I suppose one of those silly women tried to take a snap with her Brownie.'

'Snap with her brownie?' This anachronism was too much for the interpreter's English, excellent as it was. 'I do not understand.'

H.E. gestured irritably. 'Take a photograph – with a Minox, a camera.'

'No. Now it is you who does not understand.'

'Who does?' the American Ambassador asked.

Comrade Vetski interrupted with a flood of Russian. 'A Soviet writer not content with the many benefits he receives from the state, has written a book – a subversive book – a book full of lies about his Motherland – which he wishes to have published in the West, where it could do much harm to the present détente between the USSR and the Western Allies. It has been transferred to microfilm and an attempt has been made to smuggle it out of the country. How can you talk about diplomatic immunity for such a – a dastardly act?'

'Are you accusing a member of our party – ' H.E. began.

'I am not accusing. I am telling you what she has done – has tried but failed to do. You appreciate now how serious the matter is. And you cannot say that we have trumped it up because she has admitted it – in front of all the other wives. She has admitted her crime against the people of the Soviet Socialist Republic.'

'Who – ?'

But the door had opened and a bevy of stricken women poured across the hall to us. Whatever their personal relations with them may have been, no collection of husbands can ever have been more pleased to see their wives than this lot were. During the last two minutes, when Vetski had been explaining to us the nature and the importance of the accusation, there can't have been a diplomat in that room who didn't dread, at least momentarily, that it was his wife who had given way to a sudden temptation and agreed, probably in the name of freedom and human rights, to take that microfilm to the West.

I exempt myself, because somehow I knew at once that it was Lynn who had tried – and failed – to do this mad, irresponsible thing. But I hoped, against hope. I went on staring at the door as if I really expected a girl in a mauve dress and jacket, a girl with long hair the colour of a corn field, to walk in. Lynn, however, did not appear. And what for the others was a passing fear, for me became stark reality. I felt numb.

The Ambassador was splendid. He summed up the situation – what he believed to be the situation – immediately and he roared like a lion, albeit a wounded lion. It was the only course he could take if he was to save Lynn. And never once, either then or later, did he reproach me.

First he cried diplomatic immunity. Then, when that brought no response, he pleaded. He said that Mrs Almourn was a very young woman, who knew nothing of international niceties, only recently married to a diplomat and so inexperienced that she would not have understood how wrong her action was. Luckily, however, no actual harm had been done. The microfilm had been found. In the circumstances, therefore, he was certain it was best *for everybody concerned* that that should be an end to the matter. The Soviet Union would not want to escalate a moment of folly on the part of a young diplomat's wife into a great scandal and thus put themselves in the wrong. And, with the merest suggestion of a threat behind his pleading, he was back again to diplomatic immunity. It was a masterly performance.

I was grateful to the American Ambassador too. Not content with a part in the chorus of support which the others had provided, he stuck his neck out. Mrs Almourn was married to a British diplomat but she had been born in the United States, she was an American citizen, she carried an American passport, she was the daughter of Kenneth J. Charlton, a most important member of the United States Senate. His country would also take a very poor view if Lynn Charlton Almourn should come to any harm whatsoever.

'And Mr Almourn? What does Mr Derek Almourn have to say about his wife's behaviour?'

Comrade Vetski's interpreter had been working overtime, translating the ambassadors. The Comrade himself had said almost nothing but had contented himself with nodding his head to show that he understood. The rest of the Russians stood behind him, like waxworks in Madame Tussaud's. Now Vetski had asked a direct question and asked it of me. And what could I say to help Lynn that hadn't already been said? I was so desperately afraid for her.

The Ambassadress squeezed my arm and I found myself on my feet. 'If my wife has indeed done or tried to do what she is accused of – ' I began slowly.

'Her guilt is not in question. She has admitted it.'

'Then I can only ask for understanding and leniency for her. But I want to see her – now. I want to be sure that she's all right.'

The Border Commissioner, who had been studying the toes of his shoes, jerked up his head and looked at me. He opened his mouth as if to say something and shut it again.

'If it is necessary, of course we claim diplomatic immunity. But if you wish that some fine should be paid, some forfeit given I – I would be glad to take her place – to stand in for Lynn, my wife – Mrs Almourn, in any way that's acceptable to you.'

There was a silence I could feel. One of the women began to cry. She was very noisy about it.

'I want to see my wife,' I repeated. 'Now!'

'Not now, Mr Almourn, I regret. Perhaps in a short while,' the interpreter translated. His tone mimicking his master's was mild. 'First I must consult with my superiors. Your Excellencies will appreciate my position. But tea will be served and after that, I think I can safely promise, we won't keep you.'

We had to be content with that for the moment. The Russians filed out of the room and some servers came in carrying samovars. They poured tea and passed cakes; without exception everybody refused. It was meant partly as a gesture of sympathy towards me and partly as a gesture of defiance.

There was a susurration of conversation in a variety of languages. The American and Dutch Ambassadors were urging the Norwegian colonel to take action or to be firm or to do something. But he was helpless and they knew it. H.E. led the Ambassadress and me aside; he could have been at a cocktail party, wanting a little private talk.

'Marion, dear, tell us precisely what happened.'

'Where shall I begin?'

'After we left you.'

'We went to the cloakroom and tidied ourselves. Then we got into a bus and they drove us to this old wooden chapel. We had three Russian interpreters with us. They chatted us up, but not unduly. We came back and they took us to their shop where they urged us to change our money into roubles and buy souvenirs. There were some quite attractive things, ikons – modern, naturally – and those dolls which open to let you you find smaller and smaller dolls inside. Lynn bought several. I remember she had a little pile of parcels. I suppose the microfilm might have been in one of them, except that I don't understand how there was time – '

'What makes you think that was when she got the microfilm?'

'She did. Afterwards, while we were watching a film about the Ukraine, that dreadful man Vetski brought in the girl who had served us in the shop. She looked terrified, poor child, but she identified Lynn as the one to whom she had given the microfilm. Lynn denied it, as you would expect. And I said there must be a mistake because I had been standing beside Lynn all the time and the girl had had no opportunity to persuade her to take the microfilm or anything else.'

'Is that true? Are you positive, Marion?'

'Not one hundred per cent. I did move away for – a minute, not more. She would have had to have been terribly quick. When I got back they were talking about that brooch Lynn was wearing on her lapel. I saw the girl point to it and I heard Lynn say, yes, it was a British bulldog and her brother had given it to her. I don't see how there was time – but I suppose there must have been.'

'What happened next?'

'Vetski said she would have to be searched. I objected. I told him we had diplomatic immunity and he had no right to search any of us. I demanded they should fetch you. But I was wasting my breath. Anyway Vetski agreed I could go with Lynn – this was all through his interpreter, of course – and we were leaving the room when he turned on Lynn and said she had left her shoulder-bag behind, and why, and he would look in there first.'

'And it was in her bag? There was no doubt? He couldn't have slipped it in himself?'

'No. It was in an inner pocket of the bag, the sort of place that you keep travellers' cheques or a piece of jewellery when you're travelling. Besides – I'm so very sorry, Derek, but there's no doubt she knew what she was doing. When Vetski produced the microfilm she admitted it. She said she had been happy to take the work of a great man back to the free world, that there was no freedom in the Soviet Union for writers and artists, that everybody had a right to publish – oh, a lot of liberalistic stuff. It was quite a speech. She was very brave.'

'She was a bloody fool!' H.E. said and frowned ferociously. 'I'm sorry, my boy. We must all pray hard. Frankly I can't think of anything else to do at the moment.'

I had listened to what the Ambassadress had had to say in a sort of daze. My thoughts were concentrated on Lynn, where she was, what she was doing, if they were bullying her. I must have taken in what the Ambassadress was saying because later I could recall it all very clearly, but at the time it seemed singularly unimportant. The one important and essential thing was to get Lynn back across the border into the safety of Norway.

Then Comrade Igor Vetski returned with his interpreter. He stood just inside the door. He didn't need to call for attention. There was complete silence.

He said: 'Excellencies, ladies and gentlemen, your buses are outside.'

The interpreter was dead-pan but there was something about Vetski triumphant, mocking. 'I regret that Mrs Derek Almourn will not be able to accompany you.'

I started towards him and H.E. seized me by the arm and held on to me.

'Mrs Almourn, I must tell you, is presently on her way to Moscow to stand trial for the crime she has committed against the Union of Soviet Socialist Republics.'

Chapter Seven

I wanted to hit the sod, kill him, break his bloody samovars, trample on his little iced cakes! I wanted to weep.

I don't remember the journey back to Kirkenes but, as soon as we got there, H.E. went into action. In the remote hope that, in spite of what Comrade Vetski had said, Lynn might still be at Boris Gleb, he appealed for at least some symbolic action on the part of the Norwegian Border Commissioner. He talked on the Commission's secure line to the Norwegian Ministry of Defence, asking that the Embassy be advised and told to inform London, and he requested – and obtained – a plane to fly us back to Oslo immediately.

I went through the right motions. I was half out of my mind, acting like some sort of robot, but I managed to pack my suitcase and Lynn's and was meticulous about leaving nothing behind. What's more, on the flight to Oslo I slept, though God knows how I could; I strongly suspect the Ambassadress slipped one of her sleeping pills into my coffee.

The sleep helped a bit. The telephone conversation I had with my father when we got to the Embassy helped even more. Francis promised to pull every string, to use every influence, to do everything possible and impossible to 'rescue that poor, silly girl of yours'. He also promised to let the Charltons know what had happened, which was a relief; I couldn't bear the idea of talking to Lynn's family myself.

And, as the day – Saturday – progressed, everything that could be done was done. Cypher clerks were kept busy and wires humming. Diplomats and politicians were forced to sacrifice their weekend. Scrambled conversations took place between Oslo and London, Oslo and Moscow, London and Moscow, London and Washington, Washington and Moscow, Washington and Oslo.

The presence of Russian ambassadors was demanded at ministries in Oslo, London and Washington, and in their turn the Norwegian, British and American ambassadors in Moscow lodged strong protests and demanded the instant release of Mrs Lynn Charlton Almourn, as the media were to call her.

In fact nobody knew exactly where Lynn was or what was happening to her. And, although by now I could appreciate that Comrade Vetski was only part of the system and that nothing could be achieved by slowly extracting his guts, I wouldn't have minded trying. As it was there was really nothing I could do except wait for news of her.

I had been kept busy all day at the Embassy which, for a Saturday, was seething with activity. Mostly I had been assisting H.E. – I think he did it out of kindness – and by five o'clock I was dog-tired. I wanted to be home, by myself. I couldn't face any of the hospitality that was offered to me. I let Colin Kirkham, who always seemed to be performing acts of charity, drive me back to Smestad.

On the way, tactfully avoiding the subject which was uppermost in both our minds, he began to talk about the Gatlings. Martin was getting steadily better. There was no question of a relapse and it was only a matter of time before he would be fit again. Lorna, Colin said with a sympathetic grin, was like an ecstatic mother hen.

Lorna. I was happy for her and Martin, very happy – and relieved. Tomorrow I would go to the hospital. I would take her the silver brooch I had bought for her in Kautokeino. Which reminded me how much that Lapp silver had appealed to Lynn. Lynn . . .

'What?'

'I said: Are you sure you won't come and have supper with us?'

'Quite sure, thanks, Colin.'

'Well, what about tomorrow? I imagine we'll be having a picnic in the garden, that is if I'm not at the office. I chose a bad weekend to be duty officer, didn't – I mean – I mean some Norwegian friends had asked us to go sailing and it's such lovely weather.' He took a deep breath and tried again. 'We'll expect you then, Derek.'

'No – no, don't do that. I'll telephone if I'm coming. How will that be?'

He agreed reluctantly, knowing that he had bungled the invitation, knowing that I wouldn't come. To compensate he refused to drop me at the bottom of the drive and insisted on taking me to the front door and helping me with the two small, light suitcases, which was all the luggage that Lynn and I had taken to the north. I didn't invite him in. I stood in the hall and listened to him drive slowly, in low gear, down the steep gravel driveway to the road. I was glad to be alone.

I carried the suitcases into the bedroom. I didn't bother to unpack them. I went around the house and, although it didn't smell musty, I opened all the windows. The lady who did for us three times a week had aired the place yesterday and left everything clean and dusted. She had also put the post on a tray in the middle of the dining-room table. I added a glass, a siphon, and a bottle of Vat 69 to the tray and took it out on the verandah.

I poured myself a stiff whisky, sprawled my body in a garden chair and looked at the letters. I had already taken off my jacket and tie. Now I kicked off my shoes. It didn't matter what picture of squalor I presented; Lynn wasn't there to see. I drank half my whisky.

The post consisted of a bill from the doctor who had treated Lynn after her LSD trip at the Canadian Residence, a letter from my older sister which amounted to politics and personalities at Junior Minister level, and one from Virginia. Virginia had written a short, polite, bread-and-butter letter for the two weeks she had spent with us. It was dated but gave no address and struck me as being excessively formal, not the usual sort of screed she wrote to Lynn.

I wondered what Virginia would think when she heard what Lynn had done. It would be on the BBC nine o'clock news tonight and a splash in all the Sundays. The Foreign Office was issuing a formal statement with the intention of keeping everything in low key but, depending on the rest of the news, they were unlikely to succeed. I shrank from the thought of the publicity but it might help Lynn; the Russians were susceptible to world opinion.

World opinion? I must be mad. It couldn't come to that. I gulped down what was left of the whisky and poured myself another one. I still found it difficult to believe that I wasn't living in some bad dream, that Lynn wouldn't come roaring up the drive in her little yellow Fiat – or that I wouldn't wake up in a hospital room with the FBI inspector sitting by my bed.

The evening passed. When the whisky bottle was getting on for half empty I went into the kitchen, made myself some bread and cheese, ate some fruit, drank some coffee. The coffee was a mistake; it woke me up. I thought of telephoning some of my family but the effort of coping with long distance in Norwegian was too much for me. I had a hot bath, another drink and went to bed.

It was just after ten. I went to sleep at once and slept heavily but dreamlessly. I suppose it was all the whisky that I had drunk. I woke at twelve-thirty.

I tossed and turned and tossed. I pumped up the pillows. I struggled with the duvet. I listened to the ticking of the clock. I did some more tossing and turning. But the trouble was that I had shared this bed with Lynn, made love to her on it only four nights ago, and the linen was impregnated with the faint scent of her body. How could I sleep?

There was nothing for it except to take a sleeping pill. Normally I never touch the things – or any other sort of pills – if I can help it, and I wouldn't have had any at my disposal, but after that mugging in Washington Lynn's doctor had prescribed some for her which, although they weren't barbiturates, relaxed her and enabled her to sleep. They weren't meant to be addictive, but she had got pretty attached to them and we had brought a large supply to Oslo.

I rolled out of bed and went along to the bathroom. There was no point in toughing out the night when a couple of those pills would give me five or six hours of oblivion. My sleeplessness wasn't going to help Lynn. I opened the door of the medicine cupboard and stretched out my hand. I knew precisely where she kept those pills.

They were not there.

I searched, thinking that they must have got misplaced. I found aspirin, bicarbonate of soda, toothpaste, shaving cream, after-shave, a laxative, Lynn's anti-pregnancy pills, mouth-wash, eyedrops, deodorants and a few other things. I emptied the cupboard and put the contents back again.

I went back to the bedroom. It was just possible that, as we had been going away for two or three nights, Lynn had decided for safer keeping to put them in a drawer of her dressing-table where she kept her cosmetics, though it would have been logical to have hidden her anti-pregnancy pills too. The sleeping pills were not in the dressing-table. I shut the drawer irritably, and opened it again.

Lynn didn't use much make-up but there were a few things she liked and she kept a small stock of them, a new tube of the stuff she put on her eyelashes, for example, an unopened bottle of *Je reviens* and her special hand cream and others; I couldn't have said exactly what. But these were all missing. The drawer was half empty.

She must have taken the make-up – and the sleeping pills – with her to Kirkenes.

I emptied her suitcase on to the bed. I had packed that suitcase very carefully, and I had not left anything behind in the hotel room. I found neither sleeping pills nor cosmetics.

I went into the kitchen and made myself some coffee. All desire for sleep had gone. I searched, primarily for the sleeping pills but not forgetting the other stuff, in the obvious and not so obvious places. I didn't find anything that I was looking for.

Lynn must have taken them with her to Kirkenes. And she must have had them in her shoulder-bag – the whole boiling – in her shoulder-bag with the extra safe compartment for travellers' cheques and microfilm, the shoulder-bag that Virginia Urse had had especially made for her. It was as if she expected . . .

I recalled what the Ambassadress had said. I could hear the puzzlement in her voice. 'The girl from the souvenir shop identified Lynn . . . And I said there must have been a mistake. There had been no opportunity. I did move away but . . . terribly quick. When I got back they were talking about the brooch Lynn was wearing . . . bulldog . . . very British. I don't see how she had time to persuade Lynn to take the microfilm.'

There were a lot of other things as well. I sat on the edge of the bed and brooded. Finally I drew the obvious conclusion. Lynn had not agreed to take the microfilm of this supposedly subversive book across the border on some sudden liberalistic impulse. The whole thing had been carefully planned in advance. She had known what she was going to do – and she had been afraid of being caught.

Once I had faced up to this I realized two things. One was that I had suspected it all the time but had been unwilling to acknowledge my own suspicions. The other was that, if the Russians could prove it, Lynn's position was more vulnerable than I had thought or the British Government at present believed. I told myself that I had to be wrong.

By now it was almost three o'clock. The short summer night was ended. The sky, never really dark over Oslo in July, was getting appreciably lighter. The birds were awake and beginning to sing.

I put on some slacks and a sweater, made myself some more coffee and took it – and a scratch pad and pen – out on the verandah where already it was reasonably light. I wanted to jot down the known facts, the case, if you like, for and against Lynn. I had to know the worst.

My hypothesis was that Virginia Urse, probably acting on the instigation of that peace-loving, freedom-loving mystery man, Bruno, had persuaded Lynn to act as a courier between the Russian dissident and his chums in the West. Lynn would have considered it right in theory that she should smuggle the microfilm of the Russian's book across the border but in practice she hadn't wanted to do it because she was frightened of being caught.

Evidence for was overwhelming.

Lynn had been happy in Oslo until Bruno sent her flowers to remind her – so Virginia had said – that she had to go on fighting for peace and freedom.

Virginia had given Lynn the specially made shoulder-bag.

She and Lynn had known about the visit to the Arctic. Bruno? They said an American wife had told them. And Virginia had been surprised that I wasn't to be in the British party! She had assumed I would be because of the job I had had in Washington.

She and Lynn had actually urged H.E. to take me.

Their good luck – Martin's bad luck – and we were to go. At this point Lynn must have realized what she had let herself in for. She

155

had been nervous, irritable and desperately loving during the last few days. She must have been terrified but she would have been too proud, too stubborn to back out.

Afraid she might be caught, she had tried to plan accordingly. She had packed pills, cosmetics, extra money perhaps; when she mislaid her shoulder-bag at Fornebu she had refused to go without it. Although it was warm she had been determined to take her coat to Boris Gleb.

At Kautokeino she had bought that Lapp silver and made a list – for me to distribute? She hadn't bought me anything. She had said I wouldn't want a memento.

But she had reminded me more than once that she was tough, she could look after herself and I ought not to worry about her.

And the *modus operandi* had been simple. Lynn had gone to the souvenir shop. The server, having identified Lynn from a description and the gold bulldog she had worn on her lapel, had given her the microfilm with the things she had bought. This would explain what had puzzled the Ambassadress.

Lynn had put the microfilm in a 'special place' in the shoulder-bag, one that would escape a cursory examination. She should have been safe. But, as she had feared, she had been caught.

Evidence against was negative.

The whole thing was somewhat amateurish but the People for Peace and Freedom had always struck me as being an amateurish bunch. And they had relied on luck to a great extent, luck which had deserted them at the last moment.

But that was all. I had to accept that my hypothesis was proven; Lynn had planned, before she left Oslo, to smuggle microfilm out of the USSR.

And now, I thought, I knew the worst. I was overwhelmed by my fears for Lynn.

I shuffled together all the bits of paper I had used and tore them up. It had taken a lot of time and effort to produce the final analysis. Indeed it was nearly six a.m. and, one way or another, I felt awful. I went into the kitchen, threw away everything except my last copy, which I folded and put in my wallet, and decided I ought to make some breakfast.

The bacon was under-done, the eggs broken, the toast slightly burnt. It wasn't inviting. I sat and looked at my plate. I tried to force myself to eat. The whistle of the telephone had me on my feet, the chair thrown back. I leapt into the living-room.

My father-in-law, Senator Charlton, was about as welcome as the eggs and bacon. He wanted me to tell him exactly what had happened; Francis, he said, had been very vague. But when I gave him details, he blew his stack. He blamed everybody, except Lynn. He blamed the Russians for framing her, although she had proudly and publicly admitted her guilt. He blamed H.E. and me for not looking after her properly. He blamed the American Ambassador for not being more forceful. He practically blamed the Norwegian Border Commissioner for not attacking Boris Gleb and rescuing her by force, the British Admiralty for not sending a gun-boat to help, and the President of the United States for not threatening Moscow with a nuclear strike. He said that he himself would guarantee immediate action in Washington, that Lloyd was flying to London where he would be staying with my parents, and that I would have to do my best in Oslo. He implied that he didn't think my best would be much good.

I put down the receiver very gently. I had thoughts of telling him that everything was damn well his fault, that if he hadn't brought Lynn up to be a bleeding-heart liberal she wouldn't have got herself mixed up with characters like Bruno and Virginia Urse and People for Peace and Freedom and she wouldn't be in the mess she was. But I managed to restrain myself; it wasn't really true anyway. Besides, Lynn was his only daughter and, if things were bad for me, they were bad for him too, and for Mrs Charlton.

And at least the Senator had given me an excellent excuse for not eating my breakfast. The eggs and bacon had become a cold, congealed mess. I scraped them off the plate on top of my torn attempts at analysing what and why Lynn had done what she had. I made some fresh toast and a pot of tea and wondered how I could fill the hours until it was possible to visit Martin Gatling in the hospital.

Physical labour was the obvious answer. I didn't want to think any more. But it was too early to mow the lawn and the hedge didn't need clipping and anyhow I felt physically exhausted as well as mentally. A walk might help. Having washed my face in cold water and rubbed an electric razor over my beard, I set out. I went by way of the verandah and didn't bother to shut the French windows behind me.

It was a beautiful morning, warm and peaceful and quiet except for the chatter of the birds. The pale, wooden houses were still sleeping. Nobody walked in the apple orchards. I saw only one Norwegian flag, hoisted by an early riser, fluttering gently in the breeze from the fjord. At the bottom of the hill I hesitated. If I turned left I could be in Frogner Park in ten or fifteen minutes; if I turned right I could make a wide circle around Smestad Pond.

I plumped for the right and again a choice of hills. I went up and along the road that leads to the airport. There was no traffic. I reminded myself that some time today I ought to drive out to Fornebu and pick up the English Sunday papers. And it crossed my mind that this was the way that Virginia must have come early in the morning of the day that she had left us. Otherwise I wasn't thinking of anything in particular.

There is a good view from the ridge over the whole of Smestad Pond and I stood, looking down. It was a pleasant, rather than a spectacular sight. The pond is, in fact, a small lake with a colony of semi-tame ducks and enough fish to interest the local lads. But I had never seen anybody swim there before, probably because of the reeds, so I was surprised to hear a louder plop than any fish would make and see a swimmer crawl powerfully through the water.

He had gone in on the far side from where I was. There the bank is well-wooded and the edge not marshy and with fewer reeds. I watched him idly. He swam towards the middle of the pond, turned, swam back and climbed out of the water as if it were a ritual like a morning bath. He was a tall young man with blond, almost white hair. He disappeared among the trees where the light glistened on the sides of a tent. He could have been Hank or Chuck, camping by Smestad Pond instead of in my apple orchard, except of course that my old chums should have been back in the States by now.

158

I told myself that I was imagining things, that my nerves were shot, that the mugging I had undergone in that underground garage in Washington had had more effect on me than I had realized. But I didn't encircle the pond as I had planned. I went back to the house the same way as I had come.

I went in via the verandah and the French windows and, as soon as I stepped into the living-room, I realized there was somebody in the house. There were sounds coming from the bedroom, heavy breathing, the opening and shutting of drawers. It could have been a casual thief but this was a Sunday morning in Oslo and Norwegians are on the whole an honest people. I looked around for some sort of weapon. The only conceivable object was a paper weight, but I never could throw straight and anyway I didn't think a glass paper weight would be of much use against a Hank or a Chuck.

I barged into the bedroom and said: 'What the hell do you think you're doing?'

The fair-haired man, who had been on his knees in front of the little desk that Lynn used as her own, scrambled to his feet, bumping his elbow hard on the edge of an open drawer. He gobbled at me in shock.

'Why – why, Derek. Frightfully sorry, old man. But the door was open – and you were out. I helped myself, so to speak.'

I tried to hide my relief. The hair was almost as blond, the build very similar to that of Hank's or Chuck's but this was an older man, thicker, heavier, with the beginning of a paunch. He looked like an ex-boxer going to seed. His name was David Worthington and he acted as Security Officer at the Embassy. I didn't like him very much.

'You helped yourself. To what? I never leave loose cash around.'

He flushed at the insult. 'Your house was open. I shouted for you but there was no answer, so I walked in.'

'Fair enough. But you haven't answered my original question. What the hell do you think you're doing?'

'I was searching that desk, as you saw.'

'What for?'

'I don't know. Now, look, Derek, I don't like this any more than you do but – '

'Either you're mad or I am. How can you be searching for something and not know what – in my house, on a Sunday morning?' I was angry, irrationally angry because, I suppose, I had been scared, thinking he might be Hank or Chuck.

'Orders from London.'

'What?'

'I've received orders from London to search your house and – and to ask you questions. You can check with H.E. if you don't believe me.'

I sat heavily on the edge of the bed, and stared at him. It had to do with Lynn. It must – but what? I thought about sleeping pills and eyelash cream and lists of Lapp silver and the piece of paper in my hip pocket that proved Lynn had deliberately planned to smuggle microfilm across the Soviet border.

'I'm terribly sorry, David,' I said hypocritically. 'But I'm pretty strained at the moment, you know. It's about Lynn, of course. You haven't any – any news, have you?'

'No. I'm afraid not,' he said. 'I wish I had.'

He was just another Foreign Service Officer, I thought, like me except that he had been given some special training in Security, a kind man who didn't like his present job.

'What do you want to do first? Finish the search or ask me questions?'

'Perhaps we could do both together.'

'All right. But do you mind if I put on some coffee before we start?'

He didn't mind. I strolled off to the kitchen and put some fresh coffee in the percolator. I had thrown the old grounds into the bin on top of the congealed eggs and bacon. The bits of torn paper, my efforts from earlier this morning, were now completely buried and safe enough from David Worthington. Then I went into the lavatory, tore up my final accusing draft, made water on it, which, though I didn't know it, was about all that it was worth, and flushed it down the pan. I washed my hands noisily while I waited to make sure that no scrap of paper would be regurgitated. I felt like some spy character in a second-rate movie made for television.

Back in the bedroom, I said that coffee wouldn't be long. I sat on the bed and watched Worthington's search. It wasn't pleasant to see a stranger going through Lynn's clothes or reading scraps of her correspondence but, I told myself, it wouldn't do her any harm; he wouldn't find any proof that she hadn't acted on impulse which, from his questions, was what he had been told to look for.

'Would you say your wife was a secretive person, Derek?'

'Yes, moderately – but aren't all women?'

'Before you went on this trip did she behave oddly in any way?'

'No, I don't think so.' I pretended to mull over his question. 'She's apt to be a bit nervous, of course. It's a result of that dreadful experience we had in Washington.'

'M-mm. I heard about it. Nasty! You haven't been too lucky since you married, have you?'

I didn't answer that one. Worthington picked up Lynn's jewel-box and brought it over to me. 'No point in my looking in here. You tell me what's missing, will you, Derek?'

'All right.' I opened the box, which began to play a little tune and went on and on playing it.

I found myself gripping the box and staring unseeing at its contents. For some inexplicable reason the tune had jogged my memory and had made me think of Lynn's diary. Until this moment I had completely forgotten about her diary. During the night, when I had been trying to find her sleeping pills, I had looked in the middle drawer of her desk, which was where she kept it, but my mind had been on the other things. Now I couldn't have sworn whether or not the diary had been there. But if it wasn't there, where was it?

'I don't think there's anything actually missing,' I heard myself say calmly. 'Lynn was wearing her engagement and wedding rings, of course – and a gold lapel brooch that her brother gave her. And she has a small, leather case, which she always takes with her when she's travelling, with her grandmother's pearls and some other of her more treasured possessions in it. She doesn't have a lot of jewellery – not valuable stuff, I mean.'

'M-mm. By the way, I suppose your wife didn't keep a diary?'

He must have read my thoughts. It was a blow below the belt. And there was only one way to deal with it, to tell the truth.

'Oh yes. She certainly did.'

'I haven't found it. Where did she keep it?'

'In the middle drawer of that desk.'

'It's not there now.'

I swallowed. 'Are you sure?'

'Yes. There are some letters from you – love letters, not my business. And some from Hanoi, from a Lloyd. That's her brother, isn't it?'

'Yes. He was a POW for years.'

'She was lucky to hear so much from him.'

'Yes.' He was giving me time to think.

'But no diary.'

'No? Then she must have taken it with her.' I kept my voice level. 'Is it important? It wasn't a Boswellian effort, you know, David. More an engagement book than a diary really. Dinner with the Gatlings, cocktails at the Canadian Embassy. You know the sort of thing.'

'Sure.'

I wondered if he knew too that I was lying in my teeth. Lynn's diary was one of those three-year jobs, too big to fit even into Virginia's special shoulder-bag. So she had not taken it with her to Kirkenes and, as I discovered later, after Worthington had gone and I had made yet another search of the place, it was not in the house either. So where was it?

Here was yet another bloody mystery that didn't make any sense.

Chapter One

David Worthington saw me off at Fornebu.

I never knew whether this was because he didn't trust me to catch the London plane and expected me to make a dash behind the Iron Curtain or because nobody else was available and the Embassy thought it improper that I should go off alone. Anyhow I was lumbered with him. It was the final irony of what had been an unreal week.

There had been little or no news of Lynn. London had been informed that she was in the ill-reputed Lubianka gaol in Moscow but, in spite of repeated requests from both the British and the American Embassies, nobody had been allowed to visit her. Our Ambassador to the USSR had suddenly flown home for consultations and the media had built this up but the Office had refused to comment. Meanwhile, our Embassy in Moscow had received assurances that Lynn was in good health and that, while her case was being considered, she was well cared for. Unfortunately, when she was in the hands of the KGB this didn't mean very much. It was perhaps more hopeful that both *Pravda* and *Izvestia* had reserved their big guns to shoot at the dissidents in the Soviet Union, especially the writers, and had been inclined to play down Lynn's part in the affair. But again this could mean nothing.

As the Norwegian Minister, who in the circumstances can't have felt a great deal of sympathy with her, said; '*Man vet aldri hva som kan hende*, which translated means, 'There's no knowing what may happen'. I didn't find this very consoling. But then I wasn't in the business of being consoled. I wasn't in any business at all. My only job was to wait.

And I had waited, through a long, long, week.

It had come as a relief when, the following Monday, H.E. had sent for me and told me that I was to catch a mid-day flight to London. But it was worrying, too. H.E. was extraordinarily evasive. During the last few days he had gone out of his way to be kind and helpful. Now, without any warning, he clammed up on me. I couldn't understand why, unless something had happened, something that concerned Lynn. And if something that concerned Lynn had happened it also concerned me and I wanted to know what it was.

'Did the Office tell you why I was to report, sir?'

'Yes. I was informed.'

'It has to do with Lynn?'

'It's connected with her, yes, though maybe I shouldn't tell you so.'

'Has something happened to her? Please, sir.'

'No. No, Derek. She's – all right.'

'Then, what – I'm sorry, sir.'

'I'm sorry too, but I'm afraid I can't tell you any more. Better go home now. Make arrangements to be away for a week or two but try not to alert the press. We'll send a car to take you out to Fornebu and – er – incidentally, you'll be met at Heathrow. I – er – hope things turn out well for you, Derek.'

'Thank you, sir.'

And I had to be content with that. I tried to get some more information out of Worthington but he wasn't forthcoming either. I don't believe he knew any more than I did. Nevertheless, he put up a smoke-screen and I made efforts to pierce it. It helped to pass the time until my flight number was called.

We shook hands and he wished me luck. I was turning away when he stopped me. 'Derek!'

'Yes.'

He flapped his arms ineffectually, as if he were about to lay an egg. 'A word of advice. I may not be very good at this job, but you're not a very good liar. When you meet the professionals it would be wisest to stick to the truth.'

I stared at him, stunned. But there was no chance to ask him what he meant. He was already pushing his way towards the exit and I followed the other passengers to my plane. I was still wondering how much I had underrated him when we took off.

Last Sunday he had had a free run of the house at Smestad and I had answered all his questions, with reasonable honesty. Perhaps he had just sensed that I was being over-careful, trying to mislead him. The only direct lie I had told had been about Lynn's diary and it could be that had made him suspicious. He had referred to the diary again a couple of times, half hinting that it was somewhere in the house and I must know where.

In fact, I hadn't worked out the problem myself until after he had gone; and I hadn't been able to confirm my theory until the Monday morning, when the Smestad Post Office opened.

Once I had convinced myself that the damned thing wasn't in the house – I knew Lynn hadn't taken it with her to Kirkenes and I couldn't imagine her burying it by the flag pole or in some other chosen spot – it had seemed to me that there were two options, either she had given it to Virginia for safe-keeping or she had posted it, probably to Lloyd. And my tentative enquiries at the Smestad Post Office had borne fruit; Lynn had indeed posted a heavy parcel, registered and insured – to Mrs Virginia Urse at an address in London.

So two questions were answered for the price of one, as it were. I knew what had happened to Lynn's diary; she must suddenly have remembered it that Tuesday, when Virginia had already left, and dashed up the hill to the Post Office to send it after her so that, if something went wrong at Boris Gleb, no prying Worthington, or prying husband for that matter, would be able to read it. I also knew where in London Virginia was living.

The answer to the second question, a question I hadn't really formulated, was to prove absolutely vital. The answer to the first merely strengthened my belief that Lynn had set off for the north, fearing that her plan might miscarry and prepared for the worst. And the worst . . .

'Mr Almourn! Wake up, please, Mr Almourn.'

I jerked awake, my seat belt by its sudden constriction reminding me where I was. The steward was bending over me, his face close to mine. His breath smelt of peppermint. I turned my head aside and rubbed a hand across my eyes. It was only recently that

167

I had developed this disconcerting habit of dropping off to sleep at odd intervals, like an old man.

'What is it?'

'We're coming in to land, sir. If you would be ready when we taxi in, I'll fetch you. You're being met, I gather, sir.'

'Thank you.'

I was used to VIP treatment when I travelled with my father but I didn't usually get it when I was by myself. I wondered what sort of reception committee was meeting me and shelved the question of 'why'. I hoped nobody from the media had got wind of my arrival. A minute or two later we touched down.

Some minutes after that the steward ushered me through the first-class compartment and across the ramp. I was back in England.

'Good afternoon, Mr Almourn.'

'Good afternoon.'

'If you would give me your passport and your baggage slip – '

I handed them over. 'I just have a small suitcase, Samsonsite, grey with a large white letter A stencilled on it.'

'Thank you.' He passed them to his minion, who hastened away. 'If you would follow me – '

I followed. He was fractionally over six feet, and walked like a Guards' officer. His hair was red, cut short, and the back of his head was flat. He wore a navy blue suit and highly-polished shoes. He walked very fast. I lengthened my stride to keep up with him.

He knew his way around Heathrow. In next to no time, having by-passed all authorities and almost everybody else, we were sitting in an anonymous black Cortina waiting for my luggage and my passport. We didn't have to wait long. The suitcase was pushed into the boot, the passport given to Redhead who absent-mindedly, it seemed, put it in his inner breast pocket and the minion, donning a chauffeur's peaked cap, got behind the wheel. We drove in silence. The circumstances weren't right for casual conversation.

I stared out of the car window at the traffic on the motorway. The minion drove superbly, keeping to the outer lane except where it was necessary to cut in. We passed continually and were passed by nothing. We must have beaten the record into central London. But even he couldn't do much when we bogged down in the usual jams. As our progress became uneasy I shut my eyes. The combination of whisky and sleep on the plane had given me an incipient headache.

I opened them again as we reached our destination. I knew that we had arrived because Redhead leaned across and opened the car door on my side. Otherwise it wouldn't have occurred to me. I hadn't asked where I was being taken and nobody had told me. I had assumed that we were going to the Foreign Office.

'Where are we?'

'If you would get out, Mr Almourn – '

'And who the hell are you?'

'If you had asked me before – '

He was a past-master at the conditional clause and the unfinished sentence. He produced a wallet from his pocket and showed me his pass. The photograph flattered him. He kept his thumb over his signature but so casually that it wasn't until later I realized that I had never seen his name.

'Satisfied?'

'Yes, but why?'

'The Commander wishes to ask you a few questions.'

I had no right to object; it was inevitable that Intelligence should be interested in what had happened to Lynn. But their highhanded methods riled me.

We were standing on the pavement now, Redhead and I – the minion had driven off in the car – and I knew where I was, under the shadow of Westminster Cathedral. With a landmark like that they weren't making any secret of it.

'If you'll come along, Mr Almourn – '

I went along, into one of those large anonymous blocks of flats that were once common around Victoria but which have been mostly pulled down and replaced by offices. I noticed from the name plates in the hall that in this building too offices were already encroaching. We went up to the top floor which had been taken over in its entirety by the SIS.

'If you'll wait a moment, Mr Almourn – '

They kept me waiting for fifteen minutes, in a room that was short on furniture, uncomfortable and provided nothing to read.

I suppose it was something to do with psychological warfare. It merely irritated me. Perhaps that's what they wanted to achieve. If so they had misjudged my character. They would have done better to persuade me to co-operate. I was willing enough, if it would do Lynn any good, willing to do anything.

The door opened and Readhead's minion appeared. He seemed to have a variety of jobs, aide, chauffeur, and now – what? He led me along the corridor, which could have done with a fresh coat of its institutional green paint, and knocked on the end door. When a voice said, 'Come!' he went in ahead of me, stood aside and announced in his best butler's voice:

'Mr Derek Almourn, Commander.'

The room, after the dismal appearance of the rest of the establishment, was a shock. It was close-carpeted and furnished more in the style of what used to be called a 'gentleman's library' than an office. There were a lot of books around, one or two good pieces of furniture and some reputable modern paintings. I recognized a Scottie Wilson and what I thought was a Hockney. I was so busy gazing around the room that I disregarded its occupant, which was a mistake.

He had been standing, looking out of the window. He was a small, slight man, in his early fifties, grey haired, blue-eyed, with untidy eyebrows and a mouth that was a straight, lipless line. Even on the rare occasions that he smiled he didn't show his teeth. He came towards me and, thinking he was going to shake hands, I offered mine. He didn't actually refuse it. It was more that he didn't see it, that he suddenly changed direction and went to sit behind his desk. The effect, however, was the same. I felt slapped down. He waved me to a chair and shuffled through some papers.

'A-ah, yes! Mr Almourn – do you love your wife?'

'Yes!' I swallowed.

'Very much, would you say?'

'Yes, very much!'

'Besotted with her?' His voice was sharp, incisive.

I took a deep breath. 'No, that I wouldn't say.'

'Good!'

Evidently this was the end of the first skirmish because he went back to shuffling his papers. It wasn't a total rout but clearly he had won on points, which wasn't fair because I hadn't realized that the battle had begun. I hadn't even realized there was to be a battle. I girded my loins for the next attack but I was out of my league. He had decided to shift his ground and he still had the better of me. The Commander, I was to learn, was never fair.

'Now, let me see,' he said mildly. 'Do you have a good memory?'

'Yes, pretty good.'

'So you can tell me, for instance, where you were on Monday evening of the week before last?'

'I can. I was at home, in my house at Smestad.' It had taken a moment to remember, time had tended to become confused lately. 'We were giving a supper party.'

'Yes, that was the evening your colleague, Mr Gatling, was poisoned. You must have been very worried when he nearly died. Kind of you to arrange for a specialist to see him. You felt responsible, I suppose? Your wife's cooking?'

'No. Yes. I felt responsible because it happened in my house but my wife had nothing to do with it.'

'Really? Are you sure?'

'I mean – I mean, she didn't do the cooking.'

'Quite.'

'Besides there was nothing wrong with the food. We all ate and drank the same things and nobody else was ill. If you're suggesting – '

'I'm not suggesting anything, Mr Almourn. And you yourself have made the point. Only Mr Gatling was poisoned. He was having a bad time, wasn't he?' He paused but I didn't respond. 'He could have been killed by that motor-bike, couldn't he, or badly injured? Your wife doesn't cook, it seems. Does she ride a motor-bike?'

'No! She does not ride a motor-bike! Commander, I don't care what authority you've got, you've got no right to imply – '

'I have every right, Mr Almourn.'

'But if you know so much you must know it was a young man, a Norwegian student, who – who . . . It certainly wasn't Lynn.'

'And it certainly wasn't she who tried to drown Mr Gatling at Holmenkollen, was it?'

'Nobody tried to drown him. It was me, who was nearly – '

'Hasn't it occurred to you that the intended victim was Martin Gatling, and not you, Mr Almourn? The job, in fact, was fumbled.'

My blank face must have answered him. I said: 'My wife, Commander, would never do anything to harm Martin Gatling or anybody else. Why on earth should she?'

'Why indeed?' He shrugged. 'Of course she was very eager to go on this visit to Boris Gleb, and with Mr Gatling out of the way –'

'That's preposterous.'

'Is it?'

'Yes.'

'She had to go, in fact, to collect the microfilm of this book.'

'No. She didn't know about the microfilm. How could she? She acted on impulse. When the Russian girl at the souvenir shop asked –'

'It was all planned beforehand.'

'How could it be?'

'Ah, if only we had your wife's diary, perhaps we should know. Such a pity Mr Worthington didn't find it. Where is the diary, Mr Almourn? Did you find it?'

'No.'

'You didn't find it, either before or after Mr Worthington searched your house, and destroy it?'

'No.'

'Or hide it somewhere?'

'No.'

'But you lied to Mr Worthington about it? You told him it was only an engagement book. You lied to him, didn't you? Why?'

'Yes. I – I lied. A diary's a personal thing. It was none of his business.'

'And you were afraid that if he found the diary we would have proof of your wife's complicity?'

'No!'

'Whose side are you on, Mr Almourn?'

'My wife's!'

172

'Your wife's an American.'

'I thought the Americans and the British were on the same side.'

'Come now, don't be sour. You must admit it was unkind of her to wear a British bulldog as a recognition sign at Boris Gleb. She might have chosen an American eagle. You do know what a recognition sign is?'

'Yes.'

'And she has been asking to see the British Ambassador in Moscow, not the American.'

'As my wife, Lynn is British.'

'Quite. But she's not usually so keen on us, is she? Fair enough when you were just married and still in Washington – though she even got you into trouble there, didn't she? – but she made it obvious in Oslo that she much preferred the American community to the old Brits. And now she's suddenly 'one of us'. Very odd – and rather mean, don't you think?'

'No – not in the circumstances.'

'I was forgetting. You're on her side. You're not on the Russians' side?'

'The Russians?' The situation was out of hand. Everybody was mad. 'No, I am not on the Russians' side, Commander. In case you've forgotten,' I said with heavy sarcasm, 'I love my wife and she is at this very moment in the Lubianka gaol.'

There was a tap on the door and the minion came in bringing a tray with coffee pot, milk, sugar and one cup. I felt extraordinarily grateful when he set it down beside me and not beside the Commander. The Commander stood up.

'I'll leave you to enjoy your coffee, Mr Almourn – and a piece of news. The Russians may not have your wife very much longer.'

'What? You mean they're going to release Lynn? When? Soon?'

'Fairly soon.'

'But that's – wonderful. I – I – Commander, you're not lying to me for some – some reason of your own, are you?'

'No, I'm not lying, Mr Almourn. It's not definite but there's a very real possibility that your wife will be released in the near future.'

As soon as I was alone I put my head down on the desk, burying my face in my arms. I thought my own private, inarticulate thoughts. When I had regained some of my composure I drank the coffee. It tasted like nectar and ambrosia.

And Redhead came into the room. He sat himself down in the Commander's chair on the other side of the desk. He looked very military, as if he were sitting to attention. And the questions began again.

'Feeling better?'

'I'm all right.'

'Good.'

'Mr Almourn, why don't you tell us the truth?'

'What truth?'

'About your wife, who, I might remind you, is also Lord Almourn's daughter-in-law and Senator Charlton's daughter, a VIP, you could say.'

We wasted some effort on these stupidities but got nowhere. I didn't understand where the SIS wanted to get. I didn't understand why, if the Russians were prepared to let Lynn go, it mattered whether or not she had known in advance about the microfilm – not that I was prepared to admit that she had. I didn't understand why, when the SIS knew or guessed at least as much as I did, I was being questioned in this way. And I didn't like Redhead. It must have been mutual. He made me go through the whole sequence of events from the time Lynn and I left Oslo together to the time I left Boris Gleb without her.

Eventually the Commander returned. I presumed he had been having dinner; there was something replete about him, which was annoying because it reminded me that, except for a cup of their coffee, I had had nothing to eat or drink since an open sandwich and a couple of whiskys on the plane. Nevertheless, I was glad to see him. I was bloody-well bored with Redhead's questions – I wanted to go home – and it was the Commander who would have the authority to bring this stupid farce to an end. But he showed no inclination to do so.

'Mr Almourn, what day did Mrs Urse come to stay with you?'

I referred to my engagement book and told him. He put out his hand. Reluctantly I got up and gave him the book. He checked various dates with some notes that he had and held out the book to me. I didn't move. I wasn't going to get up a second time. He tossed it lightly on to the desk, within my reach, and I put it back in my pocket.

'Did you invite her?'

'Naturally.'

'Of course. She was a very close friend of your wife's. But when?'

'When? Before we left Washington. It was an open invitation.'

'But when did she take you up on it?'

'I can't remember exactly. Very shortly before she came.'

'And she brought you a book, a biography of John Day-Brune?'

'Yes, but how on earth – '

'Mr Worthington is more efficient than you give him credit for, Mr Almourn.' He gave me a lipless smile. 'The book was a pre-publication copy, wasn't it? Why do you think she went to so much trouble for your sake?'

'How should I know? She had had a bag made for Lynn.' I bit my tongue. 'She must have thought the book would interest me.'

'Why?'

I shrugged. He hadn't taken me up on the bag. 'I was Political Secretary in Washington when Day-Brune was caught. Of course I was interested.'

'You knew him personally?'

'Day-Brune? I'd met him once or twice, in London.'

'He dined at your house. He was a colleague and a friend of your father's.'

'What the hell are you getting at now, Commander?'

'In the circumstances Mrs Urse might have concluded that you would feel some sympathy for Day-Brune.'

'I have no sympathy for any traitor,' I said coldly.

'No? Ah, well! I would suggest to you, Mr Almourn, that while you have dinner you give some thought to John Day-Brune's position in relation to your wife's. *Bon appétit*.'

He was gone before I could absorb what he had said and the minion appeared to lead me back to that horrid little waiting-room, where a card-table had been set and a meal provided. It was a cold meal, but very good – avocado vinaigrette, Scotch salmon with a green salad, fresh fruit, cheeses, and a half bottle of Chablis. I couldn't have been less interested. I wondered what the KGB were providing for Lynn.

I am not a complete fool. Though some of the questions had thrown me because of their seeming irrelevance, I had followed the general drift of the SIS's reasoning. And once I had taken in the Commander's last remark, I most certainly knew what conclusion I was expected to draw from it – that Day-Brune, whom the Russians yearned to get their hands on, was in a British prison, and Lynn was in a Soviet prison, and the Russians would be happy to swap Lynn for Day-Brune.

But the idea was preposterous! The British Government would never agree. Day-Brune would be a prize beyond price for the communists, whereas Lynn, even though she was Lord Almourn's daughter-in-law and Senator Charlton's daughter, was just a – a silly young girl. For the first time I was angry with her; she had put so much in jeopardy because of a bloody, stupid act. But fear was at the back of my anger. If the British Government didn't agree . . .

While I had been thinking – if one can call thinking a process which resembled that of a tumble-drier – I had eaten very quickly. I had got through the avocado and most of the salmon when Redhead reappeared. He raised an eyebrow in surprise. I hadn't been expected to eat at all.

'If you'll come along now – '

'One moment.'

Deliberately I finished my salmon, poured another half glass of wine and drank it. I even ate a few grapes. Redhead didn't trouble to hide his dislike of me.

'Mr Almourn, it took us twenty-two months to prove our case against John Day-Brune, a lot of work and a lot of overtime. During that period at least one man – a close friend of mine, as it happened – was killed, and another badly maimed in the communists' effort to protect Day-Brune's cover. A marriage broke up because the wife had to be neglected; the job came first. And there were other consequences, which we suspect are linked, though we can't prove it. All that will be wasted, Mr Almourn, if Day-Brune is swapped for that silly bitch who married you.'

'John!'

'Commander – sir!'

'You must excuse that outburst, Mr Almourn. And please come with me.'

I followed the Commander back to his office. Redhead came with us. He stood with his back to the window and didn't speak; such a long speech without a single if-clause must have exhausted him. The Commander sat down at his desk.

'Well, now you understand the situation?'

'Yes.' I understood their latent hostility too, thanks to Redhead.

'And you appreciate that we need to know the whole truth if we are to negotiate with the Russians, just as a defence counsel needs to know the whole truth. It will do Mrs Almourn's case no good if she's made out to be a complete innocent, which is what most of the news media is doing at the moment, and then later she's shown up as – as not quite an angel.'

'Yes.' I thought for a moment. The worse Lynn's behaviour could be made to seem, the less public opinion in Britain and the States would support her. And the less pressure there would be on HMG to release Day-Brune in exchange for her. For their own private – or secret – reasons the SIS would do everything in their power to prevent the swap. Therefore the SIS had a vested interest in blackening Lynn's motives.

'And you'll co-operate with us, Mr Almourn?'

'I thought I had been co-operating.'

'But, of course.'

It was ten minutes to midnight when they gave up. I had agreed that Lynn *might* have arranged in advance to bring the Russian's microfilm across the border; such an act was not inconsistent with her character and beliefs. But I had no further evidence to offer them in support of this theory. I had not seen her diary since before we went to Kirkenes; I suggested that her shoulder-bag was large and she could have taken the diary with her or, if she had really planned everything, it could be buried in the garden at Smestad (the idea of Worthington digging up the apple orchard gave me a moment's pleasure), or, I was forced to agree, she could have given it to Virginia Urse. Mrs Urse had said she was going to stay with friends in the UK; she hadn't mentioned where and her thank-you note had given no address; I was sorry I couldn't help them to find her. And Bruno? They sprang Bruno on me as I was leaving. Bruno, I said, was an acquaintance of Lynn's from her People for Peace and Freedom days. I had never met him and knew nothing about him.

I stumbled out to the black Cortina and let the minion drive me to my parents' house. There was no need to tell him the address. I felt mentally battered, exhausted and as worried as hell. To say in the circumstances that something was wrong, desperately wrong, sounds absurd, but I sensed that, over and above the obvious, this was true. I was appalled by how much the SIS already knew and appalled by what they might still discover. I was like a man doing a jig-saw puzzle that had too many pieces, a man whose life or whose wife's life depended on its successful completion. I could only hope that for Lynn's sake Virginia would help me with it.

Chapter Two

I was late going down to breakfast the following morning. It had been after three when I finally got to sleep. My mother was drinking coffee, which is all she ever has at this time, and reading the *Telegraph*; my father, buried behind *The Times*, was consuming a large helping of eggs and bacon. They greeted me warmly but casually as if I had merely driven up from the country to spend a weekend with them. A third place was laid at the breakfast table. I helped myself to what I wanted and sat down.

'I assume this is Lloyd's place,' I said.

'Lloyd? Oh no, dear,' my mother said. 'It's for you. Lloyd has gone.'

'Gone? Do you mean back to the States?'

'No. To stay with some friends of his family, I believe. He spent two nights with us. He said he couldn't stand the public glare any more, reporters on the doorstep and photographers taking his picture whenever he put his nose out of the door.'

'Is it bad?'

'The publicity? Not really, dear. But then we're comparatively used to it. Was it bad for you in Oslo?'

'No. I was very sheltered. The Embassy saw to that.'

'The PM regrets he didn't slap a D notice on the whole affair,' my father said unexpectedly from behind his newspaper.

'I'm glad for Lynn's sake he didn't.'

'Don't be too glad. Publicity's a two-edged weapon.'

'What do you mean, Francis?'

'Later. After breakfast.'

And later, after breakfast, Francis explained. Public opinion, he said, was at the moment strongly in Lynn's favour. Every woman who ever went abroad on some package tour could imagine herself in Lynn's predicament and so sympathize with her; every man could picture his own girl-friend or wife caught in a similar situation. The mass media were also behind Lynn; there were only a few doubting Thomases. The British bulldog, in fact, was all for taking on the Russian bear on her behalf. But this, he emphasized, was because she was believed to be in no way culpable.

Francis gave me a hard look when he made the last remark and then added slowly: 'Derek, you know as well as we do, even if you won't admit it, that Lynn planned in advance to smuggle subversive material out of Russia. And naturally, since they engineered the entire matter, the communists know it too.'

'What?'

'The Intelligence chaps didn't tell you?'

'They told me the Russians had offered to swap her for John Day-Brune and that HMG was considering the matter. They also made it bloody clear that if they could put a spoke in the proceedings they would. But they didn't – '

'Can you blame them? Good God! Day-Brune's a traitor. He has done untold damage to this country and her allies. He could still do a lot more. Of course we've done our best to paper up the cracks since he was caught but he could still pass on immense amounts of information to the communists, stuff he's got stored in his head, stuff he has probably forgotten he knows. But they'll get it out of him. They'll pick him clean. And you think we should exchange him for a witless girl – just like that? Do you think she's worth it?'

Francis was striding up and down the study. His voice was hoarse with emotion. Usually he's a pretty imperturbable man and I could only remember seeing him like this once before, when the doctor told him my mother might have cancer. The memory stayed the angry retort I was about to make.

'What did you mean when you said the communists engineered everything?' I asked. 'Do you mean they knew in advance that Lynn –'

'We believe they want Day-Brune badly, perhaps for some reason we don't even know about. There was an elaborate plan – let's call it plan A – to arrange his escape from prison. That failed.

We believe they then decided to put plan B into operation. This was to acquire a suitable exchange for Day-Brune. And they made use of a set-up that was on ice – a set-up involving you and Lynn.'

'No – that's absurd!'

But my protest wasn't as vehement as it might have been. I had done a great deal of thinking in the small hours of the morning and, although I was sure I hadn't got all the facts right, I had a much clearer picture of what had been happening than when I made that analysis in Smestad. I intended to get an even clearer picture, which was why I was going to find Virginia Urse – but not, if I could help it, in the company of the SIS.

'It's not absurd,' my father said angrily. 'It wouldn't be the first time the communists have deliberately used people, our people, for their own ends. And your posting to Oslo was a godsend to them. We believe they seized their chance, arranged this trip to Boris Gleb, got Martin Gatling out of the way so that you would go with the Ambassador – they expected him to take you because you had been on the NATO desk in Washington – and fixed it so that Mrs Derek Almourn saw herself as a great liberation heroine bearing the words of the oppressed Russian writer to the free world, and thus trapped her to swap for John Day-Brune. The stupid little fool! She didn't stop to consider the consequences if she was caught, did she?'

I thought of Lynn. I opened my mouth and shut it again. I wanted to tell Francis that it hadn't been like that at all, that Lynn had done what she had done reluctantly and under great pressure – I was sure of it – and that she had been afraid of being caught, desperately afraid.

Instead I said: 'You promised me to do everything you possibly could to get her back. Are you reneging on your promise, Francis?'

'You got that promise from me under false pretences, Derek. You may not have been absolutely positive but you were as near to dammit sure that Lynn had arranged to collect the microfilm, and yet you failed to mention the fact to me.'

'That's not true. You've got the timing wrong,' I began; but he wouldn't listen.

'We *can't* let the communists get away with Day-Brune!' he

181

exploded. 'Good God, if we did, we'd deserve to be kicked out at the next election. We've made poor exchanges in the past but never as poor as this. We'll try to negotiate, of course. We'll do what we can. But we can't and we won't give up Day-Brune.'

'Who is this 'we' you keep on talking about? It doesn't include Lynn or me, does it?'

'It includes the Prime Minister of this country – your country, Derek – and his close advisers, one of whom I've had the honour to be for a long time!'

I swung away from the window where I had been staring down, half-seeing, into the square, at the policeman standing on guard outside our house, the green Mini parked by the garden railings across the street, the man walking his dog. My temper snapped. I had been counting so much on Francis but now it seemed he was prepared to let me down, to put his unspeakable politics before me, before Lynn. His 'do what we can' meant 'do damn all'. I couldn't depend on him any more.

'Day-Brune was also a close adviser to the high-paid help of my country,' I said acidly.

'Yes,' Francis said, without emphasis. 'I am aware of that.'

We stood, glaring at each other. To Francis's Private Secretary, who had just come into the study, we must have looked very alike.

'I'm sorry to interrupt, Lord Almourn, but there's a message from Number Ten. The PM's compliments and he would like to see you as soon as possible.'

'Right.'

'I shan't be here when you get back,' I said. 'My presence in this house must be an embarrassment to you in the circumstances. I'll be at Mary's, if anybody wants me.' Mary is my younger sister, married to a doctor.

'Very well.' He didn't try to argue about it. 'Say goodbye to your mother before you go. And remember this, Derek! The public were furious about Day-Brune – at the time a lot of them would have liked him shot – and they're not going to want to give him up now. What's more, although they and the media are all for Lynn Charlton Almourn at the moment and are demanding that the Government should 'take action', they'd change their tune if it became known how criminally foolish she has been. And I warn you, if it's necessary to justify our actions, they will be told. So your best bet, if you want to see that wife of yours again, is to co-operate with the SIS and with *us*, the politicians you so despise.'

He gave me a curt nod and strode out of the room. The PPS shut the door gently behind them. I went back to the window and watched as they came out of the house. I was shaking with suppressed emotions. They got into the waiting Bentley and drove off, Francis and his Secretary in the back seat, the chauffeur and Francis's personal detective in the front. The policeman, who had been full of salutes, resumed his dull watch. The man was still walking his dog. The green Mini was still parked where it had been before.

I made myself consider calmly what Francis had said. It didn't change my purpose, which was to get hold of Virginia Urse and wring the truth out of her. And it didn't change the fact that I intended to do this without the Commander or Redhead or his minion breathing down my neck.

Fifteen minutes later, having telephoned Mary and explained to my mother that I was moving out – a statement which she received without protest – I stood on the doorstep, clutching a three-suiter in one hand and a briefcase in the other. The policeman regarded me with interest. The driver of the green Mini started the engine but did not move away. The dog-owner sighted a friend and waved to him. There were no reporters or photographers in sight. A taxi cruised around the square, stopped at my signal, picked up me and my baggage and set off for Upper Wimpole Street.

It was a casual glance out of the rear window while we were going through the Park that made me wonder about the green Mini. After all London abounds in Minis, many of them green. Perhaps the one which was now bowling along some fifty yards behind my taxi, up Park Lane, through Mayfair, across Oxford Street, Manchester Square, the Marylebone High Street, Weymouth Street and thus to Upper Wimpole Street was not the same as the one that had been parked opposite our house in Belgravia. I was paying off the taxi as this Mini drove past where we were stopped, but the taxi-driver chose that moment to drop half my change on the floor and I was distracted from seeing who was driving.

By now I was suspicious of the taxi-driver too – the dog-owner could have been signalling to him and not to some unknown friend – the more so when, waiting for the door-bell to be answered, I saw him refuse another fare and drive off with his light out, empty. Of course he could have been going for a late breakfast. But I had become wary of coincidences.

I had an extra cup of coffee with Mary, who was sympathetic and did her best not to ask too many questions. I said hullo to my five-year-old nephew and enquired after my brother-in-law. Then I collected another taxi that took me down to Whitehall. I didn't see the green Mini again.

At the Office I duly reported my return; nobody seemed to know exactly why I had been recalled or they pretended not to. There was nothing for me to do. I wandered around talking to people who were friendly enough considering that I wasn't actually flying a yellow fever flag. I felt inordinately grateful to a chum of mine who insisted on taking me off to his club for an early lunch. He told me that *Tass*, the Russian news agency, had released the information that the Soviet Union was prepared to let Lynn go in exchange for Day-Brune and that the Foreign Secretary was due to make a statement to the effect that such an exchange was not agreeable to HMG but they would hope to negotiate. If I had ever had an appetite for the excellent food and wine which he urged on me, this latest piece of information would have destroyed it.

After I left him I walked to Hamleys where I bought my nephew some educational building blocks; they looked quite fun and would please his parents who had progressive ideas about children's toys. From there I walked back to Upper Wimpole Street. Mary and the child were out, James was doubtless downstairs in his consulting rooms, the place was empty. I made myself some tea and wandered around. I spent a good deal of time looking out of the window but it was impossible to spot if anybody was watching the house. I tried not to think of Lynn.

I had decided not to go to Virginia's until late afternoon, partly because I thought she was more likely to be in at that time and partly because I hoped that the SIS, if they were having me followed, would have become less suspicious by then. At ten past five I left the house and picked up a taxi, although I was only going a very short distance. When we reached Regent Mansions – a huge block of flats where an elderly cousin of mine has lived for ages – I gave the driver a pound, told him to wait for five minutes and, if I didn't reappear, to keep the change. I mentioned my cousin's name to the hall porter, who knew me by sight, and set off down the quarter mile of broad, carpeted corridor. But, as soon as his back was turned, I slipped through a service door, along a passage and out into a side street.

I thought I had been rather clever. Now I was lucky. I doubled back to Baker Street and just managed to jump on a Number 30 bus, stopped by the traffic lights, which took me to South Ken station. The address to which Lynn had sent her diary was five minutes away. It turned out to be another vast warren of flats but slightly seedy in appearance and with no porter on duty. The flat numbers were clearly marked, however, and I had no difficulty in finding Number 46. I pressed the bell-push and one of those ridiculous waterfalls of chimes sounded. Nobody answered it.

This address was the only lead I had to Virginia and I refused to face the possibility that I might not find her here. Bending down I peered through the letter-box. I could see a light shining from what was probably the sitting-room and hear some distinct but uninterpretable sounds. I put my fingers on the bell-push and held it there while a cascade of notes spilled forth.

The front door opened about six inches and was stopped short by a chain. A face looked at me, Virginia's face but not Virginia's hair. This was a blowzy blonde! I hesitated. The door began to close and a voice – thank God it was Virginia's voice – said very loudly. 'Derek Almourn! Why, did you ever! Derek, hang on a minute.'

The front door closed and, released from its chain after an appreciable interval and a certain amount of fumbling, opened wide. I had a fleeting impression of Virginia; she was wearing the same green trouser-suit that I had last seen her in at Smestad, and her hair was as short and as dark as always. Then I was enfolded in her arms and in the musky scent that she favoured. She kissed me. I felt the tears on her cheek. She clung to my hand as she led me into the sitting-room.

'Derek, it's dreadful about Lynn, dreadful. I've been making myself ill worrying about her.'

Her hypocrisy sickened me. 'Why did you let her do it then?' I said roughly. 'Or was it you who made her do it, Virginia?'

Her eyes widened and she shook her head. 'I – I don't know what you mean. But sit down, Derek, and have some sherry. I'm sorry I've no scotch.'

'I don't want anything, thank you.'

'Oh – you must.'

I hadn't planned any particular approach to Virginia and somehow the sight of her standing there and offering me sherry, when Lynn . . . The angry words jerked out of me. 'So you can poison me as you poisoned Martin Gatling in Oslo? If he had died you would have been a murderess. Do you realize that, Virginia? And you could still do a long stretch in gaol. If Lynn doesn't get back safely, I'll damn well see you do. I swear I will.'

'For heaven's sake, what are you talking about? I haven't murdered anybody, Derek.' She spoke mildly; my angry threats had made no impression on her. 'I just don't understand. You come bursting into my apartment and make these ghastly accusations. Derek, I realize you're upset about Lynn but so am I. I'm devoted to her. I'd do anything for her. I look on her as a – a sort of younger sister.'

'Then perhaps you'll help to get her out of the mess you've got her into.'

'Of course I'd help her if I could. You must know that. But there's nothing I can do, nothing any of us can do right now. Derek, leave things alone. Let them be. The Brits'll exchange her for Day-Brune and then everything'll be okay. It'll be all over. You and Lynn will be able to be happy together.'

She sounded as if she believed what she was saying but I didn't. 'Listen,' I said, 'the British aren't such fools as you think. The authorities know – amongst other things – that Lynn went to Boris

Gleb with the intention of smuggling that microfilm back to the West and I know she didn't want to do it. I know you persuaded her, Virginia – or would blackmailed be a better word? You set up the whole thing for her and you made her carry it out. And I want to know how you managed to *persuade* her, you and that blasted man, Bruno. Because – '

We both froze, staring at each other. Virginia's eyes were blank. We listened. The noise was not repeated.

Then I had recovered from my surprise. I was on my feet, in the passage, throwing open doors, bedroom, bathroom, cupboard, kitchen. My sense of direction was poor. I should have known the noise came from the kitchen. The back door was ajar. I didn't think about danger but ran across the room, tripping over something fair and furry – a cat? – and pulled wide the door, only to be met with an empty, enclosed space, the back door of the opposite flat and the cage of a service lift. I pressed myself against the metal frame and peered down but there was nothing to see, except the top of the descending lift and a clutch of cables. The whirring of the machinery was one of the most frustrating sounds I have ever heard.

My brain worked slowly. But I did react. I reached the kitchen window, flung it open and hung half out. The figure of a man had emerged below. He kept close to the wall of the building. I saw him only briefly and from an odd angle. I got the impression that he was tall and somehow stiff-limbed, with pale, bright hair. Then he was gone and I was left with an irritating memory as elusive as an almost forgotten tune. I told myself I must have imagined that there was something familiar about him.

I withdrew my head, taking care not to bang it on the edge of the window, and looked at my hands. They were black with dirt from the sill. I washed them in the kitchen sink, dried them on a paper towel and started back to the sitting-room. Out of the corner of my eye I caught sight of the thing I had tripped over when I ran into the kitchen. I bent and picked it up. It wasn't a cat as I had half supposed but a blond wig, the wig Virginia must have been wearing when she first opened the door to me. Carrying it I returned to her.

She was as I had left her, sitting in the same chair and looking quite composed. In her hand was a small, blunt revolver, which appeared to give her command of the situation. She smiled at me, thin-lipped, reminding me of the SIS Commander who had questioned me last night.

'Sit down, Derek.'

I sat, not because I was afraid – I couldn't imagine Virginia actually shooting me – but because there was a lot I needed to know. I hadn't finished with Virginia yet; in fact I had scarcely begun.

'Tell me,' I began, 'who was that – '

'No, you tell me!' she retorted. 'First how did you know where to find me?'

'The Post Office at Smestad gave me your address. Lynn sent you her diary to keep for her. She must have forgotten it when you were there.'

'And I never even knew she kept a diary. Very silly of her! But clever of you to work that out, Derek. I thought, when I got the packet, that it might just occur to you.'

'I had some help from the Intelligence man at our Embassy.'

'Intelligence? Ah –yes. Your people don't know where I am, do they?'

'Not at the moment.'

'You didn't tell them? You swear?'

'I didn't tell them. But they'd like to know all right and what you're doing here, going around in disguise.' I threw the wig at her feet. 'I suppose you wear dark glasses too when you go out.'

'It's no crime to wear a wig and I'm doing nothing criminal,' she said calmly. 'I'm merely waiting – out of the way of questions – until Lynn's safely back again. And that's what you're going to do, Derek, whether you like it or not and whatever you know or think you know, because – '

'You may have to wait for ever,' I interrupted. 'The British Government does *not* intend to swap John Day-Brune for Lynn or anybody. He's much too important.'

'But they'll have to,' she said with assurance. 'It's a pity the authorities know it wasn't just an impulsive act on Lynn's part but it won't make any difference in the long run. The people are clamouring for her return and the Government can't ignore the will of the people – not with an election coming up next year.'

'You've forgotten something,' I said, 'and that's the opposition there'll be to giving up Day-Brune in exchange – Day-Brune's treachery aroused a hell of a lot of anger and hatred in this country – and the Government will do their utmost to encourage it. They'll plug Day-Brune's importance to the security of the UK and the top secret stuff he could still reveal. And if they're driven to it, they'll reveal that Lynn deliberately – '

'No, they won't, Derek. There's something you've forgotten. Your Government will hold its hand. Because Lynn's important too. She's Lord Almourn's daughter-in-law and Lord Almourn isn't going to let the wife of his son and heir languish in a Russian gaol, is he? He's a personal friend of your Prime Minister's, a member of the Establishment and he'll pull every string he can. And Senator Charlton will do the same in Washington so that the President will pressure the Brits. Remember, Lynn's the sister of a Vietnam veteran, a war hero. The American people will all be rooting for her.' Virginia's mouth twisted as if something had amused her. 'You know, Derek, I didn't want Lynn to be used for this, believe me, I didn't, but she really is the perfect exchange for John Day-Brune, isn't she?'

I looked at her in disgust. 'Don't count on Francis Almourn,' I said. 'He made it very clear to me this morning that he's primarily a politician and secondly a father. And don't count on public opinion either. It's notoriously fickle. There won't be much sympathy for Lynn if it's made known that the communists set a trap and because of her bloody stupid ideas she let herself be manoeuvred into it. The British don't like being tricked and they'll blame Lynn for what they'll consider her stupidity – or worse.'

'Derek – what did you say?' Virginia's voice was sharp. 'About the communists manoeuvring Lynn into a trap. You're not suggesting your authorities suspect some sort of communist plot to – to rescue Day-Brune, are you?'

'Yes.'

'But what – Have they any proof?' For the first time she seemed shaken. 'No – of course not. How could they?'

'I don't know about proof,' I said, 'but my father warned me – threatened me, you could say. If they were forced to it, the politicians would have no hesitation in justifying to the country their reasons for refusing to exchange Day-Brune. Once it got to this stage, there'd be no chance of a secret deal, of some other bargain that might persuade the Russians to let Lynn go. And God knows what would happen then. Don't you see, Virginia, Lynn's best hope is to persuade HMG that she was forced to do what she did. She must show she had no choice, that she wasn't criminally foolish. This is the only thing that will weaken the Government's case and make them hesitate to tell the whole story in public. It could even make them offer more for Lynn – Day-Brune's release in five years, perhaps, when he won't be as dangerous to security as they think he is right now.'

I stopped. Virginia wasn't listening. She seemed to be lost in some private speculation. I had no idea what she was thinking about – maybe the possibility that the communists' plan to free Day-Brune might indeed fail; I didn't know how deeply she herself was committed. Whatever it was, she found it bitter. Her mouth was pursed and she chewed busily at the inside of her lip. Then suddenly she relaxed, laughing.

'You're trying to con me, Derek. And, you know, I nearly fell for it. I suppose because you're one of those horribly honest people whom it's so difficult not to trust.'

'Virginia, I am not trying to con you. I swear it.'

'I suppose your SIS put you up to it in the hope of getting some proof for this little theory of theirs about a communist plot.'

'No! Why should they? I'd told them I hadn't a clue where you were.'

'Then your father was bluffing you. They'd never dare make such an accusation without proof. And you're not going to give them any proof, Derek.'

'For pity's sake, Virginia. All I want is to save Lynn. Can't you understand that?' I was beginning to feel desperate. I was pretty sure Francis hadn't been bluffing but I couldn't remember precisely what he had said, except that he had told me to co-operate with the SIS; Virginia could be right about their need for proof. 'I don't care a damn, apart from Lynn,' I said. 'The governments can sort out the rest for themselves.'

Virginia looked at me speculatively. 'My poor Derek, you know, I really believe you mean that. If it was anybody else but you – '

'For God's sake, it doesn't matter about me. It's Lynn who matters.'

'Derek, there's nothing you or I can do for her right now.'

'You could tell me the truth. Why did Lynn agree to take that microfilm, when she didn't want to? How did she get mixed up in this – this mess in the beginning? You know, don't you, Virginia?'

'Yes, I know. What's more I'll gladly tell you, Derek, and then you'll understand why you mustn't try to interfere. I was going to tell you when – when the cat made that noise in the kitchen and you shot out of the room.'

'Well, you've begun with a lie,' I said irritably. 'It was a man, not a cat, in your kitchen. He got away in the service lift but I saw him from the window.'

I was totally unprepared for what happened next. Virginia had leapt to her feet. She held the gun pointed at my chest and it didn't waver. I could see her finger on the trigger. She was within a hair's breadth of shooting me. For the first time since I had come into the flat I felt afraid. But more than fear I felt surprise. Perhaps it was the utter amazement printed on my face that saved me.

'What did you see?'

'A man, in a dark suit, with fair hair. That's all. I doubt I'd recognize him again, if that's what's worrying you. It's a long way down to the courtyard and the light wasn't good.'

Virginia nodded slowly. She walked over to a modern butler's tray, where some bottles and glasses were arranged. She put the gun on the tray, poured herself a brandy, drank some and refilled the glass. She brought another across to me. She seemed to be trying hard not to laugh; her eyes shone, and her mouth twitched.

'Not poisoned,' she said as she gave me the brandy. 'You saw for yourself. I tasted it.' Her voice shook.

'Who was it?' I asked. 'The man in the kitchen. Who was he?'

'That – oh, that was Bruno,' Virginia said. 'Bruno!' She raised her glass as if she were offering a toast to him. Then she did begin to laugh. I couldn't understand why she found the situation so amusing.

Chapter Three

'You were going to tell me about Lynn,' I said, still kicking myself that I had come so close to catching Bruno but had failed.

'So I was.' Virginia regarded me with amused contempt. I dare say she guessed what I was thinking. 'But let me tell you about me first. Did you know, Derek, that I started life as a bastard in a poor but ever so respectable family in the Mid-West? In fact it was so respectable that none of them could forgive me for being born. At fifteen I ran away from home and came East. At sixteen I married a kinky teacher, more than twice my age. But he educated me, even helped me get a degree.'

'Virginia, please – '

'Do you want to hear about Lynn or not, Derek?'

'About Lynn, yes.'

'Then you listen to what I've got to say,' she said sharply. 'I was glad when my husband was killed – not in Vietnam as I told Lynn – in an automobile accident, because I was free of him and I collected plenty. He'd left more money than I'd expected, too. He was heavy with insurance. So I went back to College, which was where I met Bruno. Of course I didn't know him as Bruno then.'

Up to now Virginia's story had been getting less than half my attention. I had been wondering if I was wasting my time, if there was no possibility of extracting from her the information about Lynn that I needed and that only she could provide. Her mention of Bruno, however, changed all this. I was immediately engrossed by what she had to say.

'I fell for him completely and utterly. It didn't matter that he was quite a bit younger than I was or that he came from such a different background or that he was a crypto-communist. Nothing mattered. I had an idyllic year. I would have done anything for him – and I did.' Virginia stopped.

To prompt her, I said: 'You mean you became a communist?'

'I was already a sympathizer and he didn't want me to join the Party. One can often be more use outside. In a corrupt capitalist society like ours – '

'Spare me.'

'Have you ever given it a thought? You – Lord Almourn's son and heir! How did your family make its money?' She sneered at me.

'Tell me about Lynn.'

'Don't be so impatient, Derek. Let me tell you about Bruno.'

And Virginia proceeded to tell me. Bruno, it seemed, had been drafted and had not appealed against the draft, although he was a student. He had gone willingly to Vietnam. But before he went he had made her promise that if she received any orders from 'Bruno' she would do as instructed and ask no questions, and she had kept her promise; there had been a lot of orders and she had acted on all of them.

It was due to Bruno that she became a member of People for Peace and Freedom, which she described as a useless collection of weepers and moaners. Later he told her to cultivate a girl called Lynn Charlton, whose brother was missing in Vietnam and whom somebody would bring to a meeting. The Charltons had heard nothing of Lloyd since his helicopter had been shot down and Lynn, who adored her brother, was distraught. When Virginia said she might be able to get news of Lloyd through a 'secret underground source', Lynn leapt at the chance; she had always been anti the Vietnam war, like so many other Americans, and saw nothing unpatriotic in this.

Lynn was informed that Lloyd was alive and well, and had been moved to a prison camp in Hanoi. Shortly afterwards his name was released on an official POW list. She was immensely grateful to Virginia, as was to be expected, and to the unknown Bruno, from whom Virginia was ordered to disassociate herself. Lynn was to receive the impression that she, whose brother was a prisoner, and Virginia, whose husband had been killed, were on the same side, whereas Bruno was merely somebody whose help they needed. This would mean that later Bruno could bring pressure to bear on her without spoiling her relationship with Virginia. Lynn, in fact, was being hooked.

For the moment nothing was asked of her, except in the general terms of supporting the cause of world peace and freedom. She received a letter from Lloyd, which she was forbidden to show to her parents and which upset her very much. Lloyd was having a bad time. Conditions were appalling, food was minimal, he had a recurrent fever but there were no drugs, and a buddy of his had just died from a neglected wound. Lynn was horrified and naturally she appealed to Virginia; as Virginia said sardonically, they had become very close by this time.

Lynn was now prepared to give anything and do anything if it would help Lloyd. But she was only asked to contribute a little money to the People for Peace and Freedom – and there was somebody eager to meet her father, if she could arrange a casual introduction. In return the Charltons got a message from Lloyd through a Quaker mercy mission and Lynn another private letter through Bruno, in which Lloyd said that things had inexplicably improved.

The pattern was clear. There was no need for Virginia to go into more detail. Lynn was caught. As long as Lloyd was a POW in Vietnam she had to dance to Bruno's tune. However, Bruno's demands were not excessive – and all in the name of good, liberalistic ideals. Lynn didn't realize that she was mortgaging the rest of her life and, as it turned out, mine too.

'Bruno was delighted when you fell for Lynn,' Virginia said. 'He was all for encouraging it. Lord Almourn's only son, the apple of his eye! It was a gift from the gods. Senator's daughter was good but Lord Almourn's daughter-in-law was even better.'

And Lynn? What did she feel about it? I tried to say it but I couldn't. I choked on the words. Virginia regarded me mockingly. She knew what I was asking myself, the doubt that she had put into my mind. I would never again be one hundred per cent sure why Lynn had married me, and that pleased her. Virginia, whatever Bruno's feelings might be, had never liked me.

'Your marriage must have suggested all sorts of possibilities,' she continued, 'especially since the Brits had caught John Day-Brune.

Lynn, poor sweetie, believed that once Lloyd was safely home she would be free of Bruno, but she didn't understand. She was irrevocably committed. Still she tried to escape. Derek, do you remember Grant – my cousin?'

'Grant? No.' I shook my head.

'He wasn't really a cousin. He was one of Bruno's people. Lynn refused to ask the Senator, as a personal favour to her, to give Grant a job in his office. Lloyd was home now and Bruno's threat to tell her family or even to make public some of the things she had done didn't seem so important. After all they weren't that dreadful and she thought people would understand. So she refused. I begged her. I pleaded with her. I asked you to help but you wouldn't.'

'I remember,' I said. 'If only I had known – Why didn't she tell me? Or Lloyd?'

'Perhaps she would have told you, given time, but Bruno didn't give her time. Grant was kind of a test and Lynn was failing it. Bruno wasn't going to allow that. His masters wouldn't like it. They had a plan for you and Lynn, if it was needed. So Bruno arranged for a nice, pseudo mugging in the underground garage of your apartment block.'

'What? Bruno arranged that?' I remembered the FBI Inspector and the questions he had asked; they made more sense now.

'Yes – and it worked. You were beaten up and the whole thing made to look like an authentic Washington mugging. Lynn was scarcely touched – Bruno gave strict orders about that – but she was taught her lesson. Afterwards she would have asked her father for anything, a hundred jobs in his office, anything that Bruno wanted.

'God damn him,' I said, 'and you, Virginia. You knew what he was going to do. You could have stopped it.'

'No,' she said. 'No, I couldn't. I tried, for Lynn's sake. But he wouldn't listen. He said he would see to it that Lynn came to no harm herself but she had to learn discipline. I – I couldn't do anything.'

'You expect me to believe that?'

196

'It's the truth. Bruno's different than he used to be, more dedicated and more – '

'Sadistic?'

'No. More – implacable is probably the right word,' she said. 'You could say his war experiences had tempered him.'

'And what do you mean by that? Was there something odd about his war experiences?'

'You could say that too.'

'You mean something that would explain how he could be fighting in the Vietnamese jungle and yet sending you a constant stream of orders. Come on, Virginia!' I said roughly. 'You must have guessed I'd notice that discrepancy.'

Virginia gave me a sour smile. 'Clever, aren't you?'

'Tell me about Bruno's war experiences.'

'He never had any,' she said, 'not the sort you're thinking of. He was captured a couple of weeks after he got to Vietnam. Actually it was all arranged, a put-up job. Didn't you think it peculiar that a commie, who could easily have got deferred, was happy to go and fight in Vietnam? But everything was laid on. He did his war service in Moscow. And now, Derek, he has become a very dangerous man, who will let nothing and no one stand in his way. Sometimes he even frightens me.'

It was a warning. I should have paid more heed to it, but I was still trying to absorb what she had told me about Bruno. Extraordinary as the story was I believed every word of it. It made sense of so much that had been utterly inexplicable before. The truth is, I suppose, that in this peculiar world, of which Bruno and Virginia and the FBI Inspector and the characters from the SIS, and Lynn, were part, I was a complete unsophisticate. And, at this point, all I could do was flounder on.

'Now where was I?' Virginia said. 'Oh yes, Bruno had had you beaten up. That mugging served another purpose besides disciplining Lynn. As Bruno had hoped, it caused you to be posted and he couldn't have chosen a better post for you than Oslo. It meant that if Day-Brune's gaol-break failed, as it did, Bruno could immediately set about arranging for Lynn to be made available as an exchange. But your people know all this, you say. A pity! We had hoped the exchange could've been arranged on an ordinary everyday basis without them suspecting a thing. Then, when it was over, Lynn would have been free from – further duties, if that was the way she wanted it. Bruno gave her his word.'

'And you believed him?'

Virginia shrugged; she was a callous bitch. 'Who knows?'

'You didn't think of volunteering in her place?'

'I'm an American.'

'So is Lynn.'

'For this purpose she's true blue Brit – wife of a British diplomat, daughter-in-law of Lord Almourn. Wasn't she wearing her bulldog pin when she was caught in the act?'

I controlled my temper by promising myself that, if Lynn didn't get out of Russia safely, I would kill Virginia Urse. And yet Lynn *had* worn that damned brooch and it was the *British* Ambassador she was demanding to see. My thoughts fragmented.

'You're Lynn's devoted friend,' I said bitterly, 'but you don't seem to care a damn that she's in some cell in the Lubianka gaol, terrified about what's going to happen to her, probably cold and hungry and –'

'You bloody fool, Derek!' Virginia burst out laughing. 'Lynn's in the country, at a *dacha* outside Moscow, where only the most important guests of the Soviet Union are entertained. You don't think Bruno would let her –'

She stopped abruptly. The telephone was ringing in the hall. With a triumphant glance at me, she ran to answer it. She had shut the door of the sitting-room but the latch hadn't clicked and I could have heard what she was saying. It wasn't worth trying to listen, however, even though it was now obvious that she had been waiting for this call. Whoever was on the other end of the line seemed to be doing all the talking.

Besides I was overwhelmed by what she had just told me about Lynn; I found it almost impossible to accept. But Virginia hadn't sounded as if she were lying and perhaps it wasn't so far-fetched. In the circumstances the communists could afford to be generous to Lynn; indeed it might even be good policy on their part.

I tried to imagine what Lynn might be doing at this very minute, while I was here, in Virginia's flat. I could only picture her drinking vodka and eating caviar. She wasn't thinking of me. She was surrounded by a group of men in brown suits, who all looked like Comrade Vetski.

I got up and went across to the window. It had started to rain. On the other side of a quiet street was another red-brick warren of flats similar to the one in which Virginia was staying. Beneath me a large white automobile, an American Lincoln, drove slowly by. There was a man sheltering in the entrance opposite – he could have been waiting for a friend – but almost no traffic, pedestrian or otherwise. It was the sort of peaceful backwater that can be found in the busiest districts of London. I turned reluctantly as Virginia came back into the room.

She went straight to the butler's tray and poured herself another brandy. She stared at me as if she wasn't sure who I was, as if somehow I had changed since she had left me. I sensed that something had happened.

'What is it? What's the matter, Virginia?'

'Nothing, nothing at all. Help yourself to some brandy, Derek.'

'Thank you, no. Who was that on the phone?'

'Nobody you know.'

Virginia looked hurriedly at her watch and I wondered if she wanted me to go. But she had just offered me more brandy. So she must be waiting for somebody to come or something to happen. Or was I imagining the whole bloody lot?

'Derek – for God's sake, help yourself to a brandy and sit down! Don't you want to know the rest of it? About Norway – Hank and Chuck and Martin Gatling?'

Instinct prompted me to say 'no' and to get to hell out of the place. I knew enough now to put up an excellent case for Lynn having been blackmailed, and the Commander and his chums from the SIS could surely make Virginia talk; I had given up any hope that she would make a voluntary statement for Lynn's sake. But she was offering me more information, tempting me to stay and, although I didn't understand her motives, I couldn't refuse.

I did as bidden, poured myself some brandy and sat down. 'All right, Virginia,' I said. 'I should like to hear about Norway.'

'Well, Bruno suspected Lynn might be difficult about Borisoglebsk – it was quite an assignment for her to undertake – and he decided to remind her that she hadn't escaped him by leaving the States. On the contrary. So he sent her flowers and arranged for her to take a little trip.

'Take a little trip?'

'LSD, when she thought she was a bird at that Canadian reception. You can't have forgotten.'

'So that *was* meant for Lynn! I thought it might be some – some sort of stupid joke and she had just been unlucky.'

'Oh no, Derek. It was meant for Lynn, poor sweetie. It was a warning and she knew it. If there had been somebody else suitable – ' Virginia shrugged. 'But Lynn was essential to Bruno and the plan to rescue Day-Brune.' She paused to sip her brandy. 'So I was instructed to visit with you and Lynn in Oslo and to persuade her to do what was expected of her. It wasn't a job I liked and, I must say, it wasn't easy. Besides, as you know, we had other difficulties. Your Ambassador didn't seem to want to take you and Lynn to the north and poor Mr Gatling had to be put out of action – by me eventually. Those Finns were a hopeless pair. They never seemed to get a thing right – not a thing.'

'Finns? Do you mean Hank and Chuck?'

'Yes.'

'And did their mistakes include half drowning me instead of Martin Gatling?'

'Yes. At least I made some credit out of that by using it as an extra warning to Lynn. But those boys were real fools. Fancy asking to camp in your yard when they had been told I would contact them by Smestad Pond.' Virginia shook her head. 'They must have been crazy. Incidentally, I had been having a talk with them the last morning of my visit with you, when you met me at the bottom of your drive. You must have thought *me* crazy going to look at ducks at that hour.'

I didn't answer and Virginia again looked at her watch. 'Derek, I – I've got the most frightful headache.' She passed her hand over her brow in a theatrical gesture. 'I'm afraid I'll have to go to bed.

I'm sorry the way things have turned out, truly I am, but there's nothing I can do to help you.'

'I don't need your help, Virginia. But Lynn does.' I was prepared to make one last appeal. 'Please, please tell the British authorities what you've told me. If they know the truth about Lynn's part in this affair they'll be far more sympathetic towards her and they'll make the communists a far more generous offer, not Day-Brune – nothing will make them let Day-Brune go, not for some years at any rate – but there must be someone else, or something else that the communists would accept instead. And the public, the British and the American, would back Lynn for almost anything, except Day-Brune.'

Virginia was standing up. She wanted me to go now but I didn't move. I didn't believe in her sudden headache. She wanted to get rid of me for some other reason.

'And what would happen to me, if I agreed to what you're suggesting, Derek?'

'You would be protected. I swear it. And if there's anything else you want, money – '

Virginia laughed in my face. 'My poor Derek, I'm not going to tell your authorities anything and nor are you.'

'And how do you propose to stop me?'

'By telling you the truth about Lynn, this wonderful truth you want me to tell your SIS.' She was regarding me now with what I can only describe as pity, as if I were some idiot child. 'Derek, Lynn knew what she was doing, precisely what she was doing. She went to Borisoglebsk with the microfilm that I had given her already in her shoulder-bag. She wore the bulldog pin only so that the Intourist hostess could be sure to identify her. She knew the KGB would find the microfilm and that she would be taken to Moscow and would have to stay there for some weeks, until the poor old Brits agreed to exchange her for Day-Brune. That's the real truth, Derek. And do you want me to tell that to your authorities?'

'I don't believe you,' I said. 'I don't believe you.' My voice broke.

Virginia didn't bother to answer; she knew I did believe her.

The things Lynn had done, like taking her sleeping-pills and special cosmetics, making a list of that Lapp silver, carrying an unnecessary coat, even some of her remarks about being able to look after herself, these were all explicable once one accepted that Lynn expected to spend some time in the Soviet Union and wasn't just afraid she might be caught. And there was that business of the shoulder-bag at Fornebu when she had threatened to faint, to pretend to be ill, anything rather than go to Boris Gleb without the bag that Virginia had given her – and the microfilm.

'Damn you to hell,' I said thickly. 'You and Bruno. He forced her to it, but you – you persuaded her to be your friend and you didn't raise a hand to help her.'

'You're wrong there,' Virginia said. 'I didn't want her to be used. She was frightened and nervous and I was afraid she might break. But it was too late by then and actually she did real well. Bruno said she would. He said he knew he could rely on her.'

I thought of the implications – not the personal implications; I couldn't face those yet – but the implications of the fact that Lynn's culpability was of an order of magnitude that neither I nor Francis nor probably the SIS had dreamed. I felt sick.

'You do understand, don't you, Derek?' Virginia said gently. 'You can't mention anything I've told you this evening, not to a soul – not if you hope to see Lynn ever again. You could argue that she did it all for her brother's sake till you're blue in the face, but the Brits would never forgive her, and nor would the Americans. And whatever might happen to Lynn, one thing's for sure – it would be the end of your marriage. You understand?'

I nodded. I couldn't trust myself to speak. I understood only too well. I would have to wait, like Virginia – out of the way of questions – and hope that the communists would be convinced they were not going to get Day-Brune. Once they realized their ploy was pointless they might – just might – give Lynn up as a gesture of good will to the West. And they might feel they should do this before Francis and his fellow-politicians were driven to justify themselves by revealing the Soviet plot and what they believed was Lynn's part in it. It was all very complex; it was a 'you know-I know-you know' situation; it was a great deal to hope for.

Virginia was standing over me, rocking on her heels. Her shapeless face showed a mixture of emotions that I couldn't interpret. For the umpteenth time she looked at her watch. She was as impatient for me to be gone now as she had been eager to keep me earlier.

'Come on, Derek, get out and let me go to bed. This headache's killing me. You can think about what I've told you and – and, if you like, come and see me tomorrow morning. We can talk some more then.'

I got slowly to my feet and a smile split her mouth. She knew she had won. She didn't need to threaten me. I had been beaten, not by her or Bruno, but by Lynn.

Virginia followed me from the sitting-room. In the hall I stopped and turned. I had remembered Lynn's diary.

'I accept what you've told me,' I said, 'the facts. But I should like to read Lynn's diary, to know what she really felt about – about everything.'

'I haven't got it, Derek.'

'But you said –'

'Oh, it arrived safely. I gave it to Bruno. It was much too incriminating to keep around this place. I guess he destroyed it. I don't really know.'

'I see.'

'I'm sorry, Derek, truly I am. I've never liked you. I can't pretend I have. But I wish – I wish things hadn't turned out this way.'

And I was over the threshold, the door shutting behind me. As I hesitated on the mat I heard the rattle of the chain. Virginia was barricading herself in again. I walked along the passage to the lift and pushed the down button.

When the lift came I stumbled in. I went down to the ground floor, across the rather grubby hall and out into the street. The weather had changed. The sky was dark and lowering. Big thunder drops were beginning to fall. Shivering, in a thin suit and without an umbrella or raincoat, I turned right and set off in an aimless direction.

I was now within moments of being killed.

Chapter Four

Everything happened at once.

Blinded by a sudden violent squall of rain, I saw very little. I heard the roar of a powerful engine as the car accelerated and a thud as it mounted the pavement behind me. Headlights splayed on my back, surrounding me in their glare. I was aware of fear and panic. I willed myself to jump out of the way of the monster that was rushing down on me, but my feet were in lead boots. I knew I was about to die.

I was conscious of the pound of running feet, a figure hurtling across the road, the hiss of wheels on the wet surface. I could have sworn I felt the warmth of the car's engine and the nudge of metal as something or someone thrust me powerfully into the shelter of a doorway. My head shattered one of the plate-glass panels of the door, my shoulder struck the metal surround and my knees cracked sickeningly on to the stone steps.

But I was alive.

Before I blacked out I saw, or believe I saw – it's vivid in my nightmares even now, eighteen months later – the body of the man who had saved my life describe a parabola in the rain-sodden air and fall, fall with a dull heavy thud, sending up a shower of water from the gutter. The car that had tried to kill me scraped along the side of the building and fought its way back on to the road. Still going very fast, it suddenly swerved and crashed into the brick wall opposite, as a black Cortina drove straight at it. I'm certain I heard the scrunch of metal and the crash of broken glass – and the wail of a police siren.

The next thing I heard – or thought I heard – was a voice that I dimly recognized, saying: 'He'll live, God damn him!'

It seemed much later that I opened my eyes again, but I can't have been out for more than a few minutes. Somebody had carried me into the entrance hall, where I lay, my head gently bleeding into whatever was supporting it. A young man with a pink and white face, whom I had never seen before and who turned out to be a doctor visiting a nearby patient, was kneeling beside me, cutting away my hair.

'You've been very lucky,' he said.

I didn't answer. I wasn't interested in him. My gaze travelled up from the highly polished shoes, now spattered with rain, to the Gieves suit, the military stance and the familiar face of Redhead, who stood over me. From his expression it was obvious he resented my luck and the fact that I would live. He poked me gently with his foot.

'Can he walk?' he addressed the doctor. 'There are a couple of sights I want to show him.'

The doctor stopped swabbing my head and the stinging sensation eased. 'He should be in hospital.'

'Why? What's the matter with him apart from a broken crown and a few bruises?'

'Shock. Possibly concussion, a splintered bone. Besides the cuts on his head need proper cleaning. You can't expect him to walk around looking at – at sights – whatever you mean by that – in his condition.'

'Why not? How about it, Mr Almourn? Don't you want to see the results of your evening's work?'

I could hear the dislike and contempt in Redhead's voice as he toe-ed me again and would have struggled to sit up but the doctor's ministrations made that impossible. Anyway Redhead hadn't waited for my reply. Saying he would be back in a few minutes he had left us.

'What's going on?' the doctor asked curiously. 'Were you trying to escape from him?'

'No – nothing like that.'

'Almourn,' he mused, fixing a sort of dressing on the top of my head. 'That's what he called you. Are you any relation to the chap in the Cabinet, Lord Almourn?'

'Yes,' I said, resisting the temptation to deny Francis. 'I'm Derek Almourn, his son.'

'His son? But that means – the girl in Russia – Almourn's daughter-in-law?'

'My wife.'

'Holy cow!' he said, squatting on his heels and staring at me.

He was too recent a graduate to have acquired a bedside manner and anyway the setting was scarcely appropriate for it. Nevertheless, I saw no reason why I should be regarded like some strange amoeba under a microscope. I was feeling rough and I guessed the worst wasn't over yet; even though the physical danger might be past, there were other things.

'Holy cow!' he repeated, awe-struck.

'Well, you'll know where to send your account,' I said sharply.

He had the grace to blush and mutter an apology. 'That's the reason for all that,' he said, waving a hand towards the street which seemed to be a hive of activity.

'Yes,' I said.

I lifted my head gingerly and looked around the hall. There were only the doctor and myself. The man who had saved me hadn't been brought inside. He had been left lying in the gutter, in the rain, which must mean that he was dead. And it was my fault. Small wonder Redhead hated my guts. Suddenly I had had enough of the doctor. I wanted to see whatever Redhead wanted to show me.

'Help me to get up,' I said.

'You shouldn't,' he said. 'Wait for a while. The ambulance has come. They'll be attending to the others first but they won't be long.'

The others! The car that had tried to kill me had crashed. Perhaps the driver himself had died or had accidentally killed – others. How many others? I had to know. Where was Redhead?

'Help me!' I said through my teeth and this time he didn't protest.

The walls of the hall tilted and swayed as I got to my feet. I fought them mentally so that they didn't fall in upon me. The nausea subsided from the back of my throat. My vision cleared. I found myself clinging to the doctor. Fortunately he was a muscular young man – doubtless he played rugger for his hospital – and could bear my weight. With an effort I managed to stand upright, by myself, and Redhead came back.

'Good!' he said, when he saw me. 'Come along then, Mr Almourn.' He ignored the doctor.

'If he's to go anywhere you'll have to help him,' the doctor said fiercely, anxious for his patient and his own authority.

'I'll take full responsibility,' Redhead said coldly and took me by the arm.

I tried to grin at the doctor. 'Thanks,' I said. 'And don't forget that account. I mean it, you know.'

'No charge, Mr Almourn,' he called after me. 'You can have it on the National Health.'

'A worthy young man,' Redhead murmured, happy to see me worsted in even the pettiest encounter.

Resenting my physical weakness I let him help me out of the building into the street, which was floodlit by car headlights; at least it had stopped raining. My legs weren't functioning properly yet and Redhead had to support me. But my mind was clear. I saw with enormous relief two ambulance men lifting on to a stretcher with infinite care and patience the man who had saved me; I realized that he must still be alive. Redhead led me up to them. Obviously this was one of the sights I had to see.

'You've met Peter,' Redhead said. 'He was a personal friend of mine.'

'Was?'

Redhead shrugged. 'His back's broken and he probably has internal injuries. But he's young and strong. He may live. God knows if he'll ever walk again. Do you think you were worth it, Mr Almourn?'

I didn't answer. Whatever could be done for Peter, the man whom I had thought of as Redhead's minion, would be done, but I saw no reason to beat my breast and cry *mea culpa* to his boss, however close their friendship. Deliberately I turned away from the waxen face and the sack-like body that should have been my own. Redhead could think what he damned well liked.

'What next?'

'Just down the road and a few steps. Can you manage it, Mr

207

Almourn?' He used my name frequently and always as an implied insult. 'Your enemy didn't get very far.'

I would have made it if I had had to crawl. And indeed Redhead's 'few steps', in fact about thirty yards, nearly brought me to my knees. I propped myself against a pillar-box while he went to talk to the gaggle of men, fire brigade, police and one in a white coat who must have been from the hospital, all milling around the crashed cars and having a jolly discussion about something. Redhead settled the argument in about five seconds flat, while I admired the crash.

It was a stupendous smash-up. The big white American Lincoln, which I had seen earlier cruising slowly past Virginia's window, and doubtless making a recce of the best place to kill me, had slewed at right angles across the pavement and must have hit the wall of the block of flats opposite with crushing violence. It was buried nose-deep in bricks, its body distorted by the force of the impact. Its owner, a visiting pop star, still unaware that his car had been stolen, would never drive it again.

The Cortina was also scrap. The Lincoln had caught it a glancing blow, which, at the speed both cars must have been travelling, had tossed the comparatively light car across the street into a builder's skip. It was difficult to believe that either driver could be alive. But Peter, Redhead's minion, hadn't been killed and neither for that matter, had I. Besides the doctor had talked about 'others' who needed attention.

I owed nothing to the chap who had been driving the Lincoln; presumably he was one of Bruno's hirelings paid to get rid of me. Even Peter had been doing the job for which he was trained. But the driver and the possible passengers of the Cortina were different, innocent victims of an affair which was no concern of theirs. I wondered how badly they had been hurt. It was the first question I asked Redhead when he returned to me.

'Kind of you to enquire,' he said. 'Just a bruise or two. I knew what I was doing.'

'You!'

'Certainly me. I wasn't going to let that sod get away with it. And I bet on him being the chicken.'

208

'The chicken?' I supposed I was being stupid.

'You know, a version of the old game, better played in the dark. You both turn your head-lights on and drive straight for each other. The chicken is the one who swerves first. It takes a bit of nerve to hang on.'

I looked at him with awe. His voice was perfectly level, his expression as disdainful as ever but he had made the mistake of lighting a cigarette. He must have needed it. As he smoked I could see his hand shaking. At least it made him seem more human.

'Let's go and look at the chicken, Mr Almourn. At the moment he's trussed. We're going to have to cut him out of the car.'

'He's alive?'

'Yes, though it's anybody's guess for how long. Fortunately for him he's unconscious.'

My head was throbbing with pain but otherwise I felt much better. Things were staying in their proper place and no longer sliding out of my line of vision, so that up was now up and down definitely down and nothing was about to fall in on me. It made walking much easier. I scarcely needed Redhead's hand on my elbow to guide me behind the Lincoln and over the rubble of bricks. It was such a relief to feel myself functioning normally that I didn't question why he was so eager for me to see my broken enemy. I just did what I was told.

He blocked my way when we reached the far side of the car and said: 'It would save a lot of door-bell ringing if you would tell me which flat you've been visiting. You know we want to talk to Virginia Urse.'

'Virginia Urse? What has she to do with this?'

'Oh come, Mr Almourn! You wouldn't have taken that amount of trouble to give us the slip if you hadn't intended to pay her a visit. It was the merest chance that Peter caught a glimpse of you getting on that Number 30 bus in Baker Street. But if he hadn't, you would probably be dead by now. So no more games, please. Which flat is Mrs Urse in?'

I didn't answer at once. I passed a hand over my face, pretending that I felt faint. It gave me a moment to think, to realize that nothing had changed since I left Virginia. She had carried out

Bruno's orders to keep me with her until he could arrange for a simple hit-and-run accident to put an end to me, either because he was afraid I had seen him and could identify him, or because I knew too much about him, or because he believed that I wouldn't be trusted to put my love for Lynn before everything else and thus might thwart his plan to rescue Day-Brune. Maybe his reason for deciding on my annihilation was a mixture of all three of these things. Maybe, since his hireling had failed, he would make other arrangements for me. I didn't care. What I did care about was that Virginia shouldn't be forced to implicate Lynn in such a way that no British government would ever dream of exchanging her for anybody, leave alone for Day-Brune.

'Mr Almourn, I'll ask you once more. Where can we find Virginia Urse?'

'Flat 53. But it may be difficult to rouse her. She has a sick headache and she has gone to bed.'

I had spoken reluctantly, as if giving Redhead the information against my will, and had carefully not looked him in the eye. Heaven knows what he would do to me when he found out I had lied. At the moment he seemed in no hurry to do anything, so I had to assume that he had men at the back of the flats too and considered Virginia to be nicely sewn up. He was probably right. But if, knowing what was about to happen to me, she had been watching from the window and had seen Bruno's plan for me go awry, she might have decided it was sensible to disappear. In which case my lie about the flat number and mention of the sick headache – with luck the occupant of Flat 53 would be out or stone deaf or just slow to answer the door – might buy her time and even opportunity, and was worth Redhead's displeasure.

'I said: Take a look at the chap who tried to kill you, Mr Almourn.'

'Sorry.'

Redhead moved away from the car, enabling me to have a clear view of the front seat. Without much interest I leaned forward, expecting an unpleasant sight. It was a miracle, I thought, that the chap was alive at all after such a crash. But the safety belt had saved him and the fact that the Lincoln had a left-hand drive; if he had been sitting on the right side he wouldn't have had a chance. As it was he looked like a rag doll, his body crumpled, his head lolling obscenely; but there was no blood, apart from a thin trickle from the corner of his mouth, and no obviously broken bones. His internal injuries, however, were anybody's guess.

I stared at him, disbelieving what I saw, thoughts like rats scurrying through my mind. In spite of the odd angle at which his body lay, there was no mistaking him. The square set of the shoulders and the burnished cap of hair was distinctive. He had been right to want to kill me. Even from the glimpse of him that I had caught from Virginia's back window, sooner or later I would have known him again. I stared at him and continued to stare, while a paroxysm of revulsion racked me.

'You recognize him, Mr Almourn?'

I nodded. I couldn't bring myself to speak at once. With an effort I forced myself to turn away from the handsome, blank face. I leaned against the car, breathing deeply, trying to control the bile that threatened to rise in my throat.

'You recognize him, Mr Almourn?' Redhead said again.

'Yes. It's – it's Bruno.'

'Bruno?'

'Yes. I suppose he didn't have time to arrange for somebody else to kill me so he decided to do the job himself.'

'But, Bruno? It can't be. Almourn, do you realize what you're saying? Are you sure?'

'Yes. That is – Bruno. I'm sure. God help me, I wish I weren't. Virginia Urse will confirm it. Flat 46. I lied about the number before.'

'Bruno,' Redhead breathed as if it were a holy word. Disbelief had given way to joy. He was radiant. 'Almourn, this makes everything worth – '

My expression must have stopped him; he wasn't an insensitive man. And I could contain myself no longer. I pushed past him, stumbled over some loose bricks and fell on my wretched knees. My cry of pain was muffled by the vomit that poured out of my mouth. Everything was going black. I must have lost consciousness again, if only for a moment or two.

Redhead was drawing me to my feet, supporting my shivering form, wiping my mouth with his own clean handkerchief, shouting for help. Men came running. I was lifted on to a stretcher and carried to an ambulance. Somebody took off my jacket, rolled up my sleeve and gave me a shot in the arm. Almost at once a feeling of euphoria stole over me. I lay warm and cosy and unthinking under my blankets. There was a lot of activity going on outside. I could hear Redhead barking orders. But everything was slightly unreal to me.

After an indeterminate amount of time, Redhead joined me and the ambulance took us to the hospital. I remember asking him where Peter was and he said that they had taken him on ahead. I said that I would do anything I could to help. I said that Virginia was wearing a blond wig.

I must have slept.

Several hours later I was once again on the top floor of that block of flats in Victoria where I had been, unbelievably, only the previous evening. On this occasion, however, my reception had been very different and the Commander, who had shaken hands with me – it seemed I was one of them now – was treating me with every consideration.

I had walked out of the hospital against all medical advice after my head had been stitched up and various X-rays had shown that, whatever they might feel like, none of my bones were as much as cracked. Redhead had given me the option but he had stressed that the sooner I told the SIS everything I knew about Bruno, the better they would be pleased and the quicker necessary action could be taken. The Commander could visit me in the hospital but he would much prefer not to, and anyway even a private room was not exactly suitable for what Redhead was pleased to call 'a serious conference'.

Apart from the fact that I was getting allergic to hospitals, I saw their point, especially since they had lost Virginia. She must have been watching from the window, as I had thought she might, and seen the crash; she would have known that Bruno was driving the Lincoln. Presumably she had seized her chance and fled the flat.

Redhead's man, who had been guarding the rear exit, had been summoned to the front when Peter was hurt and she must have slipped through before he could be replaced. It was what I had so desperately hoped that she would do. But that was before I had known the identity of the Lincoln's driver.

So here I was, despite the doctors. My body, metaphorically wrapped in cotton wool and stuffed with pain-killers, was giving me little trouble. The anguish of my mind as the Commander delicately probed or tore at my life, since the day I had first met Lynn at that dinner party given by the British Ambassador in Washington, was a different matter. Yet even this was dulled as if by some anaesthetic hangover.

'And you're positive that until you saw him in that car you had no reason to suspect that Lloyd Charlton, your wife's brother, was in fact the man you know of as Bruno?'

'Positive. To me Bruno was somebody connected with People for Peace and Freedom, somebody who sent Lynn a porcelain bear as a wedding present and flowers which she didn't want, somebody whom she disliked and was frightened of but wouldn't talk about – essentially somebody who lived in Washington or thereabouts and who always seemed to know what was happening to her. I suppose much of this was Virginia's doing.'

'And Lloyd Charlton? How did you think of him?'

'He was my wife's brother, somebody whom she loved very much and who was a prisoner of war in Vietnam. I *knew* he was a POW. I had seen him on television in that camp at Hanoi. Why on earth should I have connected him with Bruno?'

'Why indeed? That was a clever trick, flying him in from Moscow for that interview.'

'And when he came home he was something of a hero because of what he had said during the broadcast and he had this scar down his cheek, all very authentic. I didn't find him the sort of person I was instantly drawn to but he was always pleasant to me and friendly and kind. He visited me almost every day in the hospital, in Washington, after he had had me beaten up.'

'You say you didn't recognize him when you saw him from the window of Mrs Urse's flat?'

213

'No, not at the time. But there was something familiar about him, about the way he carried himself and the top of his head, his hair. When I next met Lloyd it would have come to me sooner or later, I think, that he was Bruno.'

'So he had to kill you – if he as much as surmised what you've just told me. He couldn't let you blow his cover. It was much too precious. As Bruno he was a man of some consequence – the FBI are more than somewhat interested in him – but if he could bring off this exchange for Day-Brune his communist masters were going to love him even more dearly. He couldn't let you stop him.'

And he could no longer depend on my love for Lynn to keep me quiet, I thought bitterly, not once I knew that Bruno was the brother for whom Lynn had always said she would do anything, because then I would know she hadn't acted out of fear – she had nothing to fear from Lloyd; Virginia had confirmed his fondness for her – but out of love for him. I was not as besotted as that. There was too much on the other side of the balance.

I shifted restlessly in my chair. There was something I needed to ask. I couldn't rely on my own judgement any more and the Commander would at least give me an objective answer. Without thinking I interrupted him.

'Commander, there's something I want to ask you.'

He wasn't used to being cut off in mid-sentence but he adjusted rapidly. 'If it's about Bruno's other activities in the States, I can't tell you. I don't know a great deal myself. He was some sort of controller, I suppose. But I can tell you that Lloyd Charlton, whether under the persona of Bruno or as a communist sleeper waiting for another big job, was a very dangerous man. When we've finished with him the FBI will be delighted to have him – if he lives, of course.'

'No news from the hospital yet, sir,' Redhead said.

'That wasn't it,' I said. 'What I want to know is when you believe Lynn was told that her brother and Bruno were one and the same.'

'It would only be a reasoned guess.' The Commander spoke slowly; he appreciated the purpose of my question and, if I had any illusions left about my wife, he didn't want to shatter them, not now, when I was being a good boy. 'But I would say that they were forced to tell her when she refused absolutely to be made an exchange for Day-Brune. It was what ultimately decided her.'

'Thank you,' I said. I had worked out the same answer. Lynn might not have married me to please her brother, but that was a poor consolation; when it came to the crunch she would always put him before me – Lloyd or Bruno, it didn't matter. In the final analysis I had never meant very much to her.

The Commander was looking at his watch and exchanging smoke signals with Redhead. I sat. I was feeling very tired. The Commander gave me his thin, lipless smile.

'Mr Almourn, I have an appointment with the Prime Minister later tonight, after his dinner engagement. The decision about exchanging your wife and Day-Brune will be up to him and his advisers, a political decision, but you know how I must advise him.' He stood up and automatically I got to my feet. 'The FBI Inspector whom you met in Washington is flying over and we'll hope to see you again tomorrow. Meanwhile, thank you for your help. Richard will drive you home.' Richard, I had discovered, was Redhead's name. 'Incidentally, you may tell your father whatever you wish, but nobody else, please. I don't suppose you know, but Lord Almourn resigned from the Cabinet today because of your involvement with this case. The PM says he's adamant, but you may be able to persuade him to change his mind, now that there's no conflict of interest. We hope you can. Good night to you.'

He had gone before I had overcome my surprise and could wish him good night in return. I was stunned. Francis, whom I had acidly accused of putting politics before me, his only son, and who indeed did put politics before most things, had resigned from the job he loved for my sake. Tears stung my eyes; I felt so damned weak I could have wept. This morning I had stormed out of his house in anger. Now I could go home to lick my wounds.

Epilogue

SOMEWHERE
IN AFRICA

So the politicians disposed, with a little help from God. And everybody was happy, or almost everybody.

The diplomats had a field-day. Ambassadors received orders from their political masters in their one-time ciphers, delivered notes, referred to their foreign offices, delivered more notes. Red telephones burred continually. Certain sections of certain embassies in London, Washington, Oslo and Moscow clocked a lot of overtime, as did their respective home bases. Senior men in the British, American and Russian security services were kept busy; and, of course, the Norwegians had to be consulted. Meanwhile the heads of government and their advisers, those who would have to bear the brunt if things went badly for their side, conferred with each other and with their opposite numbers. It was a behind-the-scenes mini-crisis.

Finally, the Soviet Union realized it hadn't a hope of getting its hands on John Day-Brune. It also realized that, if it continued to make political hay from Lynn Charlton Almourn's attempt to smuggle dissident microfilm out of Russia, the world would be given proof that the communists had themselves engineered the whole business in order to get an exchange for the British traitor. However, if they cut their losses and made a grand gesture by returning Mrs Almourn to the West, the Soviet Union would still win itself a few goodwill Brownie points.

This was the solution advocated by the President of the United States, who didn't want the already shaky détente between the Soviet Union and the States to collapse completely. Nor, for obvious reasons, did he want a major spy scandal involving a supposed hero of the Vietnamese war. In addition, thanks to the information provided by Virginia Urse, who had been caught

219

boarding a Channel steamer for Le Havre, the FBI had rounded up most of Bruno's network without publicity. Bruno himself would never come to trial. Anglo-American medical opinion was agreed that, as a result of his injuries in a car accident, Lloyd Charlton would spend the rest of his life as a vegetable, and Bruno, it was known on unimpeachable evidence, was dead. The fact that Lloyd Charlton and Bruno were the same person was to become one of the most closely-guarded secrets of the decade.

As for the British Government, it was to come out of the affair best of all. The Day-Brune scandal was by now past history and, while the traitor deservedly languished in gaol, the British had made the Russians give back that foolish girl, Lynn Almourn, thus demonstrating they were not yet completely without power in the world. Their relations with the States had also improved; a very favourable trade agreement was signed between America and the EEC, and most of the credit for this went, rightly, to the UK. The PM seized his chance, called a snap election and was returned with an increased majority. Needless to say, Francis, Lord Almourn is once more back in the Cabinet.

And what about me? Well, I have exceeded my wildest ambition and become a Head of Mission before my thirty-fifth birthday. I shan't tell you the name of the country to which I am accredited. You wouldn't have heard of it anyway. It's a sliver of Africa which recently splintered from a former British colony. Its government is very proud and its people very poor, so that life is hard for them. I do what I can to help. This mainly consists of bombarding the FCO with suggestions for aid, which they ignore.

It's all a far cry from the NATO desk in Washington and superpower confrontations. I console myself with riding and trying to paint some of the most beautiful and unspoilt countryside in the world, but I must admit I find it pretty lonely. My colleagues in the diplomatic corps here are all married or, like my own staff of two, young and on their first postings. It would be easy to feel sorry for myself, but I don't blame the Office. In the circumstances I had to expect to be decently buried somewhere for what Francis calls 'a fallow period'. After all, the dust hasn't completely settled yet. Today was a bag day, and amongst the post was a thick envelope sent by Redhead. It consisted of a letter, some photocopies and a newspaper cutting. In the letter he explained that Lynn's diary had surprisingly turned up in a left luggage office about to be demolished where, it was presumed, Lloyd had put it for safe-keeping. Redhead had had a few pages copied for my interest; the cutting was self-explanatory. He hoped I would soon be back in civilization.

Perhaps I should explain. I haven't spoken to Lynn since I said a casual goodbye to her at Boris Gleb, expecting to be with her again in an hour or so. And I haven't seen her since she flew in to London on a BEA flight from Moscow, where she had been delivered like a parcel to the British Embassy. We were not to be allowed to meet until the SIS and God knows who else had questioned her; Redhead, however, had arranged that I should at least catch a glimpse of her at Heathrow. When I saw her there – she looked as beautiful as ever, healthy and tanned from her weeks at the Russian *dacha* – I knew exactly what was meant by that extraordinary phrase, 'my heart turned over', but her face was Lloyd Charlton's face, even, by a trick of light shining through a Venetian blind, to that scar down his cheek provided by his communist masters. And I knew that all I wanted to do was forget her.

Lynn must have felt the same about me. She refused either to see or speak to me during the time she was in London and, according to Redhead, demanded constantly to be sent home, by which she meant Washington. She wrote me a brief letter saying she would arrange for a divorce and later I heard from her lawyer. Lynn's letter I threw away. The lawyer's letter I gave to Francis, asking him to cope. I wanted nothing to do with it or with her.

My reaction to the photocopies was much the same; I would have liked to have got rid of them unread. I had no wish to remember my fool's happiness or its bitter aftermath. As the Minister in Washington had once said of John Day-Brune, it's the personal betrayal that really hurts.

Reluctantly I picked up the cutting, which was from one of

those ever-popular gossip columns, and learned that Mrs Lynn Charlton Almourn, daughter of former Senator Kenneth Charlton, had been seen at the Country Club dining with J. Warren Singer. Mrs Almourn's petition for divorce from the Honourable Derek Almourn would soon be heard, but Mrs Almourn denied any intention of remarriage and any romance between herself and Mr Singer. Mr Singer was a corporation lawyer and a former school friend of Mrs Almourn's brother, Lloyd Charlton, who so tragically . . .

I didn't bother to read any more. I crumpled the cutting – God knows why Redhead had sent it to me – and threw it into the wastepaper basket. Then I collected some ice from my small refrigerator and poured a generous scotch on top of it. After all it was midday, and I needed a drink if I was to read what Lynn had written in her diary more than a year ago.

But, as I read, I forgot about the whisky. I blessed Redhead for having sent me the photocopies – and the cutting; he was a better psychiatrist than I had supposed. I blessed those unpleasant Finns, Hank and Chuck, for half-drowning me in the lake at Holmenkollen. And I blessed Virginia for seizing on their mistake to threaten Lynn yet again.

Because the Commander's reasoned guess had been wrong. The knowledge that Bruno was merely a name used by her own brother was *not* what had finally persuaded Lynn to play that farce at Boris Gleb and become a hostage for John Day-Brune. On the contrary, it had appalled her, revolted her, and made her determined never again to do anything whatever that 'Bruno' asked. But, before she had brought herself to tell Virginia of this decision, I had been almost drowned and, fearing a repetition of what had happened to me in that Washington garage, Lynn had agreed to do what Lloyd wanted – for my sake and for my sake only.

It was like the lancing of a great boil.

And when I had ridden out the pain and the pleasure of the shock, I went into action. Clearly it was a gamble, but it was a gamble I had to take. I booked a first-class seat on the next plane leaving the country; I wrote in long-hand my letter of resignation from Her Majesty's Diplomatic Service; I told the senior member of my staff that I was off to Washington, DC, on urgent personal business. With regret, I walked out of my career. The odds were at least even, and if I won the future was full of promise. Lynn would prove, I hoped, a fair exchange.

All Futura Books are available at your bookshop or
newsagent, or can be ordered from the following
address:
Futura Books, Cash Sales Department,
P.O. Box 11, Falmouth, Cornwall.

Please send cheque or postal order (no currency), and
allow 45p for postage and packing for the first book
plus 20p for the second book and 14p for each additional
book ordered up to a maximum charge of £1.63 in U.K.

Customers in Eire and B.F.P.O. please allow 45p for
the first book, 20p for the second book plus 14p per
copy for the next 7 books, thereafter 8p per book.

Overseas customers please allow 75p for postage and
packing for the first book and 21p per copy for each
additional book.